RED DOG SALOON

R.D. SHERRILL

Copyright © 2013 R.D. SHERRILL
All rights reserved.
ISBN-13: 978-1493657100
ISBN-10: 1493657100

DEDICATION

To my mother, Mabel.

CONTENTS

PROLOGUE	3
THE DARK MAN COMES	9
LIES UPON LIES	22
GOODTIME EDDIE	36
MEET THE PRESS	46
JAILHOUSE RAT	68
MILK AND EGGS	80
LITTLE YELLOW CORVETTE	87
MEMORY LANE	99
A BIT TOO LATE	107
THE BEST LAID PLANS	114
OUT OF THE FRYING PAN	124
THE ONE THAT GOT AWAY	137
UP FROM THE DEEP	155
FROM THE ASHES	166
NEAR MISS	182
CHALLENGE ISSUED	203
DARK REVELATION	215
SOMETHING ABOUT BEN	224
SINS UNFORGIVEN	246
FAMILY REUNION	257
EPILOGUE	271

R.D. SHERRILL

The book is a work of fiction and is not meant to portray any real person or place, past or present

ACKNOWLEDGMENTS

To Seth Wright for his expertise in editing and cover design and Ashley Wright for her promotional prowess. And to Linda Bernhardt and Donna Anderson for their help in editing.

- FOR SOME ACTS THERE IS NO REDEMPTION, FOR SOME SINS NO FORGIVENESS -

PROLOGUE

He ran from the country church unrepentant and unforgiven, the bitter February wind slapping him in the face like an invisible hand as he dashed into the snowy night. If there was a Hell he no doubt was going there. Not just for his past deeds, but for what he was about to do. However, if he had his way this evening, Hell would have to wait until his body of work was complete, his curriculum vitae reserving him a special place in the bowels of the earth.

For now he had a date with destiny, a date toward which he willingly raced forcing aside his fear as he concentrated on the matter at hand. His fate hung in the balance. A steady mind and steady hand was key to surviving his showdown with the dark man. His personal Armageddon was just minutes away.

Sure, he considered turning his car into the wind and going the other way. He could flee Castle County forever, but somehow he knew the reaper would pursue him to the ends of the Earth until their business was done. There would be no rest for the wicked. Besides, he had invested too much, risked too much to cut and run this close to the end. He too, like the dark man, had blood on his hands leaving an invisible stain that would never wash off.

Even as he climbed into his car taking momentary refuge from the cold, he realized his antagonist was waiting for him at the old Red Dog Saloon. The dark man was looking to complete his collection of souls and finish collecting the tab they ran up long ago at the rural tavern. For the others, his fellows in sin, the price had already been paid, that price being their lives. He didn't plan the same fate to befall him. He refused to be a victim, a frightened child ducking his head under the covers after hearing things go bump in the night. He would stand up to his fears; devour them if he could. His defiance of his fate made him stronger.

His tires spun on the icy road as the rubber struggled to find grip on the snow-covered lane. The winter storm had dumped a fresh coat of powder turning the landscape into a sea of white. The bodies in the trunk helped add some weight to the rear of the vehicle, stabilizing the handling enough where he could hold it between the ditches.

If he had his way, the two corpses in his trunk would be joined by a third dearly departed soul in the next few minutes. That was if the dark man even had a soul. All would share the same watery grave in the murky depths of Castle Lake, forever concealed in the lowest reaches of the Bottomless Pit.

His last-minute stop for absolution at the church, something he found to be a wasted endeavor, put him behind schedule as he now had to hurry over the treacherous roads to make his nine o'clock appointment. His knuckles were white as he held a death grip on his steering wheel as his car sliced through the curtain of snow. Being late was not an option, not for this appointment anyway.

He threw on his brakes as he saw the turn suddenly materialize from the whiteout. His bowling bag flew forward onto the front floorboard and landed with a thud. The car slid sideways as he stood on his brakes, driving into the skid. His talent behind the wheel likely kept him from running over an embankment as he was able to collect the vehicle and continue on.

His degree of difficulty would increase; however, as he flipped off his headlights for the final leg of his journey. He couldn't afford to let the dark man know he was coming. The element of surprise was the key to his plan, and as such, key to his survival.

All he could do now was navigate the dark lane using the piles of snow on either side of the road as his guide, keeping his car in the middle of the two ditches. There would be no other traffic this evening. The people of Castle County were known for their fear of bad weather. Most locals would make pilgrimages to the grocery store ahead of such storms for milk and bread as if they were preparing for a zombie apocalypse when a dusting of snow was in the forecast. This was the biggest snow storm in memory thus insuring just he and the dark man were the only two braving the elements.

It took only a few minutes, despite his slow progress, to reach his destination, or at least the place he would park his get-away vehicle. He sat in the driver's seat for a moment still clutching his steering wheel as he considered what he was about to do. Then, preparing himself for the shock of the biting cold, he opened the door. The chill was even worse than it was minutes earlier when he started his journey. He wasted no time opening the rear door and pulling out his hunting rifle complete with night vision scope. He didn't always give the deer a fighting chance, enjoying a good night hunt from time to time. But then, illegal hunting was the least of the crimes he had committed over the course of his lifetime.

He immediately began climbing the snowy hill before him, refusing to pause to give himself time to rethink what he was doing and perhaps back out. His frozen breath poured from his face as he puffed with the strain of each step. The frigid air ripped through his lungs like little daggers as he pulled himself toward the crest of the hill. The snow was starting to slow but the bitter wind still swept the loose powder across the landscape making the ascension a chore. The accumulation reached high on his ankles, the overflow cascading into his shoes where it immediately began freezing his feet. His toes were going numb despite his thick socks. This was no way to spend Lincoln's birthday.

After what seemed like an endless climb, he reached the

pinnacle of the hill. He kept himself low against its face as he slithered the last few feet, parting the snow with his unprotected hands. He paused as he reached the peak which overlooked the valley where the infamous Red Dog Saloon stood more than twenty years ago. He took a moment to blow into his tingling hands, trying to return some feeling to his fingers. He had to be quick about his mission. The cold would not allow him time to procrastinate.

Wiggling his fingers, his top knuckles already frozen tight, he slid his rifle through an opening in the snow and peered through his scope into the valley which lay a few hundred feet below his vantage point. His night vision scope relayed an eerie greenish rendering of the flat valley as he panned it from left to right looking for any signs of movement. It didn't take him long for his cross hairs to find their target.

There he was! It was the dark man waiting for him in the middle of the snow-covered field, atop the ashes of the former tavern. This would be their final showdown. One of them would die tonight and, from the looks of things, it was going to be the dark man.

He looked through his scope for a few moments. He was not only watching to see if the dark man made any movements but also to see if there were any others lurking in the shadows. He assumed the dark man had come alone and that he had worked alone during his murderous rampage but he couldn't be careful enough. The stakes were too high.

Satisfied no one else was witness to what was about to happen, he took careful aim at the center of mass and wiggled his trigger finger back and forth to unlock his joint. Then, holding his breath just as if he was about to drop a buck, he slowly pulled the trigger. A twinkling of an eye later the tranquil night exploded, the fire from the muzzle of his rifle blinding him momentarily as it flashed off the pristine snow while the butt of the rifle cracked against his shoulder. Had he hit his target?

He dared lift his head from behind his snowy cover, straining to see into the night with his naked eye. The darkness prevented him from seeing any movement. Falling back onto his belly, he again peered into his rifle scope. He panned across the landscape until his sights again found his target. The figure was still standing from what he could tell. The darkness of his clothes cloaked whether he was facing him or facing away. Had he missed him? If he had, why was the figure still standing exposed in the open field? Why hadn't he taken cover or, even worse, returned fire?

Clenching his teeth and closing his left eye, he took careful aim through his scope, the cross hairs lined up perfectly on his target. Then, flinching in anticipation of the eruption of sound and fire, he squeezed off another round, then another, and another and another in quick succession. The gunfire split the serene silence of the countryside like claps of thunder.

Surely the dark man was dead. He couldn't have missed with that many shots. He had laid down a veritable wall of fire.

The sniper again peered through his scope. The figure in the valley was now on his knees from what he could make out through the grainy picture. Perhaps he hadn't struck the fatal blow. A kill shot would have laid out his target. However, the fact the form was dropped meant he had found his mark. Polishing off the wounded animal would be little more than a formality. He would finish the job up close and personal. Besides, he wanted to see the face of his vanquished opponent before ending him once and for all.

With that he charged over the hill, rifle in hand like a soldier attacking out of his foxhole. He slid down the snowy hill forgetting the cold as the burst of adrenaline from the excitement of the moment made him feel invincible. He had won. He was the sole survivor in a game of life and death. All he had to do now was claim his trophy.

Reaching the bottom of the hill, he cautiously approached

his quarry. He looked for any signs of movement. There was none. His prey sat slumped on the ground.

However, his elation was short-lived as something didn't seem right as he approached the dark figure. Then he saw it as he crept a few feet from his quarry. The vanquished target was leaning against a pole! He could now clearly see the dark metal top of the pole protruding above the form, something he couldn't see through his scope from the top of the hill. What was going on?

He circled the black-clad figure that lie before him, his gun still pointed at the prone target. Then, timidly reaching out, he poked the seemingly lifeless body with the still warm rifle barrel. There was still no movement. He must be dead. Adding to the evidence was a crimson puddle which had formed beneath him.

Convinced the dark man no longer presented a threat, he reached out to remove the mask that covered the figure's face. His hands shook uncontrollably, perhaps from the cold or perhaps from the excitement of the kill. Grasping the covering, he gave it a tug. The mask fell onto the snow and into the pool of blood below.

He froze as he gazed into the dead stare of the man before him, casting aside his rifle as he dropped to his knees before the figure. The dark man had won.

THE DARK MAN COMES

-Five Days Before-

Sheriff Sam Delaney hated mornings, especially cold mornings like this one. The chill invaded his aging bones reminding him that he was not a spring chicken anymore. He hated the prospect that he was just a couple of birthdays short of fifty. It was a milestone he dreaded with a passion.

Of particular annoyance this morning was the slow pace at which his patrol car's heater cut the cold, leaving him seeing his own breath for most of his cross-county trek. His lips were already going numb from the biting cold as the cruiser's heater belched out lukewarm air doing little to stem the chill.

He navigated the winding country roads peering out through the small circle he defrosted in the middle of his windshield. The limited visibility slowed him to a snail's pace as he spent twenty minutes reaching his destination. The drive should have taken half that time. He was paying for his oversight the night before when he neglected to cover his windshield despite the frost warning. The garage at his house was reserved for his wife's new minivan. Sam had made a habit of parking his car outside his house anyway as the mere presence of his patrol car tended to dissuade speeders in his neighborhood. Having the sheriff living on your street was better than having a neighborhood watch.

His arrival this morning, however, was not time sensitive given the fact the body wasn't going anywhere anytime soon. Yes, it took a dead body to get the sheriff out of bed at such an obscene hour. His standing orders to his deputies were quite specific when it came to rousting him from his sleep before eight o'clock on any given day. Homicides, jailbreaks and major natural disasters were the only reasons for which Sam wanted to be called in before his regular business hours. After all, he had loyally served the thirty thousand citizens of Castle County for over twelve years. He had spent a fourth of his life as sheriff, first winning election after coming back to his hometown after a stint with the Army.

Arriving at the scene located off Walker Road, Sam saw the yellow crime scene tape fluttering in the wind, the parameter around the small house completely surrounded by the barrier. In the driveway sat one of his department's patrol cars, a rookie deputy in the driver's seat, his door open and the engine running as evidenced by the smoke rising from the tailpipe. Sam pulled in behind the deputy. His car was finally a pleasant temperature and his windshield finally defrosted just in time for him to get out into the cold.

The young deputy quickly hopped out of the warmth of his patrol car to greet his boss and make a quick report.

"What do we have Deputy Faulkner?" the sheriff asked as he zipped up his jacket to keep the chill at bay.

"It's definitely a homicide, sir," the deputy answered. "One of his co-workers found him this morning just after sun up."

Sam wondered what brought the co-worker to the house at such an early hour. It was way too early for a social call.

"Our victim in there is Andy Crouch," the young officer revealed. "He works second shift over at the Rockford factory. It seems he didn't show up for work last night, something that's very unusual since he hasn't missed a night in years. When he didn't call in and didn't answer his phone the foreman got worried and sent somebody over to check on him. That's when he found him lying just inside the door."

The deputy noted he had already taken a preliminary statement from the man who found the victim as to the circumstances surrounding his grisly discovery.

"And you're sure it's a homicide, not a suicide, right?" Sam asked.

The sheriff realized suicides were much easier to work than homicides since in the case of suicides you already know the killer. The rookie gave the sheriff a big grin as he assured his boss they were looking at a case of homicide.

"Oh, I think when you get in there you'll agree. There's no way this is a suicide," he declared. "Someone definitely wanted this guy dead and they succeeded."

The officer advised the sheriff that the crime lab was on their way down from their headquarters, their arrival still about an hour away. The investigators from the lab would look for trace evidence at the crime scene, perhaps providing the sheriff a starting point in his homicide probe. Given the relatively small size of Castle County, Sam depended on the help of the state crime lab on the rare occasion there was an unsolved murder, the number of which Sam could count on one hand during his entire tenure as sheriff.

"Well, let's get this over," Sam said as he walked up the steps to the small white house careful not to touch the door knob which might still contain fingerprint evidence.

"Watch out when you go in, sir," the deputy called out from behind. "It's pretty messy. You might step in something."

Sam was immediately greeted by a scene of slaughter as he pushed the door open a few inches. Blood was clearly visible splattered across the carpet and back wall of the entry way.

"You weren't kidding, were you?" Sam said given the horrific scene before him.

Sam looked back at the deputy who still stood at the bottom of the stairs. He was apparently not keen on seeing the hideous scene again. The sheriff figured it was young

Faulkner's first body, something that could make anyone a bit squeamish. Despite seeing his share of bodies over the years, the initial shock was something he hadn't gotten used to.

The stiff remains of Andy Crouch, his body likely suffering from the throes of rigor mortis and from the bitter cold, lie on the floor just inside the door. The cause of his death was apparent. An ax laid buried deep in his forehead. His eyes were still open wide suggesting his death was instantaneous.

"Yep, I think we got us a murder," Sam agreed.

Sam squeezed past the body and pool of blood, being careful not to leave his footprint in the evidence.

"The poor guy never knew what hit him," the sheriff noted.

Sam figured the victim was dead before he hit the floor. The crime scene before him suggested he'd been surprised when he answered his door, ambushed by whoever was waiting outside.

"Plus I don't think our victim was in any condition to do that," Faulkner said, pointing toward a mirrored bureau in the living room of the residence.

Given the shocking specter of the bloody victim lying in the doorway, Sam failed to notice the mirror and the red letters written on it. As the old-timers often say, "if it were a bear it would have bit him".

"Red Dog," Sam read aloud as he stepped over to the mirror.

The words were written crudely on the glass, some of the crimson ink running down to the bottom of the mirror from the letters.

"What do you think?" Sam asked the young lawman realizing this was a perfect time to begin grooming the new officer for bigger and better things in the department. "I assume this is your first homicide."

The deputy shook his head. He readily seized the

opportunity to play the part of detective despite being the greenhorn of the department.

"Looks like it was written in blood to me, sir," he responded. "Looks like whoever did this used the victim's blood to write that on the mirror for some reason."

"Yes, I'd have to agree," Sam said he took a close look at the mirror. "And it appears they painted it on here with their finger."

"Why would someone do that, sir?" the deputy asked.

"It's the proverbial writing on the wall, deputy. Whoever did this was sending a message," Sam answered.

Glancing down as he examined the writing on the mirror, the sheriff noticed a wallet on the bureau. It was lying in plain sight, close enough to the mirror that a couple of drops of the crimson fluid had dripped on it.

"Seven hundred dollars and all of his credit cards," Sam noted as he looked through the wallet. "It doesn't look like this was a robbery. I mean if you're taking time to use the man's blood to scrawl out a message on the mirror, I think you'd notice his fat wallet right there."

Sam worked his way back out of the one-bedroom house careful not to disturb anything. He shut the door behind him, leaving the scene sealed for the crime lab.

"So he didn't show up for second shift meaning this probably happened sometime before seven last night," Sam said.

He was familiar with Rockford's schedule since he had worked there for a short time after his time in the army.

"That means he was lying here all night until someone found him this morning. Who was it that found the body?" Sam asked.

The deputy reached in the car and pulled out his notes.

"It was a guy named Eddie Young," the officer began. "He said our victim was just a regular guy who liked partying a lot. As far as he knew he didn't have any enemies, at least no one who'd want him dead. He said the guy worked at the plant for nearly twenty years and was a good employee. Aside from his drinking he was just your regular everyday guy."

Sam took Eddie's number and address with plans to contact him later. He realized nothing more could be done at the scene until the crime lab arrived, his tromping about making it more likely he might contaminate the crime scene. A trip to his office and a hot cup of coffee would be his next move.

"I need you to watch the place until the crime lab gets here and then I'll send out someone to relieve you," Sam directed. "And one more thing, keep what was written on the mirror quiet. We don't want that getting out to the public quite yet."

"Yes sir," the young officer responded. "What do you make of it, sheriff? The only Red Dog I know of was the old bar that used to sit off East Ridge Highway but that's been gone, well, since before I was born. Folks just use it when they give out directions and tell you go out to the old Red Dog and take a left."

"Some things never die," Sam declared as he walked back to his car, the sun finally getting high enough to offer a faint ray of warmth on the otherwise cold morning. "The old Red Dog will always be there."

Given the fact Eddie lived between the crime scene and Sam's office, the sheriff figured he may as well make a stop on his way to headquarters to pick his brain for any details the young deputy may have not elicited. After all, he was already wide awake and any chance of returning to his slumber at this hour was null out of the question. Plus, Sam knew people often think more clearly once they are removed from a traumatic situation, their thought process clouded the closer they are to that trauma. Finding a co-worker's body with an ax sunk several inches deep in his head, like Eddie did earlier that morning, would qualify as traumatic in Sam's book. It was certainly no way to begin one's day.

The sheriff pulled into the driveway and made his way to the door. His first knocks on the door of the double-wide trailer weren't answered despite Eddie's truck parked outside his residence. Surely he hadn't gone to sleep already, especially after what he had just witnessed. Sam knew it would be hard for a man to lay his head down and fall into slumber after witnessing such a heinous sight.

After nearly a minute of knocking by the sheriff, Eddie made his way to the door, the tall, dark-headed man with a scraggly graying beard still dressed in his factory uniform.

"Come on in," Eddie invited with a slight slur in his voice.

He motioned the sheriff into his messy living room where the smell of liquor hung heavy. The host walked with a slight wobble.

"Care for a drink?" Eddie asked.

"It's a little early for that don't you think?" Sam replied as Eddie refilled his glass with straight bourbon, taking a big swallow as he sat down on his couch.

"It's never too early," Eddie retorted. "Don't worry sheriff, I'm not drunk yet. I'm just taking the edge off."

The sheriff didn't really believe Eddie to be a suspect in the murder. Instead the lawman was more interested in small details he might be able to provide. Sam had learned by experience that sometimes it just takes one nugget of information to turn a case.

"So tell me what happened this morning Eddie," Sam began, hoping the liquor wasn't already clouding his memory.

"I don't know, sheriff," Eddie replied as he took another swig of his drink. His hands were noticeably shaking.

"When we couldn't get ahold of Andy at work we got worried since he never, and I mean never, misses work," Eddie explained. "Since me and him go back a long way, the foreman asked me to drop by and check on him."

Eddie paused and swallowed hard as he recalled the

events of the morning.

"When I first pulled up, I noticed the door was open a bit and his truck was in the driveway. That seemed odd on such a cold morning for a man's door to be open like that, you know," Eddie recalled. "I went up and pushed the door but there was something behind it. When I stuck my head inside the door, there laid Andy, his skull split wide open by that ax."

Eddie finished his drink in one big swallow and slammed down his glass.

"It was the most horrible thing I ever saw, sheriff," Eddie declared, looking at the lawman, his eyes bloodshot either from the bourbon or perhaps from mourning the sudden loss of his friend.

"You didn't see anything else? Think about it now. Did you see anything at all that you haven't mentioned?" Sam quizzed. "Take your time and think. It could be important."

"No sheriff. When I saw Andy lying there I went right back out and called the law," Eddie responded. "I didn't know if whoever did it might still be around."

Sam believed Eddie's recollection yet at the same time he seemed almost overly nervous even given what he had just witnessed. Perhaps there was something else on his mind, something he needed liquor to help cope with.

"So did you see anything inside, anything on the wall, anything unusual at all?" Sam asked.

The sheriff wondered about the bloody writing on the mirror. Had Eddie noticed it? If so, why had he not mentioned such a glaring detail?

"No sheriff," Eddie said sheepishly. "Like I said, when I saw him lying there I just backed out. I mean we not only worked together but we'd been friends for a long time, pretty well since high school."

Sam was already aware Eddie and the victim were old friends since Sam had grown up in the same county with them. Castle County was the kind of place where everybody knew, or at least knew of, everyone else.

"Yeah, I thought you two were friends," Sam said as he stood up to leave "As a matter of fact, you two go way back. Seems like I remember seeing you all hanging out together back at the old Red Dog and that's been more than twenty years. Time flies doesn't it?"

Eddie's face went pale white with the sheriff's reference to the Red Dog. His odd reaction caught the sheriff's eye. It was as if Eddie was suddenly at a loss for words, the wind seemingly knocked out of him.

"Something wrong, Eddie?" Sam asked.

The lawmen realized he must have hit a nerve with his reference to the Red Dog. He now suspected his witness had seen more than he was telling.

"Um, no sheriff. It's just been a long morning," Eddie stammered nervously as he stood up to escort the lawman to the door. "I appreciate you coming by though. If I think of anything else I'll call you first thing. I promise."

Sam stepped out the door giving Eddie a long look. The sheriff could tell he was being hustled away. Eddie's demeanor suggested he was eager for the lawman to leave.

"You do that," Sam said as he left.

Why was Eddie not telling everything he knew about the murder of his friend? The question would bother the sheriff all the way to his office that morning, leaving him to mull Eddie's odd behavior over his first cup of coffee.

Eddie looked through his curtains, watching as the sheriff's cruiser disappeared out of sight. He poured another drink. His buzz was just starting to arrive. It couldn't get there fast enough. Eddie needed the liquor to calm his uncontrollable shaking, his hands trembling like leaves in the wind. While a two-fisted drinker, Eddie rarely started so early but today was special. He needed it before he made the call.

He sat silently by his phone for a moment trying to focus

his thoughts and decide what he was going to say. While known as the big mouth amongst his group of friends, the morning's events left him uncharacteristically quiet. Fear had robbed him of words. The horrifying scene of his friend's skull sliced wide open and his blood used as human ink to spell out an unmistakable message left Eddie petrified. Deep down in his very soul Eddie knew the meaning of the message.

Eddie gathered his courage and picked up the phone. His fingers shook so much that he had to concentrate to peck out the numbers. The alcohol made the square digits on the dialing pad a moving target.

He waited impatiently as the phone rang, nervously rapping his fingers on the coffee table.

"Foster Motors," came a voice on the other end of the phone.

The voice was one Eddie knew to be that of Bart Foster, the ringleader of their old running group. He was now a successful car salesman and semi-reputable businessman in Easton, the county seat for Castle County.

"Hello? Anyone there? Foster Motors," Bart said as he was about to hang up since he heard no one on the other end of the line.

"Hey Bart," Eddie stammered. "This is Eddie Young."

Going quiet on the other end for a moment, Bart hesitated as if deciding if he wanted to take the call.

"Oh, Eddie, how's it been?" Bart responded in a contrived pleasant voice. "It's been a while."

"Yeah ... it has," Eddie agreed. "It's been a lot of years."

Bart didn't know why Eddie was suddenly calling him. They hadn't spoken, except in passing, in many years. The businessman assumed his old pal wanted something from him.

"To what do I owe the honor?" Bart asked. "Are you ready to trade vehicles? I have some real beauties, all low mileage on the lot. I'll give you the old friend's discount."

Not really knowing how to transition the conversation, Eddie cut to the chase.

"Andy's dead," Eddie blurted out. "Did you hear me? They found Andy this morning. He's dead."

Putting on a calm tone, since it had also been a long time since Bart had any dealings with Andy aside from selling him a truck several years ago, the businessman spoke up.

"Oh, I'm sorry to hear that," Bart said. "What happened?"

"What happened?" Eddie asked excitedly. "What happened is he was murdered last night."

"Murdered?" Bart responded. "Who would want to kill Andy? He was a good guy."

Bart was actually right. Andy was likely the best person when it came to their former running group. He was the only one who seemed to have an inkling of a conscience back in their younger days.

"I don't know," Eddie admitted as he put his head in his hands, running his hand through his thinning hair with the receiver still to his ear. "I found him this morning after he didn't come in to work. He had an ax buried in his head."

The revelation concerning the heinousness of the crime came as a surprise. Even with that, Bart still wondered why his long absent friend would be notifying him like he was next of kin. He would have read about it in the newspaper the next day even without the advance call. The way Bart figured it, Andy had gotten himself into trouble and someone had come calling to settle the issue once and for all.

"That's horrible," Bart replied, still using his pleasant businessman's voice as he eyed the man outside checking out some of the cars on his lot. "Is there anything I can do?"

"I don't think you understand, Bart," Eddie said. "It doesn't just involve Andy. It involves all of us - the old gang."

"Okay Eddie, you're not making any sense and I have a customer I need to wait on," Bart replied. "Why don't you call me back later when you're a little less, you know, drunk."

"The killer wrote the words Red Dog!" Eddie yelled into the phone. "It was written in Andy's own blood! Don't you understand? Someone knows! After all this time, someone knows! What are we going to do, Bart?"

Bart forgot about his customer as his mind raced. Memories attacked his consciousness, pictures appearing before his mind's eye like snapshots in time as if it had just happened yesterday.

"Are you sure?" Bart asked.

"I saw it with my own eyes!" Eddie confirmed with his voice quivering. "Well, what are we going to do?"

Taking charge as he always did back in their "wild days," Bart responded in an authoritative voice, hoping to snap the drunken Eddie back to reality.

"The first thing is you need to stop drinking," Bart ordered. "And keep your mouth shut. You haven't told anybody else have you?"

"No. I talked to the sheriff but didn't tell him I even saw the writing," Eddie retorted.

"Let's keep it that way," Bart said. "You need to keep your mouth shut. I don't want you talking to anybody and that goes doubly true for Sheriff Delaney. Let me check this thing out."

Eddie was almost to the point of tears as he fought to hold it together amidst the fear that was gripping him.

"Who could it be?" Eddie asked with his voice pleading for an answer - an answer Bart didn't have.

"I don't know, Eddie," Bart admitted. "It's been a long time, over twenty years as a matter of fact."

"It seems like yesterday," Eddie shot back, his tone worrying Bart.

"Now listen to me, Eddie," Bart began sternly. "You sit tight and toss the liquor bottle. I'll find out about this thing. We got to hang together, just like we did back then. Do you understand me?"

"Yeah, yeah Bart, I understand," Eddie sheepishly responded.

He poured himself another drink despite his old friend's admonition. Eddie wasn't about to put down the bottle. Liquor was the only true friend he had left.

Bart assured Eddie he would contact him as soon as he discovered anything. Then, plastering a smile on his face, he went out to meet his customer, hiding the fact behind his salesman's grin that a long-buried ghost had returned from the grave to haunt him.

LIES UPON LIES

Sam had been a lawman for over a decade and during that time acquired what amounted to a sixth sense when it came to knowing when people were hiding something from him. As such he knew Eddie was keeping something close to the vest. His body language told on him when Sam mentioned the words Red Dog. What could have caused such a reaction? What was Eddie hiding? And better yet, why would he be hiding something from law enforcement when they were trying to find who killed his friend?

The sheriff poured his second cup of brew as sat at his desk considering the events of the morning, enjoying the warmth of the Columbian blend, plotting his next move. Sam realized that the quicker a suspect was generated, the better chance there was of keeping the murder from the cold case file. He prided himself in the fact that in his twelve years as Castle County Sheriff there were no unsolved murders on his ledger. But then it wasn't like the rural county had a ground swell of killings. It wasn't exactly the wild, wild, west.

What homicides that had happened on Sam's watch usually had to do with men feuding over a woman or someone getting shorted on a drug deal. And, even those cases were few and far between and were easy to solve. When you got down to it, Castle County was a good place to raise a family. Its rural values were pervasive throughout the community. Sure, the county had its rebels and scofflaws just like any town its size but overall most people in Castle

County were just good, decent, God-fearing folks. Unfortunately, given the morning's discovery, one of them was also a cold-blooded killer.

Hopefully the lab boys would be able to shed some light on the murder. They were poring over the crime scene even as Sam sat in his warm office. While real-life crime scene investigation was not nearly as cut and dry as one would see on television, the trace evidence technicians were adept at finding the rare nuggets needed to make a case. Sam knew if the killer left anything behind, they would find it. And, given his experience, a criminal always leaves a piece of himself behind whether it's fingerprints, hair, footprints, tire tracks or even his own blood. Sam was yet to see the perfect crime.

The sheriff decided to do some background work on the case while waiting for the preliminary crime lab report. He would begin with the records department which was just a short stroll down the hall from his office.

"Are you the only one here?" Sam asked as he poked his head in the door seeing Carly, his tall brown-haired records clerk, dressed in a well-fitting knee-length skirt.

The shapely clerk was raised up on her tiptoes filing papers in the top drawer of a cabinet. He had come at a perfect time. She was dressed for success.

"Yep, sheriff, it's just me this morning," Carly responded, shooting her boss a broad smile. "I'm all alone."

"Oh really, you don't say?" Sam said. "This must be my lucky day."

He looked down the hall, making sure no one was nearby before shutting the door behind him. Shooting the clerk a sly grin, he boldly approached and removed the papers from her hands, placing them on top of the cabinet.

"How's the husband doing nowadays?" Sam asked.

"He's all work and no play," Carly responded, biting her lip as Sam took her in his arms. "What about you? How's the wife?"

He drew Carly to him, kissing her on her cheek, his hands

wrapped around her waist, whispering his answer as he worked his way down her neck.

"That old hag, she ain't no fun either," Sam retorted. "We ought to run away together."

The sound of the door opening surprised the couple as Sam was still working his clerk's neck. Carly tried to quickly push him away as she saw her assistant clerk, Wanda Robertson, come in. The clerk, letting out a disgusted sigh, wasted no time speaking up.

"Why don't you two get a room?" Wanda said as she stood at the door watching the intertwined couple. "Sometimes it's hard to believe you two are married to each other the way you carry on. Men usually reserve that for their mistresses, sheriff."

Sam smiled at Wanda, not bothering to take his hands off his wife's hips.

"My fuddy-duddy wife won't let me get a girlfriend on the side so I guess I'll have to settle," Sam quipped as Carly gave him a flirtatious slap across his cheek.

"That kind of crap will get you a sexual harassment suit," Carly warned her husband of over twenty years as she went back to filing papers.

Carly, still a head-turner even after she celebrated her fortieth birthday a short time before, was a key part of the operation at the sheriff's department. His wife knew where to lay her hands on any document, record or warrant in the whole building. Sam hired his wife for the job shortly after being elected the first time. He beat the county's new nepotism policy which would have prevented him from bringing his wife on board. She was the best hire he ever made.

"To what do we owe the pleasure of the high sheriff coming down here to the dungeon?" Carly asked as she finished putting away the files. "Why aren't you out finding the hardened criminal that killed poor Andy Crouch?"

"Hey lady, you stick to filing the papers and I'll stick to

enforcing the law in Castle County," Sam retorted.

"Speaking of which, do you have anything on our victim?"

Walking over to another filing cabinet, Carly reached in and pulled out a file handing it to her husband.

"That's his jacket," Carly said. "It's pretty light."

Sam thumbed through the small file and discovered some petty arrests over the years, most alcohol-related. A couple of public drunks, a drunk driving conviction and a marijuana arrest were all that showed up in his file.

"How about Eddie Young? Do we have anything on him?" Sam asked.

His wife again demonstrated her uncanny ability to immediately fish out any file from the stacked-up records room. Sam wasn't even sure where he left his car keys.

Eddie's record was much like that of Andy's. All of his arrests had to do with alcohol. One of his public intoxications came on the same evening as one of those in Andy's record suggesting the pair were partying together that night.

"How far back do we go in here?" Sam asked.

"In theory a person's record should go from when they reached legal age but in reality we don't have a whole lot prior to you taking office," Carly admitted. "Your predecessor didn't have a top notch records clerk like me."

"True, you're a shoe-in for employee of the year," Sam winked as he handed her back the file, waving good-bye as he headed back to his office.

"I'd sure hope so," Carly chirped as he walked away. "I'm sleeping with the boss."

"The early report is back," came the voice of Sam's Chief Investigator Bo Davis, the stocky red-faced country boy filing in beside the sheriff as he walked back down the hall toward his office. "The crime lab guys are heading in to your office right now."

"Did they find anything for us?" Sam asked.

"Don't know," Bo responded with his southern drawl. "I

did a walk around out there and didn't find nothing. Talked to the neighbors and they didn't hear nothing either. It's pretty quiet out in those parts and noise carries down in that hollow where our boy lived. Whoever did it did it real quiet-like but then busting open a man's skull with an ax don't make much noise."

Sam and his investigator arrived at his office just as members of the state crime team walked in. Their faces told the sheriff their search was uneventful.

"Well, do we have anything?" Sam asked in a hopeful voice.

"Nothing," responded lead detective Bryce Gonder. "The place is as clean as I've ever seen a crime scene."

"Are you saying there's absolutely nothing?" Sam asked.

"I'm saying we went over the house with a fine-toothed comb," Gonder responded in an irritated tone. "There's not a fingerprint, footprint, tire track, or even a hair follicle there. It's almost like someone floated in there, killed the guy, and floated back out."

Disappointed the evidence techs would not be able to provide even a shred of evidence, Sam centered on the murder weapon.

"Okay, what about the ax?" Sam asked. "What do we know about that?"

"From what we can tell, the ax belonged to the victim," Gonder revealed. "He had a wood burning stove inside his house and there was a fresh wood pile around back. We're assuming the ax used to kill him was also used to chop the wood he was using for his stove. And, before you ask, the ax was clean of prints. The killer either wore gloves or wiped it clean."

"What's your guess for our perpetrator?" Sam asked. "Man, woman, big, small, what are we looking for?"

"That ax was filed razor sharp so pretty well any adult of average strength could have swung it with enough power to cause the fatal injury," Gonder answered. "The ax caught him right on top of the skull and penetrated several inches into his brain. He was dead before he hit the floor."

"Okay then, what about the blood on the mirror?" Sam asked.

"That was the victim's blood," Gonder replied. "The killer probably used his or her finger to spell out the words on the mirror. Once again, there were no viable fingerprints since it was smeared on the mirror."

Sam leaned back in his chair realizing they would have to solve the case the old-fashioned way, that being good detective work since modern science wasn't going to bail them out.

"So, in other words ..." Sam began, only to be cut off by Gonder.

"There's nothing," Gonder interjected. "Whoever did this was very efficient."

Thanking the crime scene team, Sam walked them to the parking lot before returning to his office where Bo still sat.

"What do you make of the killer writing Red Dog on the mirror?" Bo asked before Sam could even sit down at his desk. "Seems a mighty odd thing for a man to do while he's standing around a house with the corpse of the man he just killed."

"Around here the words Red Dog can mean only one thing, that being the old bar that used to sit over on East Ridge Highway," Sam said with certainty. "Now why anybody would reference a bar that has been gone for over twenty years at the scene of a murder is beyond me unless they had some long lasting issues."

"I never got to go there," Bo said matter of factly. "I always thought of trying to sneak in when I was a teenager but then the place burned down when I was still too young."

"You didn't miss anything, Bo," Sam declared. "It was a redneck saloon where nothing good ever happened. As a matter of fact a lot of bad things happened there. A decent person wouldn't be caught dead in that dive."

"What about you? Did you ever go?" Bo shot back.

"Oh yeah, I went a time or two," Sam admitted, a bit embarrassed he had darkened the Red Dog door. "But it wasn't really my cup of tea. Just a bunch of brawlers and drunks hung out there looking for trouble. Going out there was more of a rite of passage, showing your buddies you had guts enough to walk into the Red Dog."

"That takes us right back to the question of the Red Dog," Bo noted. "Why take the time to write that message after splitting a guy's head in two?"

"You just answered your own question," Sam said. "It was a message, perhaps a threat. Whoever did it felt it was important enough to delay their departure from the scene of the crime. As for their choice of words, I'm hoping an old friend can help me out on that one."

"An old friend? Who's that?" Bo asked.

"Well, I think I'm going to get me a little lunch and then I'm going to drive out and see my predecessor, Bill Foster," Sam declared. "He was sheriff in Castle County back during the Red Dog's heyday. Maybe he recalls an old feud or bad blood from back then that could have led to the murder."

Bill Foster was not only Sam's predecessor as sheriff but he had served as the county's chief law enforcement officer for nearly a quarter-century before retiring twelve years ago. His decision not to seek a seventh term of office left every political hopeful in Castle County scrambling to toss their hat in the ring. No less than ten candidates sought election to Foster's seat.

Prior to the announcement of his retirement, no one had dared run against the veteran sheriff in three elections. Whether it was due to intimidation or just reluctance to throw their money away on a hopeless campaign, no one lifted a finger to try to unseat the incumbent during his final terms of office.

The popular old-school lawman dispensed a brand of justice that while, fine for its time, had run its course with the changing of times. His retirement was well-timed. His strong-handed tactics, in the modern climate of litigation, would have surely seen Castle County sued several times over if he were still in office.

The campaign that followed Sheriff Foster's announced retirement was a free-for-all with election signs in almost every front yard in Castle County. Being well known in the community since his childhood, perhaps best known as the all-state quarterback for the Castle County Knights in high school, Sam used his name recognition to his benefit along with his recent service in the U.S. Army. That combination, along with having some of the most attractive campaign signs in the field of candidates, led to Sam winning by a scant fifty votes.

Sam's popularity, as well as his margin of victory, increased over the years to the point no one even bothered run against him in the last election. He still used the campaign signs from his first run, figuring they were still the sharpest campaign signs around. He even put a few of them up the last election despite being unopposed.

Sam had consulted with his predecessor on a few occasions since taking over his office. Most of the time it was about minor things having to do with the jail or about where fugitives may be hiding out. Bill still had his ear to the ground for a lawman that had been out of the game for over a decade. Sam figured if anyone would recall the history of the Red Dog it would be Bill Foster. He had personally answered many a call at the bar back in his day.

"Sheriff Delaney, how have you been?" the sixty-nine-year-old retired lawman said, obviously surprised to see Sam standing at his door. "Come on in here, you'll catch your death of cold."

Bill, a recent widower, had always been hospitable to folks publicly despite tales Sam had heard concerning the head-busting tactics the former sheriff sometimes used to keep the peace in Castle County.

"I'd offer you some coffee but my doctor told me to cut down on caffeine - high blood pressure and whatnot," the still fit-looking senior revealed as he pulled a couple of beers from his refrigerator handing one to his guest. "That's the good thing about being the boss. Who's going to get onto you for having a beer on duty?"

Settling down at Bill's kitchen table, the men engaged in law enforcement chat for a good twenty minutes, sipping beer and swapping stories. Sam caught his predecessor up on the changes at the department. The casual chat, however, eventually led around to Bill's curiosity for the real reason of Sam's visit.

"I know you didn't drive all the way out here on the coldest day of the year to sip beer and swap war stories with an old man," Bill reckoned.

"True, I was actually hoping to pick your brain," Sam revealed as he leaned forward in his chair, giving the former sheriff a serious look.

"Pick away," Bill countered as he went for another beer. "So what do you want to pick about?"

"The old Red Dog Saloon," Sam responded, his words freezing Bill momentarily as he leaned into his refrigerator to retrieve a beer.

His voice somewhat hesitant, Bill wondered about the significance of the old bar.

"The Red Dog? You came all the way out here to ask me about a bar that's been gone for twenty-one maybe twenty-two years?" Bill asked as he returned, twisting the lid off his beer. "Shoot, there wasn't anything to talk about even when it was open. All it amounted to out there was a bunch of trouble. The day it burnt down was probably the best day in county history."

He knew he would have to show some of his cards in order to get cooperation from his predecessor. The sheriff decided to trust Bill, hoping law enforcement fraternity would ensure his silence on the sensitive matters of the case.

"Have you heard about the murder this morning?" Sam began. "They found Andy Crouch dead."

Bill nodded his head and gave Sam a solemn look.

"Yeah, I heard about that," Bill responded. "News travels fast in a small town."

"We have reason to believe his murder may have something to do with the old Red Dog," Sam revealed. "What I was wondering is if there was something back in the day that someone could have held a long grudge for. I know Andy was one of the regulars out there."

"It's hard to say sheriff," Bill began. "There was a lot of trouble out there - fights, cuttings, you name it and it went on out at the Red Dog."

"Can you recall anything having to do with Andy Crouch or his old buddy Eddie Young for that matter?" Sam questioned. "They used to hang out with your oldest son, Bart, I believe. I think I saw them out there a time or two."

Sam's reference to Bill's son brought an immediate change in demeanor from the old lawman.

"What's that supposed to mean?" Bill snapped, his tone immediately letting Sam know he had crossed an invisible line in his course of questioning. "He was a grown man so it wasn't like I could tell him where he could or couldn't go. If it were up to me he wouldn't have gotten within a hundred miles of that God-forsaken dive."

Sam apologized for the wording of his question. He was taken aback by the extreme reaction by the former sheriff.

"No, I didn't mean anything bad. I just knew there were a bunch of them that hung out together back in the old days and thought maybe Bart might have some information he passed along about things that went on out there," Sam clarified. "I'm looking for any information, no matter how seemingly minor, which might help the investigation."

Bill paused for a second and looked blankly into space as

if he was thinking back to long forgotten conversations.

"Nope. Bart never told me anything about what went on out there," Bill declared, still a bit standoffish from Sam's mention of his son. "I'm just glad I never had to arrest my own son out there. That would have been embarrassing. Like I said, the best thing that ever happened was when the place burned to the ground."

The Red Dog burned under mysterious circumstances about twenty-two years ago. The pervasive rumor was the fire was intentionally set, however, as far as Sam could recall, no one was ever charged with arson.

"It was intentionally set as I recall," Sam began. "Did you ever have an idea who was behind it?"

Sam's question seemed to again fluster his host who remained silent for a moment as if deciding whether to answer the question.

"It's according to whom you talk to, Sam," Bill started. "Some people say old Earl Cutts decided to torch the place to collect insurance and got caught up by the inferno inside before he could get out. Others say it was payback for trouble that happened there over the years. Beer wasn't the only thing being sold out of the place so let your imagination run wild. I know from my dealings with him over the years that Earl Cutts was shady as they come. There were a lot of people who were happy when he went up along with the saloon. Some folks even say the fires of Hell itself reached up to claim the Red Dog and its owner."

"So I take it the proprietor wasn't on the up and up then," Sam said.

He already knew the former bar owner's reputation as a businessman who didn't let the law stand in the way of making a dollar. Earl Cutts' less-than-honorable reputation remained two decades after he was gone.

Eyeing Sam across the table, Bill wanted answers as to what caused the sheriff to link the killing of Andy Crouch to the old Red Dog Saloon.

"You said you had reason to believe his murder had something to do with the Red Dog," Bill recalled. "What makes you think that if you don't mind me asking, one lawman to another?"

The sheriff decided to take his predecessor into confidence when it came to the writing on the mirror.

"We found the words Red Dog written on a mirror at the crime scene," Sam explained. "I think whoever did it was trying to send a message or perhaps a warning."

"So why would you think that one is related to another?" Bill asked. "He could have written that on the mirror himself. For all you know he may have hooked up with the wrong man's girl and got himself killed. That used to happen from time to time when I was sheriff. A man would bed down with the wrong man's wife and wake up dead."

"The words were written in his own blood," Sam declared. "Whoever killed Andy used his blood for the ink to write those words."

An awkward silence fell upon the pair as Bill processed what he had just heard. Something about the former sheriff's actions wasn't sitting right with Sam. He just couldn't put his finger on it.

"And you're sure you don't know anything that could help us out on this case?" Sam asked.

"Like I told you, it was a bad place," Bill snapped as he took a big swallow of his beer. "Who knows what he got into there."

Considering his next words carefully given Bill's earlier reaction, Sam reluctantly had to ask.

"You don't mind if I talk to Bart and see if he remembers anything about it do you?" Sam requested.

"Do what you want! He's a grown man!" Bill said in a loud voice as he stood up from the table. "He doesn't know anything anyhow. Now if you don't mind I've got an appointment in town I need to be getting to."

Sam knew the conversation was over given his host's

demeanor. His sixth sense told him the former sheriff had been less than forthcoming during his visit. He had certainly hit on a sore spot when it came to his son Bart, but perhaps it was just a case of Bill being an overprotective father. Sure, Bill's son was a forty-four-year-old businessman but Sam realized, as a father of two young adults himself, that they're always your kids no matter how old they are. Still, Sam had to admit to himself that Bill's reaction was suspicious. One thing for sure, he was going to have a conversation with Bart and he was going to have it right now.

Sam wasted no time heading straight to Foster Motors. He pulled into the sales lot and immediately spotted Bart's bright yellow Corvette sitting next to the building. Sam parked beside the sports car and walked into the sales office.

"Hey, I need to see Mr. Foster," Sam announced to the woman at the reception desk.

"I'm sorry but Mr. Foster isn't in today," the woman responded, not looking up from her paper work.

"He's not? That's his car parked out there isn't it?" Sam retorted

He stopped just short of questioning the woman's honesty. He knew the Corvette was Bart's latest project which he had been showing around town for the past month. He kind of doubted Bart would be tooling around in some broken down, second-hand model off his lot when he could be driving the magnificently restored vintage hot rod. The chances were that Bart was there - somewhere.

"He must have taken another car off the lot," the woman shot back as she looked up from her desk obviously not thrilled with the lawman's inference. "This is a car lot you realize."

Suspecting he was being put off for unknown reasons, Sam played along knowing Bart couldn't avoid him forever.

"So any idea when your boss will be back?" Sam asked. "Or better yet, any idea where I might find him right now?"

"I believe he'll be out of the office for the rest of the

day," the receptionist answered. "I'll tell him you came by if you'd like."

"Sure. You do that," Sam said as he left the office.

However, instead of leaving straightaway, an idea hit him. Returning to his car he paused for a moment to scribble out a note before placing it under Bart's windshield wiper.

"Maybe that will get his attention," Sam chuckled to himself.

The note contained just two words – Red Dog.

GOODTIME EDDIE

Eddie Young didn't heed the advice of his old friend as he continued his assault on the bottle of bourbon, killing it off by the end of the day only to open a new one. Drink as he would, Eddie couldn't erase the horrific sight burned into his brain of the ax buried deep into his friend's skull. He couldn't forget looking into his friend's dead eyes, Andy's dark brown eyes still opened in terror when he found him lying in a pool of blood.

Even worse was that the bourbon couldn't dull the fear - a fear that was sitting like a knot in the pit of his stomach - that the same fate may be awaiting him. After all, they were all equally guilty for what happened, no matter how many years had passed. The message was not open for interpretation. Eddie knew exactly what it meant.

Why hadn't Bart called back? He promised to "check into things" and get back with him yet the day had passed and the sun set without his old friend telling him anything. His calls to Bart's cellphone would simply roll over to voice mail which would announce his mailbox was full thanks to the scores of frantic messages Eddie had left as the day went on without any word from the old ringleader.

Given his intoxication, Eddie was in no condition to go to work prompting him to call in "sick" for his night shift. His slurred speech likely gave him away despite his best attempts to sound sober and use his sick voice when he made the call. But then Eddie had never been the consistent one like Andy. Often called Good Time Eddie by his friends, Eddie was always looking for fun. He lost many jobs over the years when he chose entertainment over responsibility. He also lost a couple of wives the same way. Eddie, now in his forties, had never grown up. His maturity level was that of an adolescent, explaining why he was still spinning his wheels when it came to the game of life.

Full of liquor and frustration, he decided to disregard even more of Bart's advice as he sat alone in his trailer. He would call Stevie Grissom, one of their old gang. Stevie was the one member of their old group who had gotten his life together. Married with a couple of children, a dog and a cat, Stevie would rarely make appearances at their various gatherings anymore. Stevie's wife kept close reins on her husband. She didn't want him to mix with his old running buddies since their gatherings generally meant he would come back at sunrise smelling of liquor and cheap perfume. Slowly but surely she had weaned Stevie off his partying ways, turning him ever so grudgingly into a family man. In Eddie's eyes Stevie's wife was the worst kind of woman. She was a real soul-sucker who kept her husband's family jewels with her anytime he went out.

Eddie realized it was almost nine o'clock at night and likely past Stevie's curfew. However, he had just enough buzz to go ahead and dial his number, all the time hoping it would be Stevie who answered the phone. Even in his intoxicated state Eddie wasn't sure he was quite drunk enough to endure her condescending voice, let alone have to ask for permission to talk to her husband. They were in the forties for crying out loud.

"Answer, Answer," Eddie urged. He listened nervously to the phone ring until Stevie picked it up on the fifth ring.

"Stevie!" Eddie yelled in an excited voice when his old friend answered the phone.

"Eddie?" he responded. A child was crying in the background letting him know all Hell was probably about to break loose at Stevie's house. "What are you doing calling this late?"

Eddie didn't waste any time getting to his main point. His tact was already drunk away by his day hitting the bottle.

"Did you hear about Andy?" Eddie asked.

Just as he had done when he called in sick a little while earlier, Eddie tried not to sound drunk but his words were still slurred despite his attempts.

"Yeah, that was horrible," Stevie responded as his wife could be heard in the background asking who was on the phone.

"It's Eddie, dear," Stevie called back to his wife. His revelation was not taken well by Stevie's better half.

"You tell Good Time Eddie not to be calling this phone so late!" Stevie's wife yelled.

Her shrill voice was like fingernails on a chalk board to Eddie's already ringing ears.

"Some of us get to sleep at a decent hour," she screamed. "Regular people don't stay up partying every night."

Eddie continued his conversation despite the annoying droning of Stevie's wife in the background.

"Did you hear what else they found?" Eddie asked.

"No, I just heard he got hit in the head and they found him there," Stevie responded.

He cupped the receiver with his hand so his wife couldn't overhear the conversation. "Isn't that what happened?"

"Hit? He had an ax buried in his brain!" Eddie responded incredulously. "But that's not all. Are you ready for this? Whoever did it wrote the words Red Dog on a mirror in Andy's blood."

Stevie went silent on his end after hearing Eddie's news.

"Hello, Hello, you still there?" Eddie asked.

He suspected Stevie's wife had hung up the phone on him. It was something he wouldn't put past the domineering woman since she wore the pants in the family.

"Are you sure?" Stevie asked sheepishly. "It was written

in his own blood?"

"Positive, I'm the person who found him. I saw it all with my own eyes," Eddie responded as he could hear Stevie swallow hard on the other end of the line. "You know what this means don't you?"

"Someone knows, someone remembers," Stevie declared in a low voice with his wife still yelling in the background. "I knew we were doing wrong. I knew it'd come back to get us."

Stevie couldn't be more right in Eddie's mind.

"We need to meet, all of us," Eddie said. "We need to figure this out."

Stevie went quiet again as he was obviously shocked and disturbed by what Eddie told him. The news hit him from out of nowhere. His comfortable existence was suddenly threatened.

"I've got to go," Stevie said, not knowing how to deal with the problem that now confronted them.

"You can't just ignore this!" Eddie said in a loud voice. "We're all in it!"

"I'll talk to you later," Stevie responded before hanging up.

Eddie knew he couldn't just trust Bart to take care of things since he had kept him in the dark all day. Still emboldened with liquor, he decided he would take the lead. Bart had gotten them into this anyway so why trust him to get them out? Eddie was going to call every member of the gang. Together they could figure something out and perhaps come up with an answer about what was going on. He would call Glenn Satterfield next, or at least he planned to before he heard the movement outside his trailer.

Eddie strained his ears and hit the mute button on his television trying to hear if the noise repeated itself. Seconds passed but he heard only the slight breeze outside.

He was about to hit the button on his remote to turn the television back on, dismissing his scare as alcohol induced paranoia, when he nearly jumped from his seat. There was a loud bump outside his living room window. Something hit the side of his trailer! This wasn't paranoia. Something or someone was outside!

Eddie scrambled to his bedroom. He tripped over a chair and cursed as he stubbed his toe. He then headed straight to his nightstand and pulled out his thirty-eight caliber pistol from the bedside drawer. He checked the clip to ensure it was loaded, jamming the clip back into the gun before chambering a round.

"They're messing with the wrong man," Eddie mumbled to himself as he stumbled out of his bedroom and headed back to the living room. His arrival was greeted by another loud thump outside the trailer.

"You hear me! You're messing with the wrong man!" Eddie yelled as he clutched his gun, pointing it randomly around the room. "Come in here and I'll blow your head off!"

The gun shook in his hand as he tried to clear his vision. He rubbed his eyes as if that would wipe away the day of drinking. Then the noises returned, an unmistakable beating, a rapping outside, the sounds circling around his trailer. Eddie followed the sound of the pounding with his gun.

"Get out of here! I'm warning you!" Eddie yelled.

The fear was now telling in his voice. "Whoever you are, whatever you are, go away!"

His threat was answered by an even more intense pounding as the sound continued moving around the outside of his double wide. The impact of the rapping reverberated through Eddie's body as the whole trailer shook.

His threats of being armed had no effect on the intruder. Actually, his shouts only served to embolden whatever was outside. He had to try another tactic.

"Okay, I'm calling the police!" he yelled as he reached for his phone.

The knocking suddenly stopped after his announcement.

Had his threat worked?

"I'm calling them right now," Eddie shouted. "You'd better get out of here!"

Eddie was about to dial 911 to make good on his threat but was stopped by a bright flash outside his back window. A moment later his trailer was plunged into total darkness. Unable to even see his hand before his face, Eddie felt in the pitch black for his phone. His hand fumbled across the receiver. He snatched it up and put it to his ear anticipating a dial tone. However, his hopes of calling for help were dashed. The line was dead.

He would have to do this on his own, he and his gun anyway. He wasn't about to be caught by surprise like Andy had been the night before. He knew someone was there and they were coming for him. The difference between him and Andy was that Eddie was forewarned. He wouldn't go down without a fight.

Eddie caught his breath as something slammed against the kitchen window. Instinctively throwing up his gun, Eddie squeezed off a round. The deafening shot shattered the window from where the sound came.

"I'm serious!" Eddie screamed as his eyes tried to pierce through the darkness which had engulfed his trailer. "I'm not scared of you!"

The banging continued again seconds later. This time the sound came from the direction of his living room window. Eddie whirled and fired in the darkness toward the sound of the noise. Flame erupted from the barrel of his thirty-eight momentarily illuminating the interior of the small trailer. His ears rang from the second concussion of his firearm.

"Get out of here!" Eddie yelled again. "I will shoot you!"

Then came the rocking of his trailer. The double-wide swayed as it was being pushed from outside. The rapping became ever louder on the trailer's siding.

Eddie moved toward the front door and peered outside trying to catch a glimpse of the intruder by the pale moonlight. He had to have a light, something to illuminate the darkness. Feeling his way back to the drawer in his bedroom, Eddie fumbled around until put his hand on the plastic cylinder of his flashlight. He turned it on hoping for safety the light would provide. However, Eddie was again disappointed. The batteries were dead. It was his only flashlight. How had he let the batteries in his only flashlight go dead? It had sat there for years doing nothing and now when he needed it, the batteries were dead.

He walked through the darkness back to the front door. His eyes were now adjusting to the dim light provided outside by the moon. Eddie wondered what to do. How would he get out of the situation alive? While Andy was a close friend, he wasn't too keen on joining him in the realm of the dead so soon.

Eddie realized he had three options as the rapping and rocking of his trailer continued. First, he could stay inside his dark trailer and wait for whatever was outside to come inside. Second, he could go outside and try to hunt down whatever was terrorizing him. And third, he could make a run for his truck and get away. Eddie decided to go with door number three. He would run to his truck, careful not to get ambushed as he rushed out the door. Then he would drive like a bat out of Hell, leaving his unwelcome visitor in his dust. It was a perfect plan, but then there are very few bad plans when you're drunk.

He grabbed his keys off the peg by the door and prepared himself for his dash. He could see his truck in the moonlight parked about ten yards from his front door. He could cover that ground, even drunk, in no time. Plus, he had a loaded gun. What could go wrong?

Counting to three, Eddie sprung from his front door. He pushed the flimsy trailer door wide open as he stumbled down the steps, rolling onto the ground at the bottom of the short flight. Eddie didn't waste time standing up as he scrambled on his hands and knees. He crawled toward his vehicle before righting himself as he reached his truck.

The keys! Eddie looked back as he held his gun in front of him like a shield. He strained his eyes back toward his trailer.

"There they are," Eddie said to himself as he found the keys where he had fallen at the foot of his stairs. He looked back and forth and then dashed back toward his steps. He quickly retrieved his keys from the ground and ran back to his truck.

He jumped into the driver's side and immediately locked his doors to prevent his visitor from crawling in the truck with him. He looked out through his windshield but saw no movement. Perhaps he had made the run without being seen.

Momentarily satisfied no one was charging at him, Eddie concentrated on getting out of there as he plunged his key into the ignition. Nothing! His truck wouldn't start! Turn the key as he might, the ignition wouldn't answer. The engine refused to turn over despite his cursing. Eddie suspected his truck had been sabotaged. Someone had intentionally disabled his vehicle to leave him trapped.

Now his options were down to two. He could either go inside and wait for the intruder to come inside or go hunting himself. This time Eddie would go with option two. He would turn the hunter into the hunted.

Eddie stepped out of his truck and realized for the first time he was still in his short sleeve work shirt. He had neglected to change out of his work clothes in all the excitement. Plus, in formulating his foolproof plan to evade his unwelcome guest, he had neglected in his inebriated state to put on shoes when he dashed out the door.

Even as his toes began to tingle from the cold, a thought occurred to him. His camping equipment, which included a lantern and emergency matches, were inside his shed behind the trailer. He would go there first and retrieve them. Light would even the playing field. If he could only see what he was hunting he could kill it.

Moving slowly his gun at arm's length, Eddie made his way toward his shed. Even the slightest noise caused him to jump and take aim. Had the intruder gone? Or, was the interloper hiding in his shed waiting for him? If the prowler was in the building, Eddie resolved, he would shoot him dead.

Eddie stood outside the shed trying to detect any movement through its small front window. The darkness inside the building kept him from catching a glimpse inside. Turning the knob, Eddie kicked open the door hoping to surprise anything that might be inside. He hesitated for just a moment before bursting inside like a gangbuster ready to open fire. He soon realized he was alone in the small shed. The only sound he could hear was his own breathing and the beating of his heart.

He wasted no time. The cold was quickly sobering him. He found his lantern and shook it, the sloshing telling him it was partially filled with kerosene. He reached deeper into the bag and found the matches. He would have light.

Exposed in the small building and quickly feeling the bite of hypothermia, Eddie decided to dash back into his house where he would have cover to light the lantern. Cautiously looking around before emerging from the building, Eddie bolted for his front door. This time he remained upright as he cleared the steps in one jump. He then ran through his front door, taking time to close and lock the door behind him.

Eddie placed the lantern down on the kitchen table and blew on his hands trying to get feeling back in his fingertips. His short misadventure outside the house chilled him to the bone. He went to work pumping the light, the hissing sound of kerosene soon becoming audible. He laid down his gun to lift up the glass so he could light the mantel. Striking his match, the light flickered to life in the otherwise dark trailer. The light gave him a sense of relative calm. The flickering of the match soon grew as the light of the lantern bathed the kitchen in its soft white glow.

It was just as he felt the jubilation after restoring light that he felt the presence behind him. It had approached him from the darkness as he was concentrating on the lantern. Whatever had been outside was now inside with him!

Eddie turned to face the presence. His body was stricken with fear, his heart in his throat as he looked at a figure with no face standing inches behind him. It was the form of a man, a dark man, standing like a statue, no movement, not even the sound of breathing.

Eddie was afraid to speak or to even scream as he stared in horror at the faceless figure. It was then he recalled his gun on the table by the lantern. It was just inches away. He would make a move. He knew it was his only chance to avoid joining Andy.

Without delay Eddie made a lunge for his gun, reaching out with his half-frozen right hand. He felt the cold steel for an instant. The gun, however, fell from his hand as a jolt of pain raced up his arm. He could no longer feel the cold steel.

Stunned by the sudden sensation, Eddie looked at the table where the gun still lay. Beside it was his severed hand!

Pulling the stub of his arm into the light, Eddie saw his blood pumping into the air like a fountain with each beat of his heart. He opened his mouth to scream but another blow from the machete silenced his horrified cry. His head fell from his shoulders, hitting the floor before the rest of his body could fall.

MEET THE PRESS

Sam reached for his phone. The incessant ringing ripped him from his sound sleep. His wife rousted just long enough to shoot him an annoyed look before turning over and pushing her head deep into her pillow.

"Sorry sheriff but Faulkner was afraid to call you two mornings in a row so he talked me into doing it," came the voice of Bo Davis as Sam looked at his clock.

The red digits revealed it was just after six in the morning.

"You better get on out here," Bo said in a serious tone. "We got another."

Still not fully awake, Sam rubbed his eyes as he tried to force himself into full consciousness.

"Another what?" Sam asked as he sat up in bed.

"Another body," Bo responded. "It's Eddie Young."

Sam slammed down his phone in frustration. Eddie's reluctance to cooperate the day before had likely cost him his life.

Sam played back his conversation with Eddie in his mind as he drove to the scene of the most recent slaying. Why had Eddie been less than forthcoming when they talked the day before - a day that would prove to be the last day of his life? What was he hiding? Did the secret he kept lead to his death?

One thing Sam knew for sure, sight unseen, the murders were related. They were likely the work of the same killer.

There was something that Eddie and Andy had been into, perhaps much earlier in their lives, that led to their demise. Had it dated all the way back to the Red Dog days or was he way off the mark?

It was like déjà vu all over again as Sam rolled up to Eddie's trailer. Yellow tape surrounded the scene of the crime. The driveway this time had three patrol cars already waiting in it. From the looks of things Sam was a late-comer.

"Crime lab boys are just a few minutes out," Bo announced as he came out to meet his boss in the driveway. "They're going to ask for their own office space here if we keep calling them every morning like this."

"I guess I'd just be wasting my breath asking if it's a homicide," Sam said.

He already knew the answer since he didn't figure Eddie for the type who would eat the barrel of his own gun or take a handful of pills.

"Oh yeah," Bo responded with a slight chuckle. "This is murder and then some."

Bo motioned the sheriff toward the door and followed as his boss walked up the same steps he climbed the day before when he questioned Eddie.

Sam's senses were immediately bombarded by the spectacle of a slaughterhouse. The room looked like something or someone had been put through a meat grinder. The veteran lawman actually gagged at the sight of the butchery.

Sam, from just inside the door, could see the severed hand on the blood-covered kitchen table. A gun was lying beside the pale appendage. Scanning the rest of the room, he realized something was missing.

"Where's his head?" Sam asked, eyeing the rest of Eddie's body.

Sam noticed Eddie was still dressed in the same clothes he was wearing the day before when he talked to him.

"You tell me," Bo replied. "We looked everywhere. It's

not here."

Sam looked his investigator in the eye realizing the lawman was being serious.

"Who takes a head? What am I going to tell his mother?" Sam posed.

The sheriff always dreaded notifying the next of kin. "You sure it's not here?"

"Positive," Bo said with assurance. "We've swept the entire property, even into the woods out back. No head."

Sam shook his head in disbelief. He rubbed his own neck in light of the macabre scene before him. It was then he realized something was missing besides Eddie's head.

"I wonder why he didn't leave a message this time," Sam declared, surprised the words weren't spelled out again given the fact there was plenty of blood available.

Bo calmly pointed toward the other side of the kitchen counter. Sam took the silent hint and walked around the counter. There on the tile floor of the kitchen were written the words in bright red letters – Red Dog.

"We definitely have a problem," Sam said.

Bo nodded in agreement as he looked at the carnage. "The question is who's next?"

With the smell of death starting to become overwhelming, the sheriff decided it was a good time to do a walk-around outside the trailer. Sam immediately noticed the broken windows, glass lying on the ground suggesting the windows had been broken from the inside.

"Looks like our victim shot them out," Bo declared as he ran his finger into what appeared to be a bullet hole in the molding around the kitchen window. "Whatever came to get him was outside first and he knew it. It looks like he was trying to shoot whatever it was before it got inside."

"Why do you keep saying whatever it is?" Sam asked. "We aren't dealing with a what; we're dealing with a who."

"If you say so, sheriff," Bo said as he shoved a dip between his cheek and gum. "If this is a who then he sure has some unresolved issues. Oh, and by the way, there was a passerby who lives about a quarter-mile down the road who said he thought he saw something, um, I mean someone, standing outside the trailer last evening. Our passerby said the guy was dressed all in black but it was dark out except for the moonlight so our witness couldn't provide a useful description of him. He didn't put any significance with it until today when he drove by and saw all this going on."

The fact the passerby would be no help in figuring out the identity of their killer meant the sheriff had to take a different tact in figuring out what led to Eddie's demise.

"Oh, by the way, the paper has already been nosing around," Bo noted. "I saw that Cliff had our passerby cornered across the road so the press probably knows what we know about the guy he saw here last night. I've not told them nothing. Told him had to talk to you if he wanted any information."

The sheriff ignored Bo's mini-briefing as he was deep in thought recalling his conversation with Eddie the day before. Sam shared his suspicions with Bo concerning Eddie's strange behavior during his interview. Perhaps the sheriff wasn't the only person Eddie spoke with that day.

"He certainly was hiding something," Sam declared. "Maybe he made some calls. Have Kendal subpoena his phone records. Let's see who he talked to on his last day. It's worth a shot. Maybe he even talked with his killer."

If Bo was Sam's right hand man then Kendal Parks was his left hand. The two sheriff's investigators were like night and day. Bo, the pickup-driving, deer-hunting, outdoor-loving country boy was the complete opposite of the prim and proper Kendal Parks who was always immaculately dressed with never a hair out of place. Moving to Castle County from a large city where he was a codes enforcer, Kendal was the brain trust for the department. He could recall every nuance of the law and was a stickler to detail. He was meticulous with all the cases crossing his desk. His progress was often slower than Sam liked but the outcome was always rock solid with all his cases ending in convictions.

His by-the-book approach to policing often left him and Bo at odds. The pair fought like cats and dogs, both too stubborn to compromise with one another as Bo would often adhere to the seat of his pants philosophy of police work. Their differences, however, were by design as Sam used the strengths of both their approaches to law enforcement to his advantage. The end result was that very few crimes went unsolved in Castle County - up until now.

"Who found him?" Sam asked as they completed their walk around the house.

"The electric company actually," Bo said. "They got a trouble call from a blocked number just before dawn and seeing how cold it is they sent a crew right out. When they got here they found what you saw."

"So our killer wanted to make sure Eddie was found this morning," Sam surmised. "It seems like our murderer is calling the shots so far. We need to change that."

Sam realized they still needed the Red Dog connection kept from the general public, leaving it only something the killer would know.

"Who knows about the writing on the kitchen floor?" Sam asked.

"Just me, you, and Faulkner," Bo responded. "The electric crew took off when they found what was left of Eddie and called us from the road. I don't blame them for getting out of here."

"Well, like last time, we keep this our secret," Sam insisted. "The less people know the better. We don't want the press to get wind of it yet."

"So what's your next step?" Bo asked as he pledged to keep the Red Dog angle quiet.

"I'm going to meet the press," Sam retorted, his response getting a strange look from Bo. "Sometimes the best news never makes it to the newspaper. I think I'm going to pay a visit to our old friend Cliff Chapman at the Castle Herald and talk about the old days."

Cliff Chapman was the Castle Herald. He had served as their crime writer for over forty years. When it came to Castle County, the veteran reporter knew it all, only a small percentage of which made it into the pages of the small town publication. Chapman had been with the company since the day of linotype and typewriters. He saw the paper business evolve to modern computers and digital cameras in recent years.

Despite being retirement age, the short gray-haired newsman refused to call it quits as he doggedly changed with the times. His old-school brand of news writing was still apparent in his stories. Even his appearance was old-school, a pipe always in his mouth as he looked out from under the brim of his green visor like he was about to deal cards at a Saturday night poker game. Sam wasn't sure if he ever saw Cliff smoke the pipe in the all the years he'd known him and wasn't sure why the old reporter would wear the visor even on cloudy days. One thing Sam did know, however, was if it happened in Castle County then Cliff knew about it. He was about to put his faith in Cliff to the test - the subject of that test being the Red Dog Saloon.

"Well, hey sheriff. I was just about to call you," Cliff said as Sam walked into his office.

The reporter didn't hesitate for the normal pleasantries. "I hear you found another dead one this morning. Are we looking at a serial killer or what? Bo wasn't too forthcoming today. He told me I had to talk to you."

Taking a seat across the desk from the senior writer, Sam gave him a grin. He was entertained by the newsman's eagerness to get the scoop.

"It's good to see you too, Cliff," Sam said as he settled into the old steel chair which Cliff no doubt used for visitors to keep their visits short and to the point. "As for your question, I can't really say we have a serial killer but I can say for the record we think the crimes are related."

Cliff puffed on his unlit pipe, jotting down notes on his reporter's pad before shooting the sheriff a glance across the desk.

"I hear our boy is missing his head," Cliff said without segue. "I also hear someone who passed by that night reported seeing a man dressed all in black - a dark man they called him - lurking outside his trailer."

His question provided the sheriff with a bargaining chip, presenting an exchange which could benefit both of them.

"Tell you what Cliff, you help me and I'll help you. How does that sound?" Sam proposed. "I need your help on these cases but I need you to keep the subject of what we're about to talk about off the record."

"Off the record huh? Well, I suppose I could do that so long as once this is over I'm the first to get the whole skinny," Cliff responded. "What about the head?"

"Tell you what Cliff, you help me out and before I leave I'll tell you all about the head," Sam offered.

His bargain was readily accepted by the small-town journalist. Cliff was intrigued since he was rarely called upon to help solve a case.

"Deal," Cliff answered as he leaned forward interested in what was on the sheriff's mind. "So what's this matter that you need my help on? I'm all ears."

"What do you know about the old Red Dog?" Sam asked.

His question obviously set the wheels rolling in the reporter's mind. Cliff sucked his empty pipe and furled his brow.

"Wow, the old Red Dog," Cliff repeated as he reclined in his chair, lacing his hands behind his head. "Funny how that place won't die after all these years. So do you think there's a connection between these killings and the old saloon?"

"Hey, you're supposed to be providing the answers right now, remember?" Sam pointed out. "I'll return the favor in a few minutes."

Cliff nodded in agreement. He squinted almost like he was trying look back in time and access the long forgotten drawer where he had deposited the Red Dog file.

"Let's see," Cliff began. "The Red Dog was built sometime back during the 1950s off East Ridge Highway. It started out as just a little package store, not really much more than a shack. Over the years the owners kept adding a little here and a little there until it grew into a regular bar. Actually, it was quite a popular little hang out during the sixties and seventies. There were a lot of folks who would head out there on Saturday nights for dancing and drinking. They even had a Bingo game out there on Tuesdays. Back then it wasn't that bad. Sure you'd get a fight here and there, but it wasn't anything your regular bar doesn't see. It was one of those places you'd go with sawdust on the floor, peanut shells crunching under your feet, thick with cigarette smoke."

Lowering his tone, Cliff recalled a change that came over the well-known club in the early eighties.

"At some point Earl Cutts took over the place. I believe it was sometime in the eighties," Cliff revealed. "That's when things started to change. See, it was around then they passed legal liquor in Easton so bars started popping up, nice pubs folks could go to instead of the old Red Dog which was getting pretty long in the tooth by then. Plus the Red Dog was out in the country located right on the most dangerous curve in the whole county. Frankly, whoever built the place should have had his head examined. I know of at least two people who got killed out there by wandering out in the highway which was just a few steps from the front door of the bar. I mean drunks and traffic don't mix.

"Now, once the decent folks started frequenting the clubs in the city, the Red Dog turned into a hangout for thugs and rednecks. As I think you know, back during the eighties and until it burned down in the nineties, you didn't go out there unless you knew how to use your fists. It was the first place some folks stopped after they got out of the penitentiary and was pretty popular with your wannabe tough guys. Of course the fact Earl Cutts ran the place added to the issue since he didn't care much what went on, especially since he was dealing more than alcohol from behind his bar. We're talking cocaine, pot and pills. It was like a drug store.

Sam stopped the story teller for a moment, wondering aloud about any incidents that could have left bad blood over the years. Cliff scratched his scraggly beard as he considered the question for a moment.

"There were a couple of stabbings out there but those were over women," Cliff began as pressed his brain for details. "And there was Jim Cole who was beaten to death with a pool cue out there. That was reportedly over a gambling debt. They charged Sid Bouldin with it but the jury ended up hung since all the witnesses as well as the victim were drunk when the killing happened. Some even claimed Earl Cutts did it himself trying to break up a brawl before they busted up his bar. I guess we'll never know who did it for sure since Earl supposedly burned up when the Red Dog burned down."

"Supposedly?" Sam asked.

"Well, sheriff, if you'd bother reading my story on the fire you'd notice they only found his dentures in the rubble," Cliff responded. "Granted, it wasn't the most meticulous fire scene investigation in history since your predecessor did it but they did sift through what was left and didn't find any other remains. That's why my story read he was assumed dead."

"Couldn't the fire have been hot enough to incinerate his remains?" Sam posed.

"Sure, and that's probably what happened. It was a huge fire. The flames could be seen clearly all the way in town," Cliff agreed. "It really doesn't matter since Earl would be pretty deep into his eighties by now if he wasn't burned up in the fire."

"What did you mean about my predecessor?" Sam asked.

The sheriff caught the reporter's barb at the former sheriff's handling of the crime scene investigation.

"All I'm saying is no one went out of their way to figure out who torched the place," Cliff said. "They didn't even call in the fire marshal's office. They just worked it themselves, the sheriff's department that is, and shoved it in the closed case files. If you ask me they were glad Earl went up in smoke along with the old Red Dog. I got the feeling they really didn't want to find out who done it."

While enlightened by the reporter's chronicling of the history of the old bar, Sam was still disappointed as the newsman had been unable to shed any light on a connection between the murders and the long-gone tavern.

"I suppose a lot of secrets burned up along with the late Mr. Cutts," Sam surmised. "I'd hoped to find a common thread between our murders and the old bar but I guess that was just wishful thinking."

"Sorry I couldn't help you sheriff but I honestly can't think of anything that would have hung around so long, that is unless Earl Cutts has come back from the ashes to seek his revenge," Cliff chuckled as he banged his pipe on the edge of his desk as if to clean it out. "You don't believe in ghosts do you sheriff?"

"Hey, after the past couple of days I'm not so sure anymore," Sam admitted.

"Okay, your turn," Cliff countered. "I've shared my vast knowledge of local history, now it's your turn to give me the scoop on what happened out there this morning. Your men have the place sealed off tight."

"Yeah, I told them to keep the press away," Sam quipped. "Especially old farts that carry pipes. Do you ever smoke that thing?"

"Smoking is bad for you sheriff," Cliff responded as he indignantly shoved the pipe back in his mouth. "Now tell me about our latest murder. You can start with our victim's name. Your boys wouldn't even give me that."

Sam was surprised the veteran reporter hadn't been able to get the name already. He must be slipping in his old age.

"Our victim's name is Eddie Young, age forty-two, an employee of..." Sam began before being cut off by the newsman.

"Eddie Young?" Cliff asked. "As strange as it sounds, that rings a bell."

"It should. He's lived here all his life," Sam responded. "You probably had him on a couple of your court dockets."

"No, I mean it rings a bell with what you were talking about," Cliff clarified. "Eddie and our last victim, Andy Crouch, was old running buddies and frequented the Red Dog."

"Yeah I knew that," Sam said. "I went there a couple of times back in the day myself."

"It's more than that sheriff," Cliff continued. "They were part of a little clique that kind of ruled the roost out there just before the fire closed the doors permanently."

"Ah, okay. So I suppose they made some enemies then," Sam said. "Anyone in particular you can recall?"

"Actually, now that you put the two together, yes, there was something," Cliff said, his comment causing the sheriff to raise an eyebrow. "It was really little more than rumor. Nothing was ever proven but there was a lot of talk and this was right before the fire."

"Well, don't keep a man waiting," Sam said with a tone of excitement in his voice.

"Word was that not long before the fire there was an incident that happened out at the club involving the group your two recent victims were in," Cliff began. "They hung out with three or four tough guy wannabes pretty well every Saturday night."

"Any recollection who these other guys were?" Sam asked.

Sitting silently in deep thought, it was apparent Cliff was trying to rip the memory from the back of his mind.

"One of them was none other than the sheriff's own son," Cliff began, referring to Bart Foster.

Cliff's recollection confirmed Sam's suspicion that Bart was connected with the first two victims. Something in the sheriff's gut told him Bart was deeply involved in whatever was going on.

"I think another was Stevie Grissom." Cliff added after another moment of thought.

Cliff paused again in an attempt to recall the other names, his face pained as he pushed himself to remember. He reluctantly gave up, hopelessly stuck.

"I can't remember the other two, or maybe there were three," Cliff admitted. "I may not have even known them anyway, I just know there was a gang of six or seven and they were real hellions."

"Okay, so you say there was something happened involving their group," Sam interjected.

"Yes, well the rumor was that one night there were some girls went out there, young girls, teenagers," Cliff said.

The old newsman leaned forward as one often would when repeating a rumor.

"At some point the other girl, or girls, went home and left one of them alone there with that drunken group of thugs. Well, one thing led to another and the girl was raped by them, gang raped from what I heard."

"Why didn't I ever hear about this?" Sam asked. "This is the first time I've heard anything like that."

Sam had lived in Castle County all his life with the exception of his time in the military. He figured he would have heard about something as heinous as a young girl being raped at the shady night spot.

"Well, first off, there were never any charges brought so that's why you didn't see it in the pages of the newspaper," Cliff began. "And second there never was an investigation since the sheriff's son was right in the middle of it. Word was the girl was either run off or paid off and the whole thing was dropped. It wasn't long after that the bar burned down and their old gang broke up."

"Do you remember the girl's name?" Sam inquired. "Any idea where she went or who her family was or even who she was with that night?"

"I'm sorry sheriff but I've slept since then," Cliff responded, obviously irritated with his own memory. "But if it comes to me I'll call you."

"You do that if you would," Sam requested.

The sheriff was encouraged by Cliff's recollections despite the obvious holes in the old reporter's memory.

"Okay, now, about the head," Cliff asked as he looked for his reward for the information he had just provided.

"Gone," Sam shot back.

"Gone?" Cliff asked.

"Yes, nowhere to be found," Sam confirmed. "We assume the killer took it with him as a souvenir."

"Do have any idea on the murder weapon sheriff?" Cliff wondered.

"Yes, something sharp," Sam quipped as he got up to leave. "I'll call you once we have anything else we can tell you. You do the same with me if you recall anymore names. And remember, mums the word on the whole Red Dog thing. And, it's up to you, but for Eddie's mother's sake, keep the whole missing head thing on the down low if you would. He's having a closed casket and she never actually viewed the body so she doesn't know his head is, well, that his head isn't with the rest of him. It's up to you but I'd say "Dark Man Sought in Killing Spree.". I think that might sell a few papers."

"You have my word, sheriff," Cliff said, crossing his heart. "Just make sure I get the exclusive and the book rights. And I like the headline. If you ever get tired of being sheriff come down here and I'll put you to work."

Sam was intercepted by Kendal Parks as he stepped out the door of the paper. The trim, slightly balding investigator pulled into the parking lot just as the sheriff exited the building.

"I got them," Kendal said as he waved a handful of papers. "It took a little bit but I got them."

Sam scratched his head as the excited investigator jumped out of his car. What was the detective talking about?

"The phone records," Kendal reminded the sheriff. "We know who Eddie Young called and when. All he had was a landline. His cellphone was cut off for nonpayment."

His eyes lighting up given Kendal's quick work, Sam took the documents from his investigator.

"Nice work, Kendal," Sam said.

The investigator beamed with pride from the sheriff's compliment.

Scanning the paper, Sam immediately noticed several calls the day of Eddie's death to the same number. Only one of the calls took up any time.

"Do we know who this call was to?" he asked as he pointed to the frequently called number; the first call made around the time Sam visited Eddie's home.

Kendal referred to his notes and promptly provided the answer.

"That would be Foster Motors," Kendal replied. "It's actually registered to Bart Foster."

Sam ran his finger down the page of numbers and came to the last call made in the mid-evening hours. The single number reflected a call lasting about five minutes.

"Who's this?" Sam asked as Kendal again referred to the papers.

"That would be to a Karen and Stevie Grissom," Kendal replied.

His answer sent up a red flag. "Bingo!" Sam exclaimed.

"Excuse me," Kendal said, wondering what caused the

sheriff's reaction.

The sheriff didn't want to reveal his suspicions until he had a few more pieces of evidence to support the theory so he decided to keep his thoughts to himself. He also didn't want to reveal what could be a crack in the case to one investigator before the other since that could cause issues between the two lawmen who often seemed more like jealous siblings rather than fellow officers of the law.

"Nothing," Sam replied with a bit of guilt. "Well, maybe nothing, maybe something. I'll let you know when I know."

Confused by his boss' odd statement, Kendal chalked it up to overwork and the stress of having two unsolved homicides in his county.

"If you say so," Kendal said.

Stepping back in his cruiser, Kendal revealed he was going to meet with the crime lab techs back at the murder scene.

"I'll let you know if they find anything," the detective promised as he pulled away.

Now armed with a possible connection between the Red Dog and his two murder victims, Sam made a calculated gamble. He realized Bart would have been the ringleader of the group given his reputation both then and now as an alpha male. Sam would make a play for the weak link, Stevie Grissom. Perhaps the fact two of his former running mates were dead, both victims of grisly murders, would scare him into being forthcoming unlike Eddie the day before.

Sam pulled up to the Grissom home in the upper middle class neighborhood of Easton. He immediately noticed a minivan in the drive. Maybe he would have better luck than he had the day before.

Sam rang the doorbell and was soon greeted at the door by Stevie Grissom. His eyes gave him away as soon as he saw the lawman standing at his door.

"Mind if I come in?" Sam asked.

He immediately noticed Stevie's body language which told him his reluctant host was very nervous about the sheriff's visit.

Why would a good, law-abiding citizen be nervous to see the sheriff?

"Um, sure sheriff," Stevie stuttered, looking around outside as if to see if any of his neighbors were watching.

Sam stepped into the nicely decorated house. A woman's touch obvious in the décor.

"Is anyone else here?" Sam asked as he did a look around inside the well-kept house.

"No. I'm about to pick up the kids at school in a few minutes," Stevie responded in a nervous voice. "The wife is at work at the hospital. She's the administrator there."

"I see," Sam said. "So you're off today?"

Stevie responded in a quiet tone. He was obviously uncomfortable with the question.

"Well, I do some day trading from my home office, take care of the kids and things like that," Stevie replied.

"Ah, you're a house husband," Sam declared.

His description left Stevie with a look of embarrassment. He must not have cared much for the characterization.

"Don't worry Stevie; I'd do the same thing if I could," the sheriff smiled.

"So what can I do for you sheriff?" Stevie timidly asked.

"Actually it's what I can do for you," Sam replied. "I'm sure you've heard about your old buddy Andy Crouch being killed yesterday."

"Um yes, that was too bad," Stevie said. "I hated to hear that."

"Well, this morning we found another one of your friends ... Eddie Young," Sam said.

His revelation caused Stevie's face to turn white as a sheet. He wasn't prepared for the bombshell.

"We think the killings are related," Sam noted.

Stevie walked over to the kitchen table to sit down. He was visibly shaken by the news.

"I just talked to him last night," Stevie confessed with his eyes starting to well-up with tears. "We talked for a couple of minutes and then I put him off. I guess I should have took my time and listened to him. I didn't realize that'd be the last time we would talk."

"What did he call about?" Sam asked. "You know you may have been the last person he talked to."

Stevie's eyes shifted, his body language letting the sheriff know he was going to evade his question.

"Oh, nothing in particular. Just a bunch of ranting," Stevie replied.

Stevie became choked up given the realization he was likely the last person his old friend talked to.

"It sounded like he'd been drinking so I just kind of tuned him out," he noted.

Seeing Stevie was legitimately moved by the passing of his old friend, Sam pressed to establish the connection between him and the old Red Dog gang.

"You used to hang out with both of them didn't you? Eddie and Andy that is?" Sam asked.

"I suppose so but that was a long time ago, back when we were just dumb kids," Stevie responded as he refused to return the sheriff's gaze. "There's a lot that's changed since then."

"As a matter of fact I think you all had a little clique out at the old Red Dog Saloon back in the day didn't you?" Sam accused.

The sheriff's question left his host visibly shaking. Stevie rubbed his hands together nervously as he tried to repress his sense of panic.

"We did hang out there some," Stevie admitted. "It was something to do on the weekends."

Sam pressed on, detecting he was hitting a nerve. Beads of sweet began forming on Stevie's brow as the sheriff continued his line of questioning.

"Any idea why someone from back in the Red Dog day would want to see your old friends dead?" Sam asked with his eyes fixed on Stevie.

"No," Stevie stammered in an obvious lie. "What makes you think it has anything to do with the Red Dog?"

"We have evidence is all I can say... compelling evidence," Sam revealed. "We also have reason to believe whoever is doing this isn't through."

"What does that mean?" Stevie asked as he swallowed hard.

"That means we think someone is looking for payback for something that happened at the Red Dog," Sam declared. "Any idea of what that could be?"

Stevie sat silently, nervously shaking his head, denying he knew the killer's motive.

"Well someone is pretty mad ... mad enough to kill," Sam declared.

"I don't know what it would have to do with me," Stevie said. "I haven't hung out with that group in years. I'm a totally different person now."

"You know there are some things for which there's no redemption," Sam said in a serious tone.

Stevie was in a state of panic, something he was trying, unsuccessfully, to keep from his visitor. He had to get out of there or he would break down. He wasn't built for this kind of stress.

"I'm sorry sheriff but I don't know anything else," Stevie said as he stood up from the table and glanced at his watch. "Now, if you don't mind, I need to be picking up the kids. It's almost time for school to get out and you know how the traffic is around the campus."

Sam realized Stevie was heading down the same road of denial as Eddie did the night he was killed.

"Something happened at Red Dog years ago, something very bad," Sam began. "I think you know what it is."

"I don't know what you're talking about sheriff," Stevie claimed as he grabbed his coat as if he were about to go out the door.

"There was a girl," Sam blurted out.

Stevie stopped dead in his tracks. He forgot to even breathe. His worst nightmare was coming to pass. Someone knew what happened.

"A teenage girl," he pressed on. "Something very bad happened to her that night."

Stevie turned around to face the sheriff and spoke in a pleading voice. Tears were now rolling down his cheeks as he shook like a leaf.

"I have a wife and kids, sheriff," Stevie began. "I can't ... I mean she would leave me if she ever found out."

Stevie's words had confirmed his suspicions. He also knew Stevie would likely be in the crosshairs of the killer if his theory was right and the killings were payback for what happened to the teenager many years ago.

"We can protect you," Sam declared. "You just need to tell me what happened back then so we can figure out who's behind this. And better yet, who may be next."

Stevie refused his offer, shaking his head frantically.

"I can't sheriff," Stevie said. "If my family ever found out, well, let's just say I'd rather be dead. And what makes you think it's a who anyway?"

"You very well may be next if you don't let me help you," Sam said in a foreboding voice. "And I assure you, whoever is doing this is very much flesh and blood. There's no such thing as ghosts."

"I'm sorry but I just can't," Stevie said as he pulled on his jacket and walked out the door. "I've got to pick up the kids."

The sheriff followed Stevie as he quickly walked to his car and started the engine. He leaned down into his window to offer one last plea.

"You're making the wrong decision," Sam argued. "Let

me help you."

"I don't have a choice," Stevie responded as he backed out of the drive barely missing the sheriff's foot. "The decision is out of my hands."

Sam watched as Stevie sped out of sight leaving him standing in his driveway worrying that may be the last time he would see him alive.

Meanwhile, eyeing the sheriff from his rear-view mirror, Stevie reached for his cellphone, nervously dialing as he rounded the corner leaving the sheriff's sight.

"Bart we got big trouble," Stevie began in a panicked tone as his call was answered. "The sheriff just came to see me and he was asking all sorts of questions. He was asking about the Red Dog. He knows, Bart, he knows!"

"Calm down Stevie," Bart urged his old friend, caught off-guard by Stevie's frantic call. "He doesn't know anything. He's just fishing."

Stevie disagreed as he believed the sheriff knew more than he revealed during the short meeting.

"He's says whoever is doing this is out to get everyone who was involved back then," Stevie continued. "I thought this was all over. How can it come back after all this time? Is it him? Has he come back to get revenge?"

Bart was worried Stevie was going to crumble under pressure. He decided the best course of action was to reassure his nervous friend rather than demean him. Stevie, if left to be consumed by his fears, could become a weak link.

"The sheriff was just trying to scare you," Bart said in a calm voice. "It's an old cop's trick. Trust me. My father did the same thing when he was sheriff when he wanted to get people to talk."

"But Andy and Eddie ... someone killed them," Stevie said in a worried voice as he navigated his car through the streets of Easton. "I was probably the last to talk to Eddie last night and he was scared. He knew something was out there to get him."

No longer able to hold his tongue given Stevie's wild talk, Bart tried to set him straight.

"Someone, you mean," Bart corrected. "It's not a something, it's a someone."

"Regardless, what are we going to do?" Stevie asked. "Any one of us could be next."

"We just have to be careful," Bart said as he returned to his calm voice. "Eddie and Andy, they weren't like us. We're from the other side of the tracks. We just have to hang together and be careful. Give him time and he'll slip up. When he does, we'll take care of him just like we took care of the problem twenty years ago."

"Did we, Bart? Did we really take care of the problem twenty years ago?" Stevie wondered aloud. "Because to me it doesn't look like the problem was taken care of. It looks to me like the problem is back."

"We'll take care of it," Bart said with confidence. "All we have to do is stick together. Let's not turn on one another after all this time. By the way, you didn't tell the sheriff anything did you?"

Stevie's silence on the other end of the line was worrisome to Bart. What had he told the sheriff?

"Well, did you tell him anything?" Bart asked. "Tell me you kept your mouth shut."

"I didn't tell him anything," Stevie answered in a quiet tone.

His assurance was not fully convincing. Bart knew Stevie quite well and knew he wasn't the type to cope well with adversity.

"See you keep it that way," Bart warned. "One loose word and we're all sunk."

"I'm scared, Bart," Stevie confessed. "Not only is there someone hunting us like animals but the law is closing in. I've got too much to lose. I can't deal with this now."

"Keep it together!" Bart yelled as he finally lost patience

with his scared friend. "Give me some time. I'll figure it all out. Just leave it to me. I got us out of it before. I'll do it again."

"You promise?" Stevie asked. "I don't know if I can take this. It's too much pressure. I'm still shaking."

"You got it old buddy," Bart assured. "I've got your back."

"If you say so, Bart," Stevie said meekly.

"You just sit tight and keep your mouth shut, okay?" Bart said. "I'll take care of the problem."

JAILHOUSE RAT

Standing in the driveway plotting his next move, Sam realized his only play was with Bart Foster. He also knew it wasn't much of a play at all since the street-wise car salesman wasn't keen on speaking with him in the first place. Despite being the son of a former lawman, Bart didn't have the best reputation. The slick car dealer was rumored to be involved in dealing in more than used cars.

If he hadn't been able to break the weakest link, the chances of getting the shady businessman to reveal anything were slim to none. Had he reached a dead end, left to wait until the killer struck again?

His thoughts were interrupted by the ringing of his cellphone. The sheriff had doggedly hung on to his clamshell flip phone rather than give in to technology and upgrade to the so-called smart phones.

"Yeah," Sam answered in a short tone.

"Hey sheriff, it's Cliff," came the voice from the other end of the line.

"Did you remember the girl's name?" Sam asked with a tone of excitement.

"No, sorry sheriff, but I'll keep working on it," Cliff apologized. "It'll come back to me at some point."

"I hope it's within the next couple of years," Sam quipped. "Not to put pressure on you or anything like that."

Cliff chuckled at his own weak memory and offered his latest recollections, one that would prove to be fascinating to the sheriff.

"I didn't remember her name but I did recall another one of the group that was supposed to be involved that night," Cliff revealed. "Actually it was quite by accident. I was going through some old dockets here doing some winter cleaning and I came across a name and the bells started ringing. I mean it was quite a twist of ..."

"Just tell me the name," Sam interrupted, putting Cliff back on topic.

"Rhody Turner," Cliff responded.

"Our Rhody Turner?" Sam asked.

"Yep, the one and the same," Cliff confirmed. "There's only one Rhody Turner. They broke the mold after they made him."

"Thank goodness for that," Sam responded; given the fact Rhody was a regular in his jail. "That changes things quite a bit I'd say."

"Glad I could help," Cliff said. "Now remember, I get the exclusive once this thing breaks."

"Yeah, yeah, you got it but I need that girl's name," Sam urged the newsman. "Go to a hypnotist, do some chanting around the fire or anything you have to do. Just get me that name."

"It'll come sheriff, it'll come," Cliff guaranteed before hanging up.

Sam called his wife immediately after hanging up with Cliff, dispensing with the niceties.

"Hey baby, do we have Rhody Turner in jail?" Sam asked in an excited voice.

"Um, who is this?" Carly replied. "My husband doesn't like me to talk to strangers."

"How many guys call you baby?" Sam countered. "So do we have Rhody or not?"

"Yes we do," Carly announced.

Her response was what he was looking for. Sam pumped his fist. Finally he'd caught a break.

"And, he's not going anywhere soon," Carly added. "The

feds have a hold on him. He's facing meth charges for that last meth lab they caught him with."

"What's he looking at?" Sam asked. "Is this going to be a long term?"

"Given his long record, his file is one of the thickest in the drawer by the way, he could get upwards of fifteen years this time," Carly answered.

"Great!" Sam responded.

"Well, I don't know if that's how he sees it," Carly quipped.

"It gives me some bargaining room," Sam clarified. "Make sure he sits tight, I'll be back in a few minutes. I may even take my favorite clerk out for dinner tonight."

"Okay, I'll tell her," Carly laughed as she always enjoyed when her husband loved her for her brain as well as her body.

Sam called Bo on his cellphone, opting not to broadcast what he had to say to his detective on the police scanners across Castle County.

"We may have gotten a break in the Red Dog cases," Sam told his chief investigator.

The sheriff outlined what he had found out so far to his detective.

"I say we get Rhody out and work him," Sam recommended. "Maybe we can offer him a deal he can't refuse."

Joining up at headquarters, which was connected through a walkway to the county jail, the lawmen set their game plan. They would work on the assumption Rhody already knew about the deaths of his former running buddies since news traveled fast in the small town. Even inside the jail the communication network was second to none.

Sam directed a jailer to escort Rhody from his cell to the interview room. The officers waited his arrival with eager anticipation realizing the inmate was their best chance of determining who was behind the pair of grisly slayings. The officers also realized they were dealing with a professional criminal who was wise to the ways of law enforcement. Rhody had been in the system since he was a juvenile. He began his walk on the wrong side of the law as a petty thief and shoplifter before graduating to more serious crimes as an adult. His rap sheet was several pages long, full of burglaries, larcenies and drug convictions. As such, Rhody had spent much of his life behind bars, his education coming from the jails and penitentiaries in which he served his time. In layman's terms, Rhody was institutionalized and somewhat of a jail house lawyer in his own right.

Considering the other members of the old Red Dog gang, Rhody was the one who didn't seem to belong. While being partiers and immature fun-lovers that never really grew up, both Andy and Eddie made decent lives for themselves. Their crimes were only minor and usually had to do with having too much to drink. There was even more of a contrast between Rhody and the other two members of the group, Stevie and Bart, both of whom moved on after their "wild days" to make comfortable lives for themselves. Why would they choose to associate themselves with Rhody, who, even twenty years ago, was bound for failure?

In Sam's estimation, the unusual pairing of bed fellows likely had to do with their desire for a tough reputation. In modern-day terms, the group wanted to be "gangster" despite not having the credentials. By including Rhody in their clique they were involving a real-life criminal while the rest of the group were simply playing the role of criminals until they returned to their normal homes after a night at the 'Dog. In the sheriff's opinion, the old gang was a big act, each member fulfilling his desire to be feared and respected even if it were just on the weekends at a small redneck bar.

"Oh no, did you find where I hid the gold?" Rhody asked mockingly as he was led into the interview room in shackles.

The thin, scraggly-haired inmate was dressed in his old-school black and white striped uniform that all inmates in

Castle County Jail wore as standard costume.

"You're not getting nothing from me, copper," he declared with a yellow-toothed grin. "You'll never take me alive."

Rhody, sporting a smirk, took a seat in the chair opposite the sheriff as Bo stood against the wall. His arms were covered with jail-house tattoos much like a steamer trunk is covered in stickers by a world traveler. Rhody rubbed his hands together, his movement restricted inside his handcuffs. The inmate glanced around curiously at the lawmen, trying to size up what they wanted.

A single black tear drop below his right eye caught the sheriff's attention. The veteran lawman realized that such tattoos were often used by inmates to represent a life they had taken. The sheriff also knew some inmates would get the tattoos to simply give them more credibility behind bars, hoping to intimidate other inmates. Sam wasn't sure which was true of the inmate, although studying Rhody's rap sheet there were only a couple of convictions for assaults. And, all of those came from drunken brawls and drug deals gone bad. Rhody didn't have the reputation of a violent criminal. He was a meth cook.

"Okay guys, make this snappy. I need to get back to my drawing room for a game of cards by three," Rhody quipped. "I stand to win a pack of cigarettes and a shiv if luck is with me today."

Sam returned the confident smile of the inmate as he started to play his hand.

"You better smoke those cigs quick, Rhody," the sheriff said knowingly.

"Why's that?" Rhody asked. "You planning to let me out early for good behavior, sheriff?"

"Well, from what I hear, there's a couple of federal marshals coming to take you off our hands at the first of the week," Sam revealed.

The sheriff's declaration wiped the smug smile off

Rhody's face.

"Looks like you'll be leaving good old Castle County for quite a while." Sam noted.

Rhody swallowed hard as he looked at both of the officers, trying to get a feel for what they were after. This wasn't his first rodeo.

"So what? Did you call me here to give me a going away party?" Rhody asked with a nervous laugh. "Where's the cake and the strippers?"

"No Rhody, this is the feds," Sam began. "I'm afraid you'll be going away for a long, long time. They've been giving meth cookers fifteen, twenty years in prison lately. They're really cracking down on you guys."

Rhody played the threat off as no big deal.

"Ain't nothing," Rhody claimed. "I can do it standing on my head."

Sitting back in his chair, sizing up the inmate with the neck tattoo sitting across from him, the sheriff questioned Rhody's resolve.

"How old a man are you now?" Sam asked. "What, forty, forty-one, forty-two?"

"What's it to you?" Rhody countered. "You ain't never got me no birthday present."

"Well, I'm just sitting here doing some figuring," Sam continued. "Now math was never my long suit, did real bad at it in school, but it seems to me that if they put fifteen years on you at this point then you're going to be an old man before you get out."

Staring across the table at the lawman, his fingers now rapping nervously on the table, Rhody remained silent. The sheriff's words had obviously hit their mark.

"I mean before, you'd be in and out," Sam said. "The longest stint you've done, according to my records, is three years. Now fifteen years, that's going to be a long row to hoe. You say you can do it standing on your head, well, I say that's a long time to be standing on your head. And, by the time you get out, that head you'll be standing on will be long since gray, that is if you ever get out. They say meth shortens your life and we all know you've had your share of the crank."

Rhody narrowed his eyes, his fists clenched in his cuffs. The once cool and cocky inmate was now showing his anger. The sheriff had gotten in his head.

"Again sheriff, what's it to you?" Rhody asked. "You obviously have something on your mind so spit it out."

Sam looked at Bo and gave him a nod. The investigator then threw down a pair of photos on the table in front of the prisoner. The photos had instant effect. The hardened criminal's eyes were wide with shock. Before him were crime scene photos from the murders of Andy and Eddie.

"The one on the left is Eddie," Sam explained as he watched the inmate's reaction. "He doesn't have his head so I didn't know if you'd recognize him."

Staring at the pictures then looking up at the sheriff, Rhody cocked his head.

"What does it have to do with me?" Rhody asked. "I didn't do it. I've been in jail for days. You can't pin it on me!"

"For once, Rhody, you're not a suspect in a crime here," Sam agreed. "What you are, however, is a potential witness."

"A witness?" Rhody asked. "I don't know who did it and even if I did, why should I tell you pigs?"

"I was hoping you'd ask," the sheriff said. "What if I told you I might be able to help you out in your federal case? Would that interest you?"

"Well, of course," Rhody responded. "But I'm not a snitch. I'm not wearing a wire and I'm not rolling on anybody."

"I respect your loyalty," Sam countered as he looked the inmate in the eye. "The question is does your loyalty have a statute of limitations? Does it go back, let's say, twenty years?"

"What do you mean?" Rhody asked.

"The Red Dog," Sam said. "I have reason to believe something happened at the Red Dog years ago, before it burned down, and whatever that was is leading to your old friends being killed one by one. It's a good thing for you that you've got around the clock police protection."

"I don't know what you're talking about," Rhody responded as he slipped the sheriff's gaze. "I just went out there to drink once in a while, flirt with the ladies, you know, that kind of thing."

Studying the inmate, Sam was sure he was hiding something and he also suspected a little prodding might cause the hardened criminal to bare his soul, especially if the price was right.

"Oh well, that's too bad," Sam said as he stood up motioning to the guard who was outside the interview room. "I'd hoped we could help each other out. You know, I scratch your back and you scratch mine, but if you don't know then you don't know."

Sam walked over to talk to his investigator while giving Rhody a wave, instructing the jailer to take him back to his cell.

"Have a good life Rhody," Sam called out. "Drop us a letter sometime and let us know how you're doing in the federal pen."

Rhody stared down the lawman as he was led toward the door, confused by the sheriff's abrupt abandonment of the line of questioning.

"Wait!" Rhody said in a loud voice. "What if, let's say, I did remember something from back in the day. What would that get me?"

The sheriff had a bite on his lure.

"But you just said you didn't know anything," Sam countered. "Now do you or don't you? I ain't got time to be jerked around. Once the marshals come to get you it's out of my hands."

Rhody shook off the jailer's grasp, his look contrite, and his body language telling Sam he may be willing to deal.

"Let's say I can help you out with your little problem," Rhody began. "What kind of deal are we talking about?"

A smile crossed sheriff's face as he motioned for Rhody to take his seat again. He had set the hook.

"What if I could keep your case here?" Sam offered. "I mean that's still a couple or three years in the state pen but that's a lot shorter than what you're looking at in federal court. That's time you could literally do standing on your head."

Rhody shot the sheriff a serious look as he leaned forward.

"What about immunity?" Rhody asked. "I don't want to pick up a new charge by cooperating."

"I'm not asking you to testify," Sam declared. "I just want to know what happened back then. Who knows, it may even save your life since from what I understand you were just as much a part of it as your old crew."

The sheriff's statement threw Rhody off his game given the lawman's apparent insight.

"I've got to have immunity and I've got to have it in writing," Rhody demanded. "You give me that and I'll tell you everything you want to know."

The sheriff questioned his continued insistence not understanding his demand for immunity since Rhody was obviously versed in the law.

"You do realize the statute of limitations has run on what happened," Sam revealed. "I don't think immunity will be needed."

Rhody disagreed as he gave the sheriff a serious look.

"Oh for what I'm going to tell you I will need immunity," Rhody declared. "There's no statute of limitations for what I know."

Rhody's statement surprised the sheriff who thought he was ready for all scenarios. Were they talking about the same thing? As a jailhouse lawyer, Rhody should know the statute of limitations for rape was twenty years in their state.

"What are we talking about here?" Sam asked.

"When I have it writing sheriff," Rhody replied. "It's not that I don't trust you, it's just that a man has to protect his best interests."

Rhody held up his cuffed hands, motioning to the officer to take him back to his cell.

"I say James, once around the park and then home," Rhody said with a bad English accent as he stood up signifying the end of the interview.

"I've got to make a few calls so sit tight and we'll be talking again soon," Sam promised.

"You know where to find me," Rhody countered as he was led out the door.

Sam was excited for the first time in quite a while realizing they might be able to solve the case before the body count climbed any higher.

Getting a deal for a drug trafficker in exchange for information which could end a string of ghastly murders should not be a problem. Sam immediately placed a call to Easton Police Chief Denton Wood.

Sam and the city's chief of police had always been on good terms, their officers working in partnership on many cases over the years.

Sam's call to Chief Wood was prompted by the fact Rhody's case was a city case made by Easton's narcotics squad in cooperation with the DEA. Rhody was one of seventeen suspects rounded up last month following a year-long undercover sting aimed at taking a bite out of the meth business in Easton. The leaders of the meth operation, the cookers and main traffickers, were going to be taken by federal authorities for prosecution. Meanwhile the Smurfs, a term law enforcement often used for those who helped supply the ingredients for the meth, would be tried locally and face much shorter sentences. Rhody was one of the ringleaders, a cooker and a trafficker, and therefore was set for federal court. His only possible redemption was that he had not yet been indicted by a federal grand jury meaning his case could be kept locally so long as the chief went along with the plan.

But why wouldn't he? It would be like letting a nickel hold up a dollar, not jumping at the deal that could help catch a murderer. Trading a drug dealer for a killer would be a no-brainer. At least that's what Sam thought.

"I can't make that call," Chief Wood declared during his phone conversation with the sheriff. "I understand your situation and it shouldn't be a big deal but I have to consult with the mayor first."

"The mayor?" Sam asked with surprise in his voice. "Since when does he run the police department in Easton?"

Sighing on the phone, annoyed he was trapped between a rock and a hard place, Denton explained, almost embarrassed by his awkward situation.

"This meth round-up made the state headlines so it's a feather in his cap and this is an election year in the city and he's hanging his hat on the crackdown. You know, safer streets, nice place to raise the family-type thing," the chief explained. "Before I start dropping charges against one of the main movers and shakers in the meth business I need to consult just to cover my back side."

"How long is this backside-covering going to take?" Sam replied.

The sheriff was annoyed that he was being held up by the minor issue. Never in a million years would he have thought there would be an issue in getting cooperation from his law enforcement partners.

"We have a killer running around in case you haven't noticed," Sam noted.

"Can you give me until tomorrow?" the chief responded. "Like I said it shouldn't be any problem, I just want to make sure. After all, he signs my checks and I'd kind of like to keep my job. You know how paranoid folks get during election and this could be a close one."

While understanding the chief's situation, Sam still wasn't happy.

"Oh but wait, some of you don't even get contested anymore," the chief quipped about Sam's winning reelection without opposition. "That must be nice not having to answer to anybody."

"It does save a couple of bucks," Sam agreed. "Call me as soon as you find out because I've still got to work it out with the Feds before I can put it in writing."

"As soon as it's all clear I'll let you know," the chief promised as they hung up.

Sitting back in his chair, Sam looked out the window as the sun started to get low in the sky. Hopefully, his deal would come in time. Could Castle County go a night without another murder? Only time would tell.

MILK AND EGGS

Stevie's nerves were on edge all afternoon after his talk with the sheriff. His mind was going a thousand miles per hour after his talk with the sheriff. His feeling of dread grew as he saw the relative safety of the sun disappear over the horizon leaving darkness to envelope his refuge.

The family man jumped at the sound of every noise outside the house, every settling of their home causing him to cower in fear wondering if the mysterious killer was coming for him. Try as he might, he couldn't hide his deep-seated terror of the unknown. His face was telling on him.

"You're jumpy as a long-tailed cat in a room full of rockers tonight," his wife declared. "How much coffee did you drink today?"

Stevie didn't need any coffee to be hyper alert. Fear alone was keeping him vigilant. His wife, eyeing him over the cover of the paperback she was reading in the living room, made him realize his paranoia was apparent. He didn't want her to catch the scent that something was wrong.

"Yeah, that's it," Stevie agreed. "I must have had one too many I guess."

"I told you to go to decaf," she said plainly, his domineering mate always having the answers for everything. "You'll live a lot longer without all that caffeine in your system."

"Live longer, yeah right," Stevie muttered under his breath.

RED DOG SALOON

With the setting sun, Stevie's life expectancy came into question. He had never been scared of the dark before. Things had changed.

"What'd you say?" his wife asked as she looked over her bifocals at her jumpy husband.

"Oh nothing dear," Stevie innocently responded.

Given the fact he and his wife had two children, she had always forbade Stevie from buying a gun for home protection fearing an accident would happen. In the end, she wore the pants in the family so her word was law. Instead of a trusty firearm, they relied on Easton's finest that patrolled their section of the small city. After all, police response times are always quicker in the nicer parts of town and Stevie lived in one of the better neighborhoods.

Stevie played his conversation with the sheriff over and over in his head like it was on a loop. He realized Sam saw through his thinly-veiled lie given the fact he had never been much of a liar. He wasn't even a good poker player. His tells gave him away anytime he tried to bluff. Instead, Stevie protected his secrets by simply remaining quiet. The way he figured it, if he kept his mouth shut and stayed under the radar he wouldn't have to lie. His distortion of the truth during his conversation with the sheriff weighed on his conscience. How he wished he could come clean and bare his soul but he realized that wasn't possible.

Between his conscience and sense of dread, Stevie found his imagination running away with him. Giving in to his paranoia, he worked his way around the house. He looked out the windows and turned on every light, exterior and interior, for which there was a switch, knob or toggle. By the end of his mission lights bathed every inch of the grounds outside their two-story dwelling. If someone or something was coming to get him, Stevie wanted to see it coming.

He paced around the house like a sentry, walking his post as he made sure the deadbolts were secure and the alarm activated. He figured to kill him the killer would have to get inside. In the back of his mind he convinced himself if he could survive the night and break the string of homicides he would be clear, that is unless the killer picked one of the others from his old gang that evening. Regardless, he wanted to live through the night at a minimum. Perhaps he would revisit seeking the sheriff's help – tomorrow.

Along with his fear, Stevie had a feeling of frustration. After all, it had been more than twenty years since the incident for which he was sure retribution was being sought. Was there no such thing as redemption for one's actions, especially actions committed in the foolishness of one's youth? Stevie had changed, becoming a good citizen and family man. He had turned his life around and become a different person than he was back during the Red Dog days. He was even born again for crying out loud, baptized by submersion at the Baptist church where his family was regular attenders and tithes payers.

Why did he have to suffer along with those who were unrepentant for their actions? It just wasn't fair in Stevie's book. Unlike the others in the old group, Stevie had felt regret, the weight of their sin wearing on him for many years. It had been only in the past few years, with the birth of his children, that he no longer felt haunted by his past. Now the ghosts had returned with a vengeance.

He knew it would be a sleepless night. There was no way he could fall asleep given the possibility something was out there waiting for him. Stevie decided he would batten down the hatches and ride it out, locked away in his bunker. There was nothing that would make him leave the safety of his fortress.

"Stevie I need you to run to the store," his wife yelled from the kitchen.

He could scarcely believe his ears. Had she just asked him to go outside where the killer was waiting on him? This couldn't be happening.

"What?" Stevie called back feebly. "Can it wait until

tomorrow honey? It's already dark out. I've got my shoes off already."

"No. I need it tonight," she responded. "If it could wait until tomorrow I'd do it myself. I need milk, eggs and some cake mix. We're having a thing at work tomorrow and I promised to take something homemade. You don't want to make me out a liar do you?"

The store was located just a mile away but that was a mile too far since it took him outside his castle. He racked his brain trying to come up with a valid excuse to stay locked away inside his home.

However, brainstorm as he would, Stevie was at a loss to come up with a reason not to run the errand. After all, he couldn't just up and tell his wife there was a killer out there waiting to seek vengeance for something he did two decades ago. If he did then he would then have to explain what happened. That explanation would surely land him on the street and in divorce court. Stevie had to decide which he feared worse, his wife or the killer who may be waiting for him in the darkness.

"Yes dear. I'm going. I'll be back in a minute," Stevie said with a defeated tone in his voice.

A sick feeling formed in the pit of his stomach as he reached for his coat. He could almost feel the presence outside waiting for him.

Pausing for a moment to peek through the front window, Stevie took a deep breath and turned the deadbolt. Then, cautiously sticking his head out of the front door, he scanned his well-lit lawn making sure no one was lurking in the hedges before making a dash to his car parked in the drive. He pushed his fob to unlock the doors while on the run.

He wasted no time as he jumped into the driver's seat, immediately locking the doors behind him while still looking in all directions for any movement.

"Let's get this over with," Stevie said to himself as he started his vehicle.

Stopping at the edge of his drive, Stevie saw a car coming down the road. His paranoia returned with the approaching vehicle. What if it was the killer? What would he do? Stevie quickly generated a grandiose plan whereby he would race through his front yard in the family minivan and lead the killer on a death-defying chase through the streets of Easton.

His contingency wouldn't be needed as the oncoming vehicle came into focus. It was a patrol car. Stevie took a relieved breath. Maybe the sheriff had ordered a patrol of his neighborhood. Regardless, he was going to take advantage of the cruiser and use it as an escort to the store.

He quickly backed out of his drive and fell in behind the officer, following the patrol car all the way to the store before reluctantly leaving his escort to pull into the market parking lot.

"Halfway home," Stevie said to himself as he looked around to make sure no one was milling around in the parking lot before climbing out of his vehicle and briskly walking into the store.

He wasted no time collecting the items he was sent to purchase. He waited impatiently in line before checking out. Any other time a visit to the store at that hour of night would be a quick in-and-out affair. However, as luck would have it, everyone in line in front of him was apparently buying enough groceries to last the rest of the year and paying for them using coupons. Don't people ever read the sign "twenty items or less"?

With the groceries in hand, Stevie glanced at his surroundings and made a quick dash back to his van. He tossed the bag into the passenger seat not caring if he broke any eggs as he locked the doors and plugged his key into the ignition.

Nothing! The engine wouldn't turn over! His nightmare was now complete. He was a mile away from home on a frigid night with the snow just beginning to fall and there was a killer out there just waiting for him.

He turned the key a few more times but realized the issue wasn't going to fix itself. What was the problem? Perhaps the cold night had drained his battery. Sitting in his locked van for a minute, he considered his options. He couldn't hoof it home. That would leave him exposed with a killer on the loose. He would take a look under the hood first. He was in a well-lit parking lot as he took the precaution of parking right under a security light. If it were something he could fix he would fix it and be on his way. If he couldn't find the problem, he would have no option but to call his wife and have a tow truck pick up his van the next morning.

Repeating his careful scan of his surroundings, Stevie unlocked his doors and climbed out, reaching back inside to trigger his hood release. He spent another minute trying to find the secondary trigger underneath the hood before finally locating the lever.

The challenge of determining what was wrong with his vehicle was one Stevie accepted out of pride even given his fear that gripped him. Stevie was an accomplished mechanic. One of his pastimes was restoring classic cars. He prided himself on being quite the expert when it came to engines so having to call a tow truck would be admitting defeat. That would be an insult to his manhood as he saw it, or at least what was left of his manhood.

Poring over the engine, he looked for the problem, blowing in his hands as the cold quickly settled in his lungs thanks to the brisk wind. Then he found it, just a couple of minutes into his diagnosis. Luck was with him. His battery cable was loose.

He pushed the connection back on the post and hand-tightened the nut, snugging it up against the battery connection.

"That should do it," Stevie said to himself with a sense of accomplishment as he slammed down his hood, again looking around the parking lot.

He jumped back into his vehicle and wasted no time

locking his doors and again jammed the key into the ignition. It started! A sense of pride bubbled inside him taking his mind off his fears for a moment. However, as the old adage says, "pride goes before the fall". He should have checked his back seat.

LITTLE YELLOW CORVETTE

For the third day in the row the sun had scarcely broke the horizon before Sam's phone rang.

"You need to get over to Foster Motors," came the monotone voice of Kendal Parks.

The all-business detective dispensed with the pleasantries most people feel they must exchange when waking someone from a sound sleep.

Wiping the sleep from his eyes, reality set in.

"Is it Bart?" Sam asked.

The sheriff, even in his semi-conscious state, wondered if their killer had taken out the ringleader. He wasn't sure whether he felt dread or relief when it came to Bart falling victim to the killer.

"No, he's very much alive," Kendal replied.

The detective's answer was confusing since he was telling the sheriff to meet him at Foster Motors. If Bart was still among the living, why was he being summoned to the car lot?

"Who's dead then?" Sam asked. "Is it Stevie?"

"Well sheriff, to be honest, we don't know," Kendal replied. "I'll brief you once you get here. Let's just say it's ... complicated."

While Sam had hoped Castle County would go an evening without another slaying, he was realistic. The killer was becoming more brazen with each murder. With that in mind, Sam usurped the garage from his wife the night before and parked his cruiser inside the relative warmth of their two-car garage. The couple found out after buying the home several years ago that "two-car garage" is code for a garage which will barely hold one car and your junk.

Quickly making his way across town, it didn't take long for Sam to see the reason for his third consecutive morning wake-up call as he pulled into the sales lot of Foster Motors. Sitting in front of the office was one of Bart's favorite cars, his beautifully-restored yellow Corvette, a Stingray to be exact. Bart could be seen tooling about the town on most days. He liked showing off his toys and the 'Vette was his favorite plaything.

From what Sam had heard, Bart restored the car a couple of months ago along with his old friend, Stevie Grissom, who was somewhat of an expert when it came to classic vehicles. The pair were one of the few long-term friendships, from what Sam knew, which remained from the Red Dog days. The immaculately-restored Corvette was Bart's pride and joy.

That was why Sam couldn't believe his eyes when he saw the shiny yellow classic with large red letters on its hood reading ... Red Dog. So much for keeping it quiet, Sam thought as he got out of his cruiser. Several people were milling around looking at the spectacle. The number of gawkers included Cliff Chapman who was busy snapping pictures of the vandalism.

"I guess it's on the record now huh?" the old newsman said as he walked up to meet the sheriff. "I'm pretty sure that's not red paint on there."

"I suppose not," Sam sighed as he eyed the size of the letters which covered most of the long, shapely hood of the Corvette.

The reporter was right. The public appearance of the killer's bloody signature message meant there was no more keeping it something only law enforcement knew. It was now public domain. The Red Dog Killer had announced his presence to the world.

"Thought of that girl's name yet?" Sam asked. "I really need that name."

Sam figured the old reporter hadn't recalled the name but decided to ask anyway. Instead he was more captivated by the scene before him. The amount of blood needed to paint the car, if it was blood, meant whoever donated the crimson fluid was likely not still alive.

"I'm trying sheriff, honest, it just isn't coming," Cliff sheepishly responded.

Cliff was embarrassed by his sketchy memory. He had tried his hardest to pluck the name from the back of his brain. He went so far as to drink a six-pack the night before. He hoped the beer would relax him and allow him to recall the forgotten name. In the end, however, all the beer served to do was give him a buzz and leave him with a dull headache this morning.

"Well keep trying," Sam said. "It's important."

Walking over to the car, the sheriff hailed Kendal who was taking statements from some bystanders.

"Before you ask, sheriff, the red on the car has field-tested positive for blood," Kendal said.

"Do we have any idea who it belongs to?" Sam asked as he saw Bart standing at the door of his dealership watching him and his investigator talk. "I mean I don't think you can go to the paint store and buy a bucket of blood."

Rolling his eyes at the sheriff's off-the-cuff comment, the ever by-the-book detective continued his briefing.

"Not for sure, but we have a good idea," Kendal responded. "It seems Stevie Grissom went out for milk and eggs last night and never came home."

Sam already assumed Stevie was the donor of the crimson paint. The sheriff kicked himself for not being aggressive enough during his meeting at Stevie's home. Had he pushed the nervous suspect harder the day before or at least brought him in for questioning, he may have gotten him to give in. With a little more prodding Stevie may have come clean and, in turn, still been alive.

"It looks like our killer decided to go public," Kendal declared.

"Agreed," Sam replied.

The sheriff's attention was drawn to the numerous bystanders watching what was going on at the car lot. Sam couldn't help but wonder if their killer was standing nearby. Perhaps the killer had returned to the scene of the crime.

"Any idea what time this happened?" Sam asked.

"Someone found it when the sun came up this morning," the investigator replied. "Now, how long it was here before that is a mystery. I suppose it could have been anytime last night since they closed the lot at eight."

Leaning in toward his detective, Sam quietly issued his orders.

"I want you to get someone with a video camera to film the scene here and make sure the person working the camera films the people milling around," Sam directed the investigator. "Make sure to be smooth about it. If our killer is standing around, I don't want to scare him off."

Nodding to the sheriff, the detective walked over to his patrol car and pulled out the video camera he kept in his trunk.

"Hey kid, come here," Kendal said, hailing Deputy Faulkner who was working crowd control trying to keep motorists moving along.

Some of the rubberneckers were causing a traffic hazard as they slowed while passing in front of the dealership to see what was going on. .

Explaining his assignment and warning him to be low key, Kendal handed the young officer the camera and walked back to the sheriff.

"Word's got out," Kendal surmised. "Rumor is already on the street this has to do with the last two murders. They're saying it's a serial killer."

Sam realized common knowledge was wrong in this case. He understood what they were dealing with was not a deranged serial killer but was instead a revenge killer. Their murderer wasn't a thrill-killer nor was he doing it for fun. The killer, Sam believed, was out to set the score straight. For all he knew, the murders could have been planned for years.

For Sam the motive was obvious. It was the remaining targets that were unclear. Were there one or five? The one thing Sam knew for sure was that Bart was in the thick of what was going on. The question in his mind was whether Bart would be the next victim or if he was behind the string of murders. Frankly, Sam wouldn't put it past him although bringing focus onto his front door step, so to speak, didn't make sense if the businessman was involved in the slayings. Regardless, it was time to have a chat with the former sheriff's son.

Excusing himself as the crime lab team pulled into the parking lot, leaving the crime scene in Kendal's hands, Sam walked into the dealership office.

"Sheriff," Bart said coldly as Sam approached.

"We need to talk," Sam declared, not bothering to extend his hand to the businessman.

Bart motioned his guest to his posh office located in the back of the dealership. He immediately walked over to his small bar and grabbed a bottle of liquor.

"Care for one?" Bart asked as he poured himself a glass of whiskey.

"No thanks," Sam replied.

"That's what I figured," Bart retorted as he closed the bottle and took a sip of his drink. "Sit down."

"I think I'll just stand if it's all the same with you," Sam replied.

The sheriff didn't believe in pretense since he had never liked Bart. The salesmen always seemed shady. Plus, there were too many rumors about Bart's connection with the criminal element. Sam knew that "where there's smoke, there's fire" so he figured the businessman was less than reputable.

"Suit yourself, sheriff," Bart shot back as he took a seat in his large leather chair.

The businessman was not a fan of the sheriff, making their dislike for one another mutual. Bart didn't approve of the way Sam did his job. In Bart's eyes, no one could be a better sheriff than his father.

"So what can I help you with today?" Bart began. "I've got a yellow Corvette on the lot I'll sell you cheap."

Sam didn't care much for Bart's flippant attitude since they were probably looking at a third homicide.

"I guess you can start by telling me what happened at the Red Dog that has someone killing your old friends one by one," Sam said. "You do remember the old Red Dog, don't you Bart?"

Giving the sheriff a nervous grin, taking a loud sip of his drink, Bart ran his hand through his receding dark hair.

"I'm sure I haven't the slightest what you're talking about sheriff," Bart said innocently. "All I know is someone trashed my prize hotrod. I hope you guys can bring this dangerous vandal to justice."

"I think we both know what that is on your hood," Sam shot back in an agitated tone. "I'm not a doctor but I'd have to guess that someone who lost that much blood probably isn't with us anymore. By my way of thinking, your old buddy Stevie Grissom is probably the donor. You know, he's the guy who helped you restore your precious hotrod. Looks like to me someone's trying to send you a message."

Bart maintained his smile and leaned back in his chair.

"You know, sheriff, that a successful businessman like me makes a few enemies here and there," Bart began. "Maybe someone is mad about paying for the undercoating - that's a scam you know. Or maybe they didn't get what they wanted in a trade. Bottom line is that could be anything messing up my fine automobile. It's deer season for crying out loud. It's probably deer blood some rednecks drained out of a poor doe after spotlighting last night. You're seeing ghosts where they aren't any."

Sam delivered a steely glare as he stared down his host for a moment.

"So that's how it's going to be?" Sam declared.

"I suppose so," Bart retorted as he locked stares with the sheriff.

"In that case, good luck to you," Sam said. "I'm sure whoever it is out there will work their way around to you sooner than later."

Bart refused to break his staring contest with the lawman although the smile ran away from his face given the sheriff's comment.

"That sounds like a threat, sheriff," Bart said, narrowing his eyes. "Are you trying to scare me?"

"No, that's a prediction," Sam countered. "I can't help you if you won't help yourself."

Bart stood up from his desk and took a last swig of his drink. Then, slamming down his glass on his desk, he sneered at the lawman.

"It seems to me, sheriff, you aren't helping anybody," Bart declared. "It seems like there's a lot of people dying on your watch lately. I don't recall people dying left and right back when my father was sheriff."

Bart's statement ran all over Sam. He could feel the veins sticking out in his neck and the heat on his face. He was about to break red on his host.

"How about young girls getting raped at the old Red Dog?" Sam shot back. "I guess your father wasn't much good at solving that, especially when his boy was involved."

Sam's statement cut a nerve as Bart stepped from behind his desk and walked aggressively toward the sheriff. He stood eye-to-eye with the lawman.

"You better watch your mouth," Bart snarled. "You don't

need to be talking about things you know nothing about and you better not talk about my father. You aren't even in his league."

Sam now sported a smirk, realizing he had hit a chord. He could feel the hatred oozing from Bart. It was white-hot.

"At least I don't turn my head to a rapist," Sam countered. "Maybe dear old dad was into that type of thing. Did he like little girls too, Bart, or was that just a thing his son was into?"

Bart was a bright shade of red. He clenched his teeth and balled up his fists. He wanted to make his move.

"If you weren't wearing a badge I'd ..." Bart began.

"You'd what?" Sam interrupted. "This badge can come off real quick, tough guy. I'd like nothing better than for you to take a swing. But then you're the type who likes taking advantage of little girls. Fighting with a grown man isn't something you've got the guts to do unless your daddy is around to save you."

Bart eyed the lawman head to toe. He would like nothing better than to smack the smile off Sam's face. But he realized that was just what the sheriff wanted. He was baiting him. Plus, deep down, Bart knew the sheriff would wipe the floor with him in a fair fight.

"That's just what you want isn't it?" Bart said knowingly. "You'd love for me to take a swing at you. Then you could put me in your jail. Well, sheriff, I'm not going to give you that pleasure. I will, however, have to ask you to leave the premises."

"I'd love to do that but this is an active crime scene," Sam responded. "And as for having you in my jail, I'd rather have the pleasure of kicking your ass. Besides, one of your old Red Dog buddies is already a guest at my bed and breakfast. Remember your old friend Rhody Turner? Well, he's back at the jail just waiting to spill his guts about what went on out there twenty years ago. I'm sure what he has to say will be fascinating."

For the first time Sam detected nervousness in Bart, the cool customer shaken by his revelation.

"Rhody Turner?" Bart said nervously. "I wouldn't hang out with a loser like that even if he was buying the beer. He's nothing but a drug dealer and a liar."

"If you say so," Sam grinned as he turned to leave the office. "One thing I do know is he's safe as a baby in his mother's arms. I've got twenty bucks that says he outlives you, Bart. Maybe you should have punched me."

Bart was filled by a poison mixture of anger and fear as he watched Sam walk out the door. How he hated Sam Delaney. He would give anything to see the high sheriff six feet under.

His musing about wanting the sheriff dead was interrupted by the ring of his cellphone. Pausing to look at the caller identification, almost too mad to talk, Bart noticed the call was from Glenn Satterfield. He had to take it despite his overwhelming anger.

"What!" Bart snapped as he answered his phone.

"We have a problem," Glenn declared, ignoring Bart's rude answer.

"You have a problem?" Bart retorted. "Have you heard? I have one big problem right out front of my office. Plus the sheriff is nosing around here asking all kinds of questions."

"Yes, news travels quickly around Easton," Glenn agreed. "Does he know about the Red Dog?"

"He thinks he knows," Bart responded. "But we don't need to be talking about this on the phone. He's figured out I'm involved in something having to do with the old Red Dog. He just can't prove it."

"What about me?" Glenn asked. "Does he know about me?"

"I doubt it," Bart replied. "I think he's still fishing."

Giving a sigh of relief, Glenn's tone remained all business.

"I need you to come down to my office," Glenn said.

"I kind of have my hands full here right now," Bart countered as he parted his blinds and watched several officers milling around his car. "They think it's Stevie this time."

"Just get on down here right now!" Glenn yelled. "I don't care what's going on down there, drop what you're doing and get over here."

Glenn's insistence caught Bart by surprise. The car dealer was intrigued by the emotion in the usually calm voice of his life-long friend. What could be so important? Glenn wasn't the type to be over dramatic. For Glenn to be rattled meant something was amiss.

"Trust me, get down here now," Glenn urged.

"If you say so," Bart replied.

Bart hung up the phone and immediately headed for the back door. He slipped out, making sure he avoided the collective eye of law enforcement. He didn't want any further run-ins with Sam. There would be time to settle that score later.

Parking in front of Glenn's office after a short drive from the dealership, Bart hustled inside. A secretary motioned him on back to the office. She was used to seeing the businessman visit so she thought nothing of his morning arrival.

Finding Glenn's office door locked, something that was unusual in Bart's experience, he paused to rap on the door. Things were getting stranger by the minute. Since when did Glenn lock his door?

"What gives?" Bart asked as the door swung open.

Glenn reached out and pulled his friend into his office before stepping out to look up and down the hall. He then closed the door and locked it.

"What's up is we got big trouble partner," Glenn declared with his eyes wide. "We got big trouble."

"I'd say so," Bart agreed. "In case you haven't heard, my car was covered with blood spelling out the words Red Dog this morning and the going theory is that blood belonged to Stevie."

"I know," Glenn agreed.

"Of course they haven't found the body yet so I guess there's a chance it isn't him," Bart noted. "Unfortunately, he's still missing."

With an odd look on his face, a look Bart had never seen on Glenn's face in all the years they knew each other, his friend walked across the room to a small coat closet.

"He's not missing anymore," Glenn declared.

The closet door swung open to reveal the lifeless body of Stevie Grissom. Their old friend hung from the coat pole like a string of fish on the river bank.

Bart was speechless; the air going out of him like someone punched him in the gut. Both men stood silently gazing at the ghastly remains of their friend like they were looking at a piece of macabre art on a museum wall. Stevie's throat was slit from ear to ear. His skin was pasty white as if he had been drained of all his blood. He was held to the coat pole in a noose with his body encased in a see-through plastic bag.

Bart was unable to rip his eyes away from the horrible scene.

"I found him this morning when I opened the door to put away my coat," Glenn revealed. "As you might guess, it was quite a surprise."

Swinging the door shut to hide the nightmarish sight, Bart tried to gather himself. Things were happening too fast even for the calculating businessman.

"Any idea how he got in here?" Bart asked

"I'm guessing he didn't walk in," Glenn retorted. "How should I know? I go to put up my coat and there's a dead body in my closet. It's not exactly the way I usually start my day."

Shaking his head, the puzzle of how Stevie's body got into Glenn's office baffling him, Bart tried to get his head around the mystery.

"But I don't understand," Bart began. "How in the world could someone have gotten him in here without being seen?"

"The question isn't how he got in here. The question is how we're going to get him out of here without someone seeing us," Glenn pointed out. "I can't have a dead body found in my closet. I don't think I have to tell you that he's going to start stinking pretty soon."

"Settle it down, mayor," Bart replied, eyeing their surroundings trying to formulate a plan on how they were going to sneak Stevie Grissom's body out of Easton City Hall.

MEMORY LANE

Suffering through an hour of chilling temperatures on what had become one of the coldest winters in Castle County history, Sam watched as the crime lab team towed Bart's Corvette to their forensics garage for a closer inspection.

The sheriff discovered Bart must have slipped away through the back of the dealership while he and the crime team were canvassing the area. The businessman was nowhere to be found to sign the papers for the impounding of his vehicle. It didn't matter, since the car was taken as evidence anyway but his absence did further convince Sam that his words had struck a chord with Bart.

Sam was about to climb in his car when he saw a figure walking at a fast pace toward his location. It was Cliff Chapman. He was moving quicker than the sheriff had ever seen the old newsman move. Hopefully he wouldn't break a hip in his haste.

"Out for a morning jog there, Cliff?" Sam joked as the old reporter bent over trying to catch his breath.

He held up a finger to indicate he needed a second to catch his breath. Cliff took one final gulp of air before forcing out a single word.

"Gina," Cliff blurted between gasps.

"Gina?" Sam repeated.

"That's the girl's name ... Gina," Cliff clarified as he caught his breath. "The girl from the Red Dog you were asking about. Her name is Gina."

"You just now remembered that?" Sam asked.

"It just hit me," Cliff admitted. "I figured I'd better tell you before I forgot ... again."

"I don't mean to look a gift horse in the mouth but do you have a last name?" Sam asked.

Cliff's memory had been stretched to its maximum. He hadn't the foggiest of the girl's last name.

"Nope," Cliff responded. "And to tell the truth, I may not have ever known her last name. You got to remember, this stuff was all through the grapevine. I'm sorry sheriff."

Sam gave Cliff a grin and reached out, patting the old reporter on the shoulder.

"You did good Cliff, you did good," Sam said. "We've got a name and we know about what age she was back then so that's a start. If it wasn't for you, I'd still be at square-one."

Sam's compliment brought a smile to Cliff's wrinkled face. He was honored his information might play a role in helping solve the biggest crime in Castle County history.

"I'm glad to help, sheriff," Cliff said. "Now what's the red substance all over Bart's Corvette?"

"No comment," Sam replied with a wink as he climbed into his cruiser and started the engine.

"But I'm helping you solve the case," Cliff declared. "How about a little help here?"

"Don't worry Cliff, you'll get an exclusive when this is all over," Sam replied. "You might even write a book out of it."

Sam sped out of the dealership and made a beeline for his office to confer with the one person he figured could help him most in discovering the true identity of the girl named Gina.

"I need to know everything you know about girls named Gina around your age," Sam said as he walked into the records office to find his wife busy typing on her computer.

"Take a number, take a seat," Carly said, glancing up over her reading glasses not missing a key stroke. "I'm kind of busy over here, in case you didn't notice."

"Seriously honey, this is important," Sam insisted. "I need the benefit of that beautiful brain you have inside that beautiful head of yours."

Carly rolled her eyes as she stopped typing.

"Flattery will get you everywhere," Carly smiled. "So you're looking for a girl named Gina who's around my age? Do we know anything else about her?"

Sam filled in his wife about the information Cliff gave him and his suspicions the Red Dog murders may have had something to do with the unreported crime from two decades ago.

"That's so horrible to think something like that happened right here in Castle County and nothing was ever done about it," Carly said. "But, as far as girls named Gina, you may be in luck since I don't recall a lot of them around my age. They were like girls named Carly - few and far between. Now had it'd been a Lisa, Tammy or Sherry, you'd be out of luck. They were a dime a dozen and they were all bleached blondes."

"I'm looking for girls, likely a little younger than …" Sam began.

"Watch it," Carly warned.

She was still a bit gun shy from all the black balloons that were delivered to her during her recent fortieth birthday celebration. Actually, in her book, turning forty was more of an observance than a celebration.

"You know what I mean," Sam said. "Someone who was one or two years behind you in high school that left town either right before or right after graduation. Shoot, for all I know she may have even been in your class."

Carly chewed on her reading glasses as she sat deep in thought for a minute. Sam could see the wheels spinning.

"I suppose if we're talking about high school I could dust off one of my old annuals," Carly suggested. "There's a good chance that if she was around my age and she was from here that she'd be in there. The annuals had the freshman through senior classes so that covers four years."

Sam realized he could be on the verge of finally uncovering the identity of the young victim.

"Tell you what, I'll dig out my annual when I get home tonight," Carly offered as she placed her glasses back on her nose.

"No, you'll dig it out right now," Sam said impatiently.

He reached out and grabbed his wife's arm.

"Come on," Sam directed as he pulled her from her desk. "I'll drive."

It took only a few minutes for Carly to lay her hands on her senior annual once they got home. She blew dust off the hard-cover book before venturing into its long-forgotten pages. It was a walk down memory lane.

"Boy, it's been a long time," Carly lamented as she thumbed through the pages of the annual. "Can you believe those hair styles? How were mullets ever cool?"

Carly laughed as she turned the pages, commenting about old friends, her step back into the past bittersweet.

"Those were some good times," Carly said as she lost focus on her mission while waxing nostalgic.

"Honey, I'm trying to catch a killer," Sam interjected as he pointed to the annual. "Do you mind?"

Beginning from the senior class, Carly went page by page. She wrote down the last names and page numbers of all the girls named Gina. She eliminated most of them for one reason or another. Working on the same criteria, Carly backed up all the way through the freshman class.

"Okay, here's what we have," Carly declared after about thirty minutes of meticulous study.

She produced three possibilities from her careful scanning of her old high school classmates' pictures.

"We have a freshman, Gina Kirby. We have a junior, Gina Porter. And, we have a junior, Gina Jones," Carly said. "I can account for everyone else named Gina."

Sam carefully studied the pictures of the three girls and immediately eliminated the junior class member Gina Jones who he knew lived in Castle County for several years after high school. She had moved to California to marry a man she met on the Internet. She was a friend of a friend so Sam was confident she wasn't the girl he was looking for.

"So we're down to Gina Kirby and Gina Porter," Sam said as he rubbed his chin. "That's a pretty good start. Now to figure out which one it is."

Sam gave his wife a kiss on her forehead, thanking her for a job well done as he snatched the annual and hustled her back out the door.

Speeding back to the office like there wasn't a second to waste, Sam called in his investigators and explained what he had learned.

"The girl you're looking for isn't Gina Kirby," Bo declared as he looked at the annual over the sheriff's shoulder.

"Why do you say that?" Sam asked. "Are you sure?"

"Yeah. We kind of dated back in school," Bo said matter of factly. "She wasn't bad looking."

Sam looked at the investigator, trying to decide if he was serious. He would have been a few years younger than her.

"Hey, what can I say? I was a real cougar magnet back then," Bo grinned. "She moved out of town with her family the next year but she would have only been about seventeen then. I think her daddy took a job up north so I think you can cross her off your list."

"That just leaves us with Gina Porter," Sam said.

He looked at the picture of the cute brown-haired junior and wondered what had become of the girl.

"That is if our Gina didn't miss picture day," Kendal spoke up. "I hate to rain on your parade but that's a real possibility."

"Stop it with the negative vibes," Sam snapped. "This is the girl we're looking for. Something in my gut tells me she's it. Regardless, we need to find this girl as soon as possible. Once we locate her we can figure out, for sure, whether she's the girl from the Red Dog."

The lawmen fanned on their mission to find what became of Gina Porter. In the meantime, Sam intended to work the Rhody Turner angle. He realized the con could provide the key to cracking the case.

Sam grabbed the annual and walked over to the copying machine, printing out a grainy but large picture of Gina Porter. He then took a walk through the hall leading to the jail portion of the sheriff's office. Sam directed the guard to open up C-block where Rhody was being held.

Since the sheriff made few trips into the block, his progress to Rhody's cell was delayed as inmates took the opportunity to express grievances with their accommodations ranging from cold food to the lack of recreation time. Sam finally reached his destination and found Rhody sitting on his bed staring at the wall.

"Got that paper?" Rhody asked as he kept his eyes fixed on the wall.

"I'm working on it," Sam replied. "I should have it later today."

"I hear our boy Stevie bought it," Rhody revealed without a hint of emotion. "That's too bad. He was a good guy."

"News travels fast in here, doesn't it?" Sam noted. "We're not sure it's Stevie, but it could be. Of course, you could have stopped that if you'd cooperated."

Sam's statement got the inmate's attention. Rhody glared at the sheriff who was leaned against his cell door bars.

"Don't blame me for your not being able to stop whoever it is. That's on you, sheriff," Rhody snapped. "As for me, I have a perfect alibi for once."

"Yep, this is one crime you actually didn't commit," Sam agreed.

"So, what's with the visit? The high sheriff doesn't usually go slumming," Rhody noted. "Like I said, until I get something in writing, we got nothing to say."

Pulling out the piece of paper from his pocket, Sam motioned for the inmate.

"Hey, a deal is a deal," Sam agreed. "You'll get your paper. But while we're waiting, take a look at this."

Rhody rose from his bunk, curious about what the sheriff was holding.

"You bring me some porn?" the inmate asked with a wry smile on his face as he walked over to the bars.

"You tell me," Sam said.

With that, the sheriff held up the picture in front of Rhody's face. The image caught Rhody unprepared. The expression on the hardened criminal's face told Sam all he needed to know.

"Never saw her before in my life," Rhody growled.

The inmate snatched the picture out of Sam's hands and ripped it to pieces before throwing them back in the sheriff's face.

"Now if you don't mind, I'm expecting a call from my old lady here in a few minutes. Come back when you got something for me," Rhody said in a dismissive tone.

"It's a date," Sam grinned.

He had gotten what he came for without the inmate having to say a single word. His eyes couldn't lie.

Sam walked back to his office, confident he was on the right trail. Now, if they could only locate the whereabouts of the mysterious Gina Porter they would be in business.

"There you go," came the voice of Kendal Parks as the sheriff stepped back into his office.

"What's this?" Sam asked as he took the piece of paper his detective as holding.

"It's what you asked for," Kendal replied. "It's the last known address of Gina Porter, former resident of Castle County"

"Impressive," Sam admitted.

The address on the paper was located only a couple of

hours drive from Easton.

"I've got to say that was pretty quick," Sam said.

Smiling with a sense of pride that the sheriff appreciated his detective work, Kendal explained.

"Hey, it's not that hard nowadays," Kendal admitted. "You can find almost anyone on the Internet."

"Still, that's pretty good detective work," Sam noted.

"She had a Facebook account, sheriff," Kendal confessed. "Most people have them. I just did a search and it gave me about a couple of hundred Gina Porters. Then I narrowed it down and there it was under the subject heading of education. She went to school at Castle County High School. Then I simply started cross-referencing what I got there and came up with an address over in Shelby."

"Have you tried to make contact yet?" Sam asked.

"Nope, I thought you'd want the honors since you're the one who developed all of this," Kendal replied. "I couldn't find a phone number, just an address. As for Facebook, her page has been dormant for over a year."

"Well, this is more than we had half an hour ago," Sam said. "I think I'm going to take a drive up to Shelby. While I'm gone see if you can get with our contact at the DEA and see if they'll go along with our plans for Rhody."

"Will do sheriff," Kendal replied. "Let me know what you find out up there. I'm curious."

With address in hand, Sam wasted no time getting in his car and pointing it in the direction of Shelby. He was possibly two hours away from busting the case wide open, either that or finding out he was working on a dead end. He realized he was in a race against time since he kind of doubted the killer would sportingly wait until his return to Castle County to take his next victim.

A BIT TOO LATE

"We can't just walk him out of here like 'Weekend at Bernie's'," Mayor Glenn Satterfield pointed out.

He and Bart stood looking at their friend's corpse as it hung nicely in the closet like a suit of clothes.

"We're going to have to be patient," Bart declared. "We're going to have to wait until tonight after city hall is closed. Then, we can sneak him out and get rid of the body."

Glenn questioned the feasibility of Bart's plan. He wasn't comfortable with disposing of a body like a hit man getting rid of the evidence. However, he knew he couldn't afford the suspicion that would come with him contacting police about their grisly discovery.

"But we're in the middle of downtown Easton," Glenn pointed out as he walked over to his office window which overlooked the hamlet. "What are you going to do, just throw him over your shoulder and stroll out the front door?"

Bart gave his slender friend an irritated look, assuring him his plan was doable.

"Trust me on this," Bart said. "You just need to make sure the cleaning woman don't come in here and find our friend hanging in the closet. If that happens, well, you're on your own."

"Oh, thanks for the support," Glenn retorted.

The worried politician flopped down in his chair and ran his hands through his perfectly groomed head of hair.

"Hey, I'm going to help you get rid of a body so don't be

giving me grief," Bart shot back.

His next words surprised even his longtime friend.

"It isn't like it's the first time I've done something like this," Bart darkly revealed.

Choosing not to pursue the meaning of Bart's reference, Glenn moved on to the next problem on his agenda - a problem that rivaled even the body in his closet.

"We have another problem," Glenn pointed out. "And this one may not be so easy to solve."

"Yes, I know, Rhody Turner," Bart said. "The sheriff was bragging about that to me before I came over here."

"I don't guess I need to tell you what it means if he talks," Glenn said. "The police chief is asking my blessing in a plea deal for him in return for his cooperation in the murders. I don't have any option but to give it my stamp of approval otherwise eyebrows will be raised. Plus, if word got out I impeded the biggest murder investigation in the history of Castle County, well, it wouldn't be very good come election time later this year."

Bart realized he had resources that could help get rid of the problem if Rhody were on the street. However, given the fact he was locked up tight in the county jail, the potential snitch would be hard to get to. That didn't mean the situation was impossible. It was just more difficult.

"So do you think he'll talk?" Glenn asked in a worried tone as he incessantly flicked the end of his pen.

"Think?" Bart replied indignantly. "I know he will. He'd sell out his own mother for a deal."

"Well, we can't have that," Glenn said as he stood back up and walked over to look out the window.

Glenn's words were an understatement. If Rhody were to reveal everything he knew he, the mayor and everyone else involved back then would be exposed. It would be only a matter of time until all of them were rounded up once the ugly truth was known. Rhody couldn't be allowed to talk. If he did, they would be joining him on the other side of the jail bars.

"I may have an idea of how we can keep our old friend quiet," Bart revealed as a far-fetched idea struck him. "It may be our only chance."

"Well, don't keep me in the dark," Glenn eagerly urged. "How do you propose to get to Rhody while he's locked away in the county jail? The sheriff already knows he can help him so he's not about to let him go waltzing out the front door."

"You leave that part to me, just make sure you don't give authorization for the deal until the end of the day. By then the federal offices will be closed," Bart replied. "As for what I have in mind, well, the less you know the better."

Again the darkness of Bart's reference kept Glenn from asking about further details. He still had plausible deniability.

"You just make sure no one comes into this office," Bart ordered. "And turn down the heat in here. A little ice wouldn't hurt either. And for crying out loud, make sure that closet door stays closed."

Agreeing to meet back at city hall after dark, Bart left to put his plan into action while Glenn sat in for a long day at his office with his dead friend.

Sam attacked the roads to Shelby, not shy about using his lights and siren to shorten his trip. He realized daylight was limited, especially if he were to spend four hours on the road going back and forth. He had to minimize his drive time given the fact there was no reason to believe the killer wouldn't be on the prowl again. Plus, in the back of his mind, Sam believed there were more members of the old gang than the ones he knew about. That meant there were potential victims who weren't even on his radar. For some reason, Sam had the feeling that the killer was saving the best for last, that being none other than Bart Foster.

He pulled into Shelby in less than ninety minutes, something Sam suspected was a record drive time from Easton. The sheriff plugged the address to Gina's last known location into his GPS as he reached Shelby. Slowing his pace as he wound through the streets of the small city, Sam found himself in a nice section of town. The well-manicured sidewalks and tree-lined streets gave the neighborhood a friendly feel.

The lawman looked at his GPS after a few minutes in the small town and realized he was almost upon his destination. The last known address for Gina Porter lie around the next turn. Just then the snow began to fall, the forecasted winter storm moving in sooner than expected. If forecasters were right, the entire portion of the state would be under several inches of snow in the next couple of days.

The target on his GPS revealing he was at his destination, Sam turned into the drive and was met by a gate guarding the entrance, its grand arch announcing he had just arrived at Shelby Mental Health Institute.

What the ..." Sam muttered to himself as he drove up the drive to the large modern-looking building. "This can't be right."

Perhaps the usually reliable Kendal Parks was wrong for once. After all, no one is perfect. Sam double checked the address his detective had written down to confirm he was at the right location.

"I came this far," Sam muttered to himself as he parked his car and headed inside.

The facility, much to his surprise, had an inviting atmosphere. Skylights and plants inside the building combined to give it an open, airy feel. It wasn't like any mental institution he had visited before. The dankness he anticipated was replaced by a well-lit entry parlor painted in light colors. Employees wore khaki pants and blue shirts instead of the antiseptic hospital white he expected.

"May I help you officer?" came the pleasant voice of a

young woman who sat smiling at him behind the front desk.

"I sure hope so," Sam responded, just then remembering he was wearing his badge on his belt but was otherwise dressed in civilian clothes as he often did while on duty. "I'm looking for a woman and all I have is an address that led me here."

"What is the woman's name?" the receptionist asked.

"It's Gina Porter," Sam replied.

The name had an immediate impact on the young lady. Her friendly tone turned serious. She looked as if she'd seen a ghost.

"Did you say Gina Porter?" the woman asked.

"Yes, Gina Porter," Sam clarified. "Is there something wrong?"

Holding up a finger asking him to wait, the woman picked up the phone, placing one hand over the receiver so Sam couldn't hear what she was saying. Moments later she hung up.

"Officer, if you don't mind you'll need to speak with our facility administrator," the woman said. "She'll be with you in just one moment."

Sam waited in the lobby for about a minute before he saw a well-dressed, middle-aged woman emerge from the back office area. She paused to speak with the receptionist who pointed toward him. The woman then walked over.

"Hello officer, I'm Agnes Marks, administrator here at SMHI," the woman said, extending her hand.

"Hi, I'm Sheriff Sam Delaney from over in Castle County," Sam replied. "I'm looking for a woman named Gina Porter."

"Step into my office if you would, sheriff," the woman said in a low voice.

Entering the administrator's office, Sam took a seat as the woman closed the door behind them.

"I take it I'm in the right place," Sam spoke up.

He already realized something was amiss. The mere

mention of Gina Porter's name seemed to have upset the apple cart.

"Yes, I guess you could say that," Agnes said as she took her seat behind her desk.

"So what do I need to do to speak with Miss Porter?" Sam asked. "It's a matter of official business for a case I'm working on."

"I'm afraid that won't be possible, sheriff," Agnes replied.

"And why is that?" Sam countered. "I could get a warrant."

"Because Gina Porter has been deceased for nearly three months," Agnes replied.

"Dead?" Sam repeated in disbelief.

He was crestfallen. His trail had just dried up.

"Yes, she passed away quite suddenly," Agnes confirmed.

"So she was a patient here?" Sam asked.

"For about four years," Agnes replied. "Until the time of her death."

He rubbed his forehead, feeling a headache coming on. The frustration of the dead end was driving up his blood pressure.

"Can you tell me what she was here for?" Sam asked.

"I'm sorry but that's confidential," Agnes apologized. "You'll need a warrant for that. We have HIPAA to deal with so I can't release that kind of information. I hope you understand my situation."

"Okay, can you tell me what she died of, or is that secret too?" Sam asked.

He was a bit irritated by the administrator not providing the reason for her stay. She was dead for crying out loud. She didn't need privacy anymore when it came to her medical condition.

"That's a matter of public record, written right on her death certificate. I can help you with that," Agnes retorted.

"The cause of her death was suicide."

"She killed herself?" Sam confirmed. "I mean, she did it here?"

"Unfortunately, yes," Agnes replied soberly. "We pride ourselves on protecting our patients both from harm from without and within."

"Do you mind me asking how she did it?" Sam inquired.

Pausing as if to decide whether to share the information, the administrator leaned toward the lawman.

"Well, I'm not sure I'm really supposed to tell this so keep it between us," Agnes warned. "She slit her own throat."

"Do you know why she did it?" Sam asked.

"I've said too much already," Agnes replied. "If you want anything else you'll need to get a warrant."

"I understand," Sam replied. "I may just do that."

Again leaning across her desk, Agnes spoke in a low voice.

"I would suggest you do," Agnes said.

Her eyes darted about as if she feared someone might be listening. Something about their conversation was making the administrator very nervous.

"You'll find her records ... enlightening," she noted.

Sam thanked Agnes for her help and made a beeline for the courthouse. The fact she had stopped just short of outright urging him to check the late Gina Porter's clinical records intrigued the lawman. She wanted to tell him more. He could sense it.

His quick trip to the courthouse was to no avail as the only judge was already gone for the afternoon, his request for a warrant for the medical records delayed until the next day. He resolved to return to swear out the warrant and even spend the day if need be.

For now he would head back to Castle County. With any luck he would be sitting down with Rhody Turner soon to hear his version of the events of twenty years ago.

THE BEST LAID PLANS

"Hey baby," came the flirty voice of Tia Wray, the on-again, off-again girlfriend of Rhody Turner. "How're they treating you in there?"

Rhody rolled his eyes as he stood at the jail phone bank in the common area of the institution. It was jail. How did she think he was doing?

Their tumultuous relationship had stretched over the past couple of years. The couple spent more time broken up than together. Actually, Tia generally just came around when Rhody was cooking - meth that is. Her taste for the drug drew her to him like a moth to the flame. Being he was nearly twice her age, Rhody enjoyed the benefits of dating a much younger woman. Under normal circumstances, a girl like Tia would have been way out of his league. If it took giving her the first cut of his meth cook, then that was a price he was willing to pay. Besides, it wasn't like Rhody was a one-woman man anyway.

He had found long ago there was no shortage of women who were looking for a "bad boy" like him. They were drawn to the danger the professional criminal brought to the table. Rhody never had a problem luring a woman. Keeping one, on the other hand, was a problem explaining why, other than a marriage that lasted just two months many years ago, he had remained a single man. It was also hard maintaining a long-term relationship when he was constantly in and out of jail.

But then it wasn't like Tia was a catch either. Her loyalties went to where the party was happening. If it wasn't Rhody then she was in the company of some other low-life. She had always been attracted to losers and drug dealers. Whether it was low self-esteem or a deep-seated need for self-destruction, she had stepped on the wrong path as a teenager and never looked back despite many interventions by her family.

While bouncing from place to place, always staying within arm's length of bad influence, there was something about Rhody that made him her favorite forbidden fruit. Whether it was the tattoos that covered his body, his long scraggly hair or his total disregard for the establishment, she was fascinated. For whatever reason, Tia broke with her tradition of throwing them aside when they were in lock-up, choosing to continue her relationship with Rhody even after his arrest and incarceration. However, her newfound loyalty would not extend to waiting for her man while he rotted away in prison for a decade or more. She wasn't the type to wait by the sea until her man came home.

"How do you think they're treating me?" Rhody responded in an irritated tone. "It's jail. Everything sucks here - the food, the people, and the guards. You name it and it sucks."

"Oh I'm sorry baby. I sure wish they allowed conjugal visits in there. I would so take your mind off it," Tia replied. "I sure miss being with you. I can't hardly stand being apart like this."

He rolled his eyes realizing there wasn't much he could do about his situation. Rhody was annoyed she would even go down that road. It was almost like she was teasing him, leaving him with no outlet while stuck behind bars. He was surprised she even knew the word conjugal, let alone used it in a sentence.

"I miss you too," Rhody replied. "Maybe we'll be able to see each other soon. I'm working on something on this end that might get me a lot less time."

"Why wait baby?" Tia asked. "I've worked it out."

He looked around to make sure no one was nearby who could overhear, cupping his hand over the receiver.

"The walls have ears," Rhody cautioned.

He realized all calls to and from the county jail were recorded. A sign hanging right above the phone bank where he stood even bore the warning. There were ears everywhere in jail.

"Don't worry, I know the drill," Tia replied.

She had spent a few nights in the county jail herself. She knew the realities when it came to life behind bars.

"It's all been arranged," she chirped. "All you have to do is go with the plan."

The plan, as she put it, dated back to before Rhody was arrested weeks ago. The grapevine had it there was something going down, something big, and Rhody's name was being thrown about as one of those likely in the middle of it. Given his record and the likelihood he may be going away for a long time, he decided to formulate a plan. He wasn't about to waste the rest of his life in a jail cell.

It had started as a thumbnail sketch, a rough draft if you will. Since then the plot had been honed and perfected to the point he was convinced it would work. He had spent a considerable amount of time in the county jail and knew its strengths and its weaknesses. Rhody began making preparations in earnest after he was arrested and learned he would soon be delivered into the hands of federal authorities. He realized once federal marshals came for him it would be too late. If he were to make his move, it would have to be while he was in Castle County Jail.

However, since he had a lifetime of experience with the system, Rhody realized simply springing himself from the cage was only half the trick. He knew he would need help from the outside to put as much distance between himself and Castle County as possible. Too many times inmates would risk life and limb to escape confinement only to be found a couple of blocks away, hiding in the basement of their girlfriend's home. Then escape charges would be added to their tab for their brief taste of liberty. They would also be permanently listed as a flight risk, meaning they would always be placed in maximum security making escape even less likely.

Rhody wasn't about to make that mistake. If he were going to make a run for it, he was never going to look back. Castle County would forever be a memory. That was where Tia came in. Well, actually, Tia was merely the necessary evil. It was her uncle in Costa Rica that interested him the most. Her uncle, much like Rhody, had long been involved in activities contrary to the law. That was what brought him to the Central American country over a decade ago. Nowadays he was making a comfortable living for himself and was in need of someone of Rhody's talents.

Rhody was a realist despite being a career criminal. He knew his sins would catch up to him eventually. Now, as things stood, it wasn't just his recent illegal activities that were catching up to him, it was also his sins of more than twenty years ago. Rhody figured it was time for a change of scenery, a reset of the game of life. He had worn out his welcome in Castle County long ago.

Rhody knew the decision he was about to make would forever affect his life. Should he go with his plan and make a break for it or should he stay and work a deal with the sheriff? There were risks either way. If he went with his plan to bust out of the county jail, there was always a chance he could get caught. Of course, so what if he did? He was already looking at spending most of the rest of his life in prison. What's another year or two?

On the other hand, if he stayed and worked a deal, he would still be looking at a few years in jail. While he wasn't on a road crew breaking boulders, it was still jail. The upside was if he were to work a deal he could stay in Castle County after being released. But then what was left for him there? He would still be one misdeed, one dirty drug test, one blunder from violating his probation and going back to jail. Plus, in his hometown he was known to law enforcement. Down there he would be just another American import. Rhody considered the immediate future. Did he want to spend the next three years in the county jail or sunning on a beach in Costa Rica?

"What time?" Rhody asked.

He was going to roll the dice and go for it. He was going to escape from Castle County Jail. It was Costa Rica or bust.

"Tonight at midnight," Tia answered.

"Do we have what we needed?" Rhody asked.

"Yes. I worked it out with a mutual friend," Tia responded. "All you have to do is be where you're supposed to be at that time."

The meeting place had been prearranged as both knew their call may be monitored.

"So we're a go then," Rhody said. "They'll be something waiting there for me?"

"Yes. It's been taken care of," Tia confirmed. "All you have to do is take care of your part."

"I'll owe you a big one for this," Rhody promised.

"You can thank me when you see me baby," Tia retorted.

"Soon, baby, soon," Rhody pledged as they said their goodbyes.

It was time to call in some favors and put the wheels in motion for his jailbreak.

"I want around the clock surveillance on Bart Foster," Sam directed after calling his staff together immediately after getting back to Easton. "He's the one person, outside our own Rhody Turner, who we know is connected with all this. And, since Rhody is safe as a baby in his momma's arms inside our jail, there's a good chance Mr. Foster could be our killer's next target."

"In other words sheriff, we're using Bart for bait," Bo

pointed out.

"I guess you could say that," Sam admitted. "But then he wouldn't accept police protection even if we offered so we're going to give it to him anyway. We're just going to have to do it at a distance and without him knowing about it."

"Then, if the killer kills him we've got our culprit," Bo interjected.

The detective's comment drew a cold look from the sheriff and snickers from his fellow officers.

"No Bo, we try to get the killer before he kills him," Sam corrected. "I know that might not be a popular order but we're sworn to protect even jerks like Bart Foster."

"If you say so," Bo responded.

"We need a man on him wherever he goes and I also want someone conducting surveillance on his home. We're going to need a couple of teams so we'll pull a couple of men off the night shift this evening," Sam ordered. "This goes into operation immediately and continues until further notice."

Ending the planning meeting by briefing his staff on what he learned during his trip to Shelby that day, Sam revealed his plans to return the next day to examine Gina Porter's sealed records.

Even as Sheriff Sam Delaney was laying plans involving him, Bart Foster was finalizing his own plans - his with the mayor of Easton.

"Could you burn a candle or something?" Bart asked as he entered the mayor's office.

He was immediately struck by the scent of their old friend's rotting flesh which was starting to escape from the closet. The decay had accelerated during the course of the day despite the fact the mayor's office felt like a walk-in cooler.

"I can't smell anything," Glenn replied as he took a

couple of deep breaths.

He was already acclimated to the smell. It was the same overpowering scent that offended Bart's nostrils the moment he walked into the office just before the end of regular business hours at Easton City Hall.

Bart rolled his eyes and got right to business, his day full of planning about to come to a head.

"In a few hours it won't matter," Bart began. "All you have to do is stick to the plan and everything will be fine."

Glenn questioned Bart's optimism. His view of the world was influenced by spending an entire day closed up in the same room with their dead friend.

"Will it Bart?" Glenn asked. "Say we get Stevie out of here without a hitch and say we convince Rhody not to spill his guts, what then? There's still something out there and that something is after us. What do we do? What can we do? What's to stop this thing before it gets all of us?"

Bart shot him a steely glare, snapping at his old friend.

"It? Really Glenn? It? Are you really going there?" Bart asked incredulously. "Surely the high mayor of Easton isn't suggesting there are ghosts and goblins at play here. Tell me you aren't saying that."

Slow to return Bart's gaze, the mayor looked at the floor before timidly lifting his eyes.

"He said he'd get all of us, even if he had to chase us to Hell," Glenn responded. "What if it is him? Who else could know what we did? What if the dark man is him?"

Bart was surprised by his friend's willingness to believe a supernatural force was to blame for the killings. He had to nip the mayor's imagination in the bud.

"What we're dealing with here is flesh and blood, a human being just like you and me," Bart declared confidently. "There are no such things as ghosts or evil spirits that come back to seek revenge. We have someone who knows what happened. That's it, nothing more."

"But who?" Glenn interrupted. "Who would know except

the people who were there? And, in case you haven't noticed, that number is shrinking pretty fast."

"Somebody ran their mouth," Bart surmised. "Someone talked to the wrong person."

Glenn shook his head. He didn't agree with Bart's simplistic explanation.

"What if you're wrong? What if it is him come back like he said?" Glenn asked in a worried tone.

"Then there's nothing we can do," Bart replied. "He will drag us to Hell with him. If you're right then we may as well eat, drink and be merry."

A sick look came over the mayor's face with Bart's comment. Glenn was on the verge of achieving his lifetime goals. The present situation threatened to ruin everything as well as perhaps lead to a grisly death.

"Trust me. We're dealing with a human being," Bart said as he placed his hand on Glenn's shoulder. "And sooner or later he's going to mess up. All we have to do is give him enough rope and he'll hang himself."

"But … " Glenn began.

"There's a reason whoever it is went after those three and not us," Bart interrupted. "They were the easy ones. They were soft. I don't know about you Glenn but I'm not like them. I'm not soft. And something else, I'm not scared either. That's just what he wants. He's using fear as a weapon. That's why Stevie is in your closet. It's all mind games."

Glenn reluctantly accepted Bart's reasoning and sat down at his desk, putting his head in his hands.

"Okay, what do we do?" Glenn asked in a muffled voice.

Bart wondered why he always had to be the calm one. Why was he the one in the group who had to come up with the solutions to their collective problems? Why couldn't anyone else carry their own weight? It was like he had to do everything.

"Okay, you need to listen close because we're going to be

on a tight schedule tonight," Bart said as he coaxed the mayor's head from his hands. "At exactly eleven-thirty tonight I'm going to pull up to the curb outside your office and blow my horn once. You need to have your window up so you can hear it."

"Do you want me to come down and meet you and let you in?" Glenn asked. "Are we going to carry him down together? Maybe we can wrap him in a carpet or something in case someone happens to come up on us?"

Bart corrected the mayor. He was annoyed that Glenn was getting ahead of himself before he could reveal his plan.

"No, it's nothing like that," Bart said. "When I pull up, I won't be in my car. Let's just say I'll be in a car that has been borrowed without permission so I can't afford to stay parked out front very long. I'd hate for one of your boys in blue to come up and run the tag. That's why we have to get him into the car quick."

"So we'll use the elevator," Glenn suggested.

"I was thinking of something even faster," Bart responded with a wicked smile.

"Faster than the elevator?" Glenn asked. "I don't know of any way faster than that."

Bart knew a way.

"When you hear my horn blow, you're going to toss our friend out the window," Bart directed. "I'll have the trunk already open so it'll be quick."

"What? You want me to just hurl Stevie's body out of the third story window of city hall?" Glenn asked in a surprised voice. "That's insane. Do you hear yourself?"

"It isn't like it's going to hurt him," Bart dryly responded. "He's already dead."

"But ... " Glenn began.

"There aren't any buts about it," Bart interrupted. "I'm the one taking all the risks out there. All you have to do is throw him out and I'll do the rest."

Pausing to consider Bart's strange plan, Glenn still

RED DOG SALOON

wasn't sold. What if someone saw him tossing a body from his third story window at city hall? It would certainly hurt his reelection chances.

"Look, it's going to be like ten degrees tonight and the snow is going to start. There shouldn't be a soul on the street," Bart argued. "This may be our only opportunity. The way I look at it is we either go with my plan or you're going to need to invest in a lot of air fresheners."

Glenn relented knowing he had no option but to follow Bart's plan, just like he had twenty years ago.

"Eleven-thirty sharp?" Glenn clarified.

"Not one minute earlier, not one minute later," Bart confirmed as he extended his hand.

They shook on the deal as they stood in the middle of the mayor's office. They were now both part and parcel of the unholy alliance.

"My light will be on when you get here," Glenn noted.

"Don't be calling attention to yourself," Bart cautioned. "We don't want people getting curious about why the mayor is burning the midnight oil."

"Don't worry. I've been leaving it on at night lately to make people think I'm working late," Glenn admitted. "Some nights I even leave my car parked out front and walk home to make it look like I'm working all night. Hey, it's an election year."

Bart shook his head in disbelief.

"You politicians are sick," Bart declared despite the improbable plan they had just hatched to dispose of their friend's body.

Bart paused at the door as he turned to leave.

"Eleven-thirty sharp," he repeated.

"What about our other problem?" Glenn asked.

"Don't worry, I've got that under control too," Bart grinned as he closed the door behind him.

R.D. SHERRILL

OUT OF THE FRYING PAN

The flu had cut a swath through Castle County Jail over the winter. The illness had spread like wildfire through the inmate population. Rhody Turner was one of the lucky ones, avoiding the bug as it worked its way through the cellblocks. Being a loner, Rhody tended to do his time in self-imposed solitary. Sure, he would participate in a poker game here or there and become somewhat social if another inmate was sharing smuggled drugs with his fellow prisoners even though he knew what orifice most drugs came from that made their way into the institution. But, for the most part, Rhody believed in just doing his time without becoming part of a clique when at the county jail. It was his solitary nature that likely spared him from the flu epidemic.

Rhody saw many of his fellow inmates suffering through the throes of the flu while avoiding it himself. The chills, fever, and the vomiting were par for the course. He also noticed the tell-tale symptoms would usually get the sick inmates sent to the infirmary and into isolation. Jail administration tried to stem the outbreak by quickly separating the sick inmates from general population. He would use those observations to his advantage this evening.

Lying around his cell during the early evening hours, Rhody held a sock, heated with warm water from his faucet, against his head. He made sure to point out to the trustee, who served him supper, that he was not feeling well. His head blazing after two hours of the warm compress, Rhody made his play. He called for a nurse, using his best sick voice, around seven o'clock. Moments later he stuck a finger down his throat and brought his supper back up. It was a necessary evil even though supper consisted of his favorite - spaghetti with mystery meat meatballs.

With a temperature of one hundred two, vomiting and chills, Rhody was diagnosed with the flu by the jail nurse. She immediately administered antibiotics and ordered him moved to sick bay. Given the flu epidemic had been almost stomped out, they would take no chances when it came to Rhody. A doctor would not be available until morning so he would be held in medical isolation until then. That would be more than enough time for the cagey inmate. The first hurdle was cleared. Rhody was out of his cell.

The move to sick bay was a major part of his plan since there he was away from the prying eyes of the guards. In the cell block, any movements could be monitored by the correctional officer who sat in the crow's nest, casting a watchful eye on the inmates in general population. Sick bay was a closed area. While still well within the confines of the jail, guards would have to physically walk up to the door and look inside. And, given it was the evening hours, Rhody knew the nurse along with a guard would only check on him roughly every three hours. This left him a wealth of unsupervised time.

Rhody selected the time of his jailbreak carefully. Much like your average prisoner, he fantasized, plotted and planned an escape. He used his many idle hours in his cell to think on such things. While, for most inmates, such plans remained simply a whimsy, for Rhody it was set in stone. During his many stays at the county jail, he discovered the facility's weaknesses. He also knew the method of operation for its employees and knew shift change happened at midnight. That would provide him with an extra bit of confusion as the torch was passed between the second and graveyard shifts. Rhody wanted every advantage he could get, thus his careful choosing of the time of his departure. However, he would have more hurdles to clear before midnight if he was to keep to his schedule.

While Rhody was setting his plan into motion, Bart was also hatching his own. It all began with taking delivery of a recently stolen sedan. His discreet contacts in neighboring Pickett County were always good at performing certain jobs that were often afoul of the law. Their first duties this evening were providing him with the stolen automobile. They would also be providing a bit of assistance later on in the evening.

Bart realized he only had to avoid suspicion for a few minutes to accomplish his mission. The snow was beginning to fall and the mercury had already dipped below twenty. There would be very few prying eyes, especially after the false call he would make, sending police to the opposite side of town just before his drive over to city hall. Provided Glenn stuck to the plan, things should all go off without a hitch. Bart wasn't so sure his old friend could hold up to the pressure. He was showing signs of cracking and that was worrisome and surprising.

Glenn had normally been strong like him. The pair were the alpha males of their group. Where they led, the others would follow. Perhaps politics had made Glenn soft. Bart now wondered if his old friend could even be trusted.

Bart headed through the snow in the stolen car. The big flakes which had fallen for hours were now starting to cover the ground. It would only be a matter of time until the roads became slick and made driving treacherous. He had given his surveillance team the slip hours earlier using one of his friends from Pickett County to lead his tail away while he remained hidden inside his dealership.

Bart assumed he was being watched. After all, why wouldn't he be? He was the only connection, aside from

Rhody, that Sheriff Delaney had between the murders and the old Red Dog. It would be foolhardy not to keep him under observation if for no other reason than to use him as human bait. Bart knew his father would have done the same if he was still sheriff. Now, as he headed toward city hall, the sheriff's stakeout team was watching his home on the other side of town, wrongly assuming he was inside.

Bart eyed his watch as he parked his car on the other side of the park from city hall. It was moments until zero hour. He could see the mayor's light glowing and could make out a figure pacing back and forth inside. The window was already open. Perhaps Glenn would be able to hold up his end of the bargain after all. Picking up the cellphone which came with the stolen car, Bart called in a fiery crash on the East Street Bridge. The howl of sirens sounded almost immediately as police and emergency crews raced toward the scene. It was go time.

Glenn had been pacing for quite a while. He was too nervous to sit still. That had been his routine for the last hour. He would pace around his office and pause for a moment to look out his window. Now, on what seemed like the millionth time he looked across the deserted downtown, he saw a single flash of headlights. It was Bart.

It was time to pull Stevie from his temporary tomb in the closet. He had dreaded this moment all evening. Glenn spread out the black tarp on his floor in front of the closet and reached inside the closet, pulling Stevie from the spot he had been hanging all day.

Glenn gave the body a tug and was able to muscle the lifeless carcass out of the closet and onto the tarp. He now realized why they call it "dead weight." The body of his lifeless friend was heavier than he expected. Glenn was particularly disturbed by the fact the body was no longer stiff, the cadaver feeling soft like a piece of meat. The entire situation combined with his open window sent a chill down his spine as he rolled Stevie into the tarp like a cocoon. At least he would no longer have to look at his face. The expression on his dead friend's face was forever burned into his brain. He was sure, however, that he would see it again in many future nightmares.

No sooner had he rolled Stevie into the tarp than he heard the sound of a car horn from the street just below his window. The single beep told him Bart was ready.

"Just do it," Glenn muttered to himself as he latched onto the tarp containing Stevie's remains.

The mayor let out a grunt as lifted the dead weight and lugged it to the window. He could see Bart standing next to his car, looking nervously up and down the street. Bart began motioning for him to toss the body down to him.

"I can't believe I'm doing this," Glenn said under his breath as he gave the body one more tug.

Glenn felt a tweak in his lower back as he deadlifted Stevie's remains onto the lip of his window. He again took inventory of downtown to make sure no one was lurking in the shadows. Then, with one last push, the body fell free.

Bart backed toward the car that sat on the curb when he saw the mayor release the wrapped body. He didn't want the falling mass to land on him.

The body hit the concrete like a bag of wet cement. Bart couldn't help but wince seeing the body bounce as it slammed against the frozen sidewalk. A fall like that would have proven fatal under normal circumstances.

Bart took no time powering his cargo into the trunk, pushing the body to the back before slamming it shut. He looked up and gave a salute to the mayor as he jumped back into the stolen car and sped away. Glenn breathed a sigh of relief as he watched the car containing Stevie's body take off. Meanwhile, in the speeding car, Bart swallowed hard. His mission was only half completed.

RED DOG SALOON

Even as Bart was speeding away from city hall with the body of Stevie Grissom stashed in the trunk of a stolen car, Rhody Turner was crawling into the drop ceiling above sick bay. The last visit from the nurse came minutes before. His temperature was now stabilized, meaning there wouldn't be another visit by the nurse for several hours.

After lifting himself into the ceiling with a blanket in tow, Rhody found himself facing a utility tunnel which led into a crawl space that lay between the interior and exterior walls of the jail. He pulled himself through the narrow opening. He slithered through the tight chamber and emerged just below the cell bars which faced the outside on the exterior wall. The exercise yard lay just on the other side of a layer of concrete block.

He wedged himself between the wall and the bars on the exterior wall. The interior walls shielded him from view of the guards. He then pulled out his shiv and began chipping away at the concrete that surrounded the metal bars. Other inmates had started the project over time. Part of the block was already chipped away leaving the bars loose. Rhody could hear the noise of inmates as they began a small uproar on the other side of the wall.

It was all part of his plan. His friends in the cellblock would create noise to cover the sound of him behind the wall. It was like a team game, the inmates all working together to get one of their own to the other side of the wire. It was almost like they were escaping vicariously through Rhody.

He chipped the concrete inch-by-inch until he could see open space begin to appear around the metal bar. The progress encouraging him, the smell of freedom becoming stronger, he began feverishly hacking on the now-crumbling concrete. He could almost feel the sun of the Costa Rican beach on his face.

Unwittingly aiding Rhody in his escape were the members of the Castle County council who decided to go with the low bid when giving the jail building contract almost a decade before. Against the recommendation of Sheriff Delaney, the county commission avoided raising taxes by hiring an inexperienced firm to build the jail. Given the fact the contractor had never built a jail before, he ignored suggested specifications, opting to cut corners. One of his cuts involved skimping when it came to building in proper support within the exterior walls. In short, the contractor built a hollow jail, something that was discovered over the years by inmates in the facility.

The metal bars now moving, Rhody gave them a hard pull. The concrete let go of its hold on the metal. With one last tug, Rhody ripped the bars out of their place, the force of his pull almost sending them falling into the crawl space below him. Such a blunder would have surely given him away. A loud sound like metal bars crashing to the floor would easily be heard on the other side of the wall even over the sounds of the inmate uproar. However, holding on to the dangling bars by just his index finger, he was able to salvage his mission. He breathed a sigh of relief as he laid the dislodged bars on the concrete ledge next to him.

Now the question was if he could squeeze through the hole he made by removing the bars. He would be working on faith since he would have to go out feet-first on his belly so he could lower himself into the exercise yard from the second floor. Anyone walking into the fenced yard would easily be able to see him once he emerged from inside the wall.

Chipping a few more inches of concrete away, Rhody realized it was now or never as he tossed his blanket in the exercise yard. He pushed himself above the hole and hung his legs outside the opening before wiggling through the gap. He became wedged in the jagged opening a couple of times but kept pushing himself outward. The lean inmate held his breath to get his stomach past the jagged remains of the wall. He could feel the concrete ripping his chest and back almost like the wall was eating him as he continued his slithering back-and-forth. Then, with one last push, he was able to push his chest free leaving him hanging a story above the exercise yard. Without pause, he let go of the ledge and landed on the frozen ground below. The impact jarred his teeth as his legs buckled beneath him. The next instant he was lying on his back in the exercise yard, looking up at the snow. He struggled for air as the impact knocked his breath out. The fall from the second story hurt worse than he imagined. Sitting around in his jail cell twenty-three hours a day had left him out of shape. The meth probably had something to do with it too.

He was almost free. Now all he had to do was mount the fifteen-foot-high fence and crawl over. The only issue was the fence was topped with razor wire.

Rhody ran across the exercise yard and threw his blanket up over the razor wire as he began scaling the metal fence. His progress was quick as he reached the top of the fence within a few seconds. Now came the razor wire. While the blanket provided some protection from the sharp wire, it didn't provide complete insulation. Rhody found that out as he felt his arm slashed by some of the razor that cut through the blanket.

He ignored the pain and the rush of blood from his arm as he continued pulling himself over the top, another sharp pain cutting through his leg as the razor wire dug in. Not deterred, the smell of freedom in his nostrils, he slung his leg over the top of the wire and straddled the fence. He hoped the razor wouldn't grab his man region. Sitting atop the fence like a roosting pigeon, he grabbed the top of the wire for support and tried to find his balance atop the span. It was then he not only felt, but he even heard, the razor slit his hand. The sound almost made him sick to his stomach.

The pain was not enough to stop him. He was halfway over the fence. He went to pull his left leg over the wire but found himself held fast. His black and white jail pants were snarled on the wire.

He felt panic set in for the first time as he sat fully exposed atop the wire. He fought to pull his pant leg free. His violent movements atop the wire had an unintended consequence - they attracted the attention of the drowsy guard in the crow's nest who had been haphazardly watching the exterior surveillance camera.

"Prisoner in the wire!" the jailer yelled, pushing the button to the announcement system, alerting the other correction officers.

However, much like the county commission had tacitly helped with Rhody's escape by not having the jail built to proper specifications, they were also responsible for understaffing the facility. There were just four jailers to guard nearly two hundred inmates.

Rhody was soon bathed in light, the flood lights filling the exercise yard. Realizing it was do or die, Rhody made a daring move. He undid his pants and pulled his legs through the pant legs, the razor ripping the front of his left leg. The move worked as he was free of the razor wire even as he saw a jailer running around the corner of the exercise yard.

He dropped to the outside of the fence, pant-less with just his boxers covering his lower half. The escapee hit the ground running and disappeared into the darkness before the jailer could identify him. The fugitive dashed into the woods that surrounded the jail, slapped in the face by frozen branches as he ran. Rhody was a free man, but for how long? Being discovered before he got away was not part of his plan. His get-away vehicle better be there on time or his goose was cooked.

He emerged from the woods about a hundred yards from the jail. He could see searchlights scanning the darkness. The yells of the jailer for him to "halt" fell on deaf ears. He knew guards didn't have the green light to shoot fleeing prisoners. If they wanted him back, they would have to catch him.

Keeping to his plan, the escapee made his way to the railroad tracks on the other side of the woods as he heard sirens coming from the direction of the jail. Rhody stumbled onto the tracks. The bitter cold was already robbing him of the feeling in his exposed legs. Time was limited. If he didn't get to cover soon he would be faced with the choice of surrender or freezing to death. How he wished he had the blanket he left hanging in the razor wire.

Rhody began to run once he mounted the tracks. He knew his ride, if it were in fact there, was waiting at the first crossing. He had to get there before the police or his escape would be foiled. The cold air ripping his lungs like shards of glass, the fugitive pushed himself as he ran along the track. The cross ties nearly tripped him several times as he ran through the darkness.

Then he saw an outline. Something was sitting on the tracks. Was it his ride or was it the police just waiting for him to come to them? It didn't matter. This was his only chance. Almost to the car, Rhody saw the red glow of a taillight. It was a signal. It was his ride! He had made it. However, raining on his parade was the wash of blue lights that were coming from the left on the other side of the woods.

"In the trunk, fast!" growled the driver as he popped the trunk.

The desperate escapee wasn't about to stop and argue the point. Rhody dove for the trunk without hesitation, slamming the lid closed above him. The car immediately accelerated leaving him immersed in the pitch darkness of its trunk. The sudden acceleration threw the fugitive against the back of the car. The sound of spinning wheels and quickly approaching sirens filled his ears. They were being chased!

What followed was an assault on the already bleeding escapee as he was thrown left and right against the hard metal of the trunk. The getaway driver drifted around corners at top speeds as he tried to elude his pursuers. Half-dazed from the pummeling he was taking in his uncomfortable refuge, Rhody tried to find something to hold on to in the cramped trunk. At one point he felt the car roll onto two wheels as the driver rounded a corner at break-neck speed.

"Was that a gun shot?" Rhody asked himself as he heard a blast from behind.

Police had opened fire on the fleeing car as the driver put space between him and his pursuers. The wheels of the sedan came off the road as he topped a hill traveling over a hundred miles per hour. While not sure their escapee was inside the car, police were taking no chances as they intended to stop the fleeing vehicle. The driver, however, was an expert. He weaved through the side roads outside Easton like a professional.

Bruised and battered from the wild ride, Rhody realized a few minutes later that the sounds of the sirens were getting fainter. He was getting away. A short time after that the sirens were a distant memory. All he could hear was the drone of the car's engine.

Now the only question in Rhody's mind was how long he would have to remain cramped inside the trunk. While considerably warmer than being outside, the trunk still presented a chill on his exposed legs. Plus, the trunk stank. Whoever was doing the driving likely didn't bother cleaning out his car. He probably used it to carry garbage to the dump considering the stench Rhody was noticing now that the chase was over. Judging from the scent, the driver may have actually left a bag in there.

Rhody rolled over and began feeling in the dark. His hands fumbled across something plastic deep inside the trunk. It wasn't a garbage bag though. It was something larger. Rhody probed further and discovered there something really large taking up the back of the trunk. He hadn't noticed it earlier in all the excitement. What was that smell? It was starting to fill his nostrils with a sickly scent.

His curiosity now peaked, Rhody began pulling at the plastic. He found a seam and spread it open. The smell now flooded the closed trunk, filling it with dank air gagging the fugitive. Then it hit him. The smell wasn't garbage. It was rotting flesh! There was a body in the trunk!

The hardened criminal let out a blood curdling scream. His cries were drowned out by the loud roar of the engine. Reaching to push the package away, his hand slipped inside the open tarp. He felt human flesh against his palm.

"Let me out of here!" Rhody yelled as he pounded the trunk lid with all his might.

His fear combined with the stench of the body robbed him of his breath as he struggled to breathe. He had to get out! He continued yelling and beating on the trunk lid with his bloody hand for several minutes until he felt the car slow down and come to a stop.

"Let me out!" Rhody yelled again.

He could hear the engine still idling but no one was answering his shouts.

"Do you hear me?" Rhody screamed. "Is anybody out there? Let me out!"

Again his cries were unanswered as he resumed his beating on the inside of the trunk even as he heard a door close. Was someone coming to let him out or were they coming to kill him? Something was wrong. Things were no longer going according to plan.

That, of course, was a matter of which side of the trunk one was on. For Bart, who stood outside the stolen blue sedan, things were proceeding smoothly with the exception of the heart-stopping run from the law. It reminded him of the old days when he would lead his father's deputies on high speed pursuits through Castle County. He was caught on rare occasions. On those few nights, the rebellious youth would simply be taken home, his punishment usually being the business end of his father's belt. After all, you couldn't just throw the sheriff's son in jail. That experience many years ago made Bart a bit of a professional when it came to evading the law. Even as a successful businessman, Bart still possessed many of his criminal skills.

Now came the easy part, provided his calculations were right. He had only a couple of feet clearance on either side of the guard rail. Too far one way and the car would slam into the rail, stopping it dead. However, if he aimed it right, the car would squeeze between the barrier and into the dark void.

Bart walked over to the top of the drop off, ignoring the yells and pounding of Rhody from the trunk. He could just make out the water seventy feet below at the bottom of the sheer cliff. It would just squeeze through.

"Sorry old buddy," Bart muttered to himself as he reached inside and knocked the car into gear before stepping back to watch it heading toward the cliff.

"We're moving again," Rhody said to himself as he momentarily stopped his pounding.

Those would be his last words. Bart's estimate was right. The car rolled over the sheer cliff and took a nose dive into the frigid water below. Despite the impact with the water having the same force as a head-on collision at highway speeds, Rhody would not die on impact. It would be the freezing water stealing away the last pocket of air in the locked trunk some five minutes later that would end the escapee's life.

Bart lit a cigar and casually leaned against Hurricane Bridge. He took a puff of the Dominican as he saw lights coming from across the high span. It was his ride.

"Perfect timing," Bart said with a grin as he hailed his associates from Pickett County.

THE ONE THAT GOT AWAY

"We got one over the wire," Jail Administrator Chuck Lance shouted over the phone.

The call arrived at the Delaney home just as he was about to nod off following his long day. Sleep had become a luxury the sheriff couldn't afford.

"Who is it? Do we have someone on it?" Sam asked in a drowsy voice.

First a chain of unsolved murders and now a jailbreak. What would happen next? While unusual, jailbreaks were not unheard of at Castle County Jail. The sheriff knew full well the Achilles heel of his jail caused by the cutting of corners in its construction. He also knew the inmates had been probing for its weak spots. A few had been able to break through the unreinforced block over the years.

In most cases, the inmates would be caught before even getting over the razor wire. On rare occasions, prisoners were able to breach the fence and get to the outside. However, in the dozen years Sam had been sheriff, not one inmate had been able to make it on the outside for more than a couple of weeks. Castle County Jail was a regular Stalag Thirteen.

Most escapees would turn up somewhere in Castle County while a few serious fugitives would be captured in nearby counties, usually nabbed while doing something stupid. While annoyed by the jailbreak, Sam had confidence the escapee would turn up in short order.

"We don't know who it is yet," the officer revealed. "We're doing a head count right now. The prisoner was already over the fence by the time the jailer got out there so he wasn't able to see his inmate number on his outfit. As far as we know it's just one inmate."

The timing of the escape seemed odd to the sheriff since the inmate decided to make a break for it on what was one of the coldest nights in years. Sam was more concerned for the inmate's safety given the dangerous cold than he was getting him back in custody. Most inmates in Castle County Jail weren't dangerous. The lion's share of the inmate population was drug addicts, drunks and petty thieves. The dangerous offenders were sent to the state penitentiary to serve their sentences.

"Do we have any idea how he got away?" Sam asked as he pulled on his clothes. "Do we have any idea where he is?"

Lance revealed his suspicions as he spoke up, trying to be heard over noise in the background.

"We had a deputy who went in pursuit of a suspicious vehicle just a block from here right after the escape," Lance explained. "The driver led them on a high speed chase around town until he gave them a slip. We think he may have been in that car but we can't be for sure. It was a blue sedan last seen heading west on the outskirts of Easton. The tags came back stolen. Just in case he wasn't in there, we have our officers searching the woods next to the jail. But, if I were a betting man, I'd put my money on that blue sedan. Our boy can't stay out too long in the elements, especially since he left his pants hanging in the wire."

Sam couldn't help but chuckle given the image of the pantless inmate running around somewhere. The headlines in the local paper would no doubt be hilarious once they got wind of their semi-nude escapee.

Now dressed and ready to head out the door, Sam prepared himself for the manhunt ahead. It was going to be a cold night. Everything would be okay so long as the escapee wasn't ...

"It's Rhody Turner!" Lance barked over the phone. "He was in sick bay and was able to get through a crawl space above the drop ceiling and chisel through the block wall. The other inmates were causing commotion to help cover the noise. They are still brewing it up right now as you can hear."

The news was too much for the sheriff to fathom. His one shot at breaking the cycle of murders was gone hours before Rhody was going to tell all when it came to the secret of the old Red Dog.

"One inmate!" the sheriff yelled at the jailer. "All I ask is that you keep one inmate safe and sound for me for one night and what happens? How in the world could you let Rhody Turner get away? Of all the inmates, why did it have to be Rhody Turner?"

"I'm sorry sheriff. We were short staffed," Lance responded. "You pulled off one of our jailers to help on that surveillance thing you all were doing and we had another jailer call in sick with the flu."

The sheriff ground his teeth together, realizing the cracker box jail provided to him by the county was more to blame than anything. He slammed down the phone and headed to the jail.

Sam found the jail and surrounding areas lit up like Christmas when he arrived ten minutes later. Officers were just completing their sweep of the area around the jail. Aside from his pants, they found no trace of the escapee. That left the blue sedan as the most likely mode of departure for the fugitive.

"We know that car hasn't left the county," Bo said as he briefed the sheriff on the progress of the manhunt. "We radioed ahead to Pickett County. That's the direction the sedan was heading. They had officers standing by on their side of the lake and never saw a car by that description enter their county."

"So he's still in Castle County?" Sam asked. "Or so we believe anyway?"

"It would appear so, sheriff," Bo said. "The question is, where he is hiding out?"

"The real question is who helped him," Sam pointed out. "He had help from the outside. If we find out who that was then I think we figure out where he's hiding out."

That's when Rhody's statement during their meeting at his cell that afternoon struck him.

"He was getting a call from a girl," Sam declared as he snapped his fingers. "He mentioned he was getting a call when I talked to him. I bet that's what we're looking for."

The jail kept electronic records of calls coming in and going out of the facility. The records included recordings of both sides of the conversations between inmates and the callers. Sam suspected the call Rhody received contained references to the pending escape and perhaps clues as to the identity of the woman.

"Pull that recording," Sam ordered. "I want to hear it right now. Perhaps it will shed some light as to where our boy is hiding."

Bo headed down the hall to the computer bank and logged into the central system where the records were stored. He returned ten minutes later to find the sheriff and several of his staff looking over a map of the county.

"Sheriff, we have a problem," Bo declared with an odd look on his face.

"Problem? What kind of problem? We have enough problems already. We can't have any more problems," Sam said, on edge given recent developments.

"It's not there," Bo revealed.

"What do you mean, it's not there?" Sam asked as he stood up from the map. "It has to be there."

"I mean it's gone, sheriff," Bo responded. "The audio from the whole afternoon is missing."

"But how can that happen?" Sam asked.

He had always assumed the program to be secure.

"Well, it's a server-based system that can be logged onto just like any network so long as you have a password," Bo said. "It seems someone logged onto the system and deleted the entire file for this afternoon."

Stunned by what he was hearing, the sheriff was determined to get to bottom of things. He could feel himself about to lose control.

"So this was an inside job?" Sam boomed. "I want to know who logged in and I want them in my office right now! Heads are going to roll!"

Bo looked nervously around the room as his face took on a slight shade of red.

"Can we trace whose password was used to do it?" Sam asked.

"Um yes, we already know," Bo said nervously. "It was yours, sheriff. Whoever did this signed in to the system using your password."

Sam stood speechless, exasperated by the revelation, his staff joining his silence. They were all afraid to speak up, sensing the sheriff was about to blow his top.

The awkward silence was broken moments later as Kendal burst in the room. He paused just long enough to eye the unusually quiet group before blurting out his business.

"There's a car in the water down at the Bottomless Pit," Kendal revealed. "A witness said it went off the Castle County side a few minutes ago."

Silence still hung momentarily over the group as they looked at the excited investigator.

"It was a blue sedan!" Kendal exclaimed.

This time he got a rise out of the lawmen. The sheriff was able to step back from the edge of rage. There was a ray of light at the end of the tunnel.

"Is it still there, I mean on the surface?" Sam excitedly asked.

"No. According to our witness it sunk pretty fast but they have a good location where it went under," Kendal noted. "It was Mitch Reagan who saw it."

Some people called Mitch Reagan a fishing nut while others just called him a nut. The retired rocket scientist spent most of his waking hours either on the lake or talking about going to the lake. If there were any justice in the world, the lake would be named in his honor once he died. However, so long as the fish were biting in Castle Lake, Mitch Reagan would likely live forever.

While Sam didn't realize it, he had caught a break courtesy of Mitch Reagan. Had he not decided to take to the lake on the coldest night in years to try one of his deep water lures, the car would have likely stayed in the depths forever with no one the wiser.

Mitch developed the lure himself and had been aching to try it. The lure, he explained to those who would listen at the neighborhood bait shop near his lake house, was developed for deep water fishing during cold weather. And, what better night to test out his new invention than on Castle Lake on a night the mercury was supposed to hit single digits?

That was what brought him under Hurricane Bridge. He had fished for about an hour and decided to get out of the wind and snow for a moment to pour himself a cup of hot coffee from his thermos. It was at that moment he heard a car approach above him. However, instead of crossing the bridge as he anticipated, it sounded like the car had stopped just short of the bridge. That, Mitch thought to himself as he sipped his coffee, was odd since all that was up there was a sheer cliff with no access to the water. However, before he could dwell on the subject he heard the car start back up. Then, much to his surprise, he heard a noise above him. A second later he heard a loud splash only a few yards away from the bridge, the splash close enough to spray him with the frigid water of Castle Lake.

The old fisherman pulled out his spotlight and

illuminated the form in front of him. The light caught a blue sedan as it quickly slipped below the water. Its windows were all rolled down from what he could see. Despite being surprised, since one doesn't see a car fly off a sheer cliff every evening, Mitch actually considered how unusual it was for a car to have all of its windows down on such a freezing evening.

His consideration didn't last for long as the car submerged like a diving submarine, remaining on the surface for only a couple of minutes. It did remain afloat long enough for him to tell there was no one inside the car's interior as he motored closer to the sinking car before it slipped under the black water for what would be a lengthy decent. He reckoned someone was dumping a stolen car since driverless cars aren't common things.

The water in Castle Lake was part of a reservoir system meaning depths reached well over one hundred feet in some areas. The particular area where Mitch saw the car enter the water was a place many fishermen called the Bottomless Pit due to the depth of the water there. Some areas below the bridge were rumored to be as deep as two hundred feet. Whether the depth was rumor or fact, the Bottomless Pit had seen its share of incidents over the years, most having to do with daring divers who risked life and limb to leap from the arch bridge. At its high point, the bridge spired eighty feet above the lake making for a dangerous jump even for a professional cliff diver. The bridge claimed several lives over the years, amateurs learning one wrong move meant death when diving from such a height. The bridge, despite a newly installed safety railing system, had been the scene of a handful of suicides over the years. Some nicknamed the bridge Lover's Leap given the grieving lovers who had said farewell to the cruel world by jumping from the bridge's heights. The bridge had even been the scene of a murder, well, at least the disposal of a pair of murder victims who had been tossed from the top of the bridge, bricks weighting their legs.

It took divers and recovery personnel the better part of a week to find the bodies that were submerged nearly one hundred feet down even after a snitch told them exactly where the bodies had been dumped over the side of the span. The Bottomless Pit definitely presented issues, especially during the dead of winter and during a snow storm which was only going to increase in intensity.

"I need your boats in the water first thing this morning," Sam yelled into the phone as he motored toward Hurricane Bridge.

On the other end of the line was John Bray, director of the local rescue squad that specialized in water recovery operations.

"It's not even getting past freezing tomorrow, sheriff," Bray replied.

He wasn't keen on paging out his men on such a bitterly cold day given the fact it was a recovery not a rescue operation.

"I say we do it first of next week," Bray suggested. "It should be a little warmer then."

Sam knew he couldn't wait that long to determine if his escapee was in the submerged sedan so he turned the screws on the rescue squad director.

"I need that car found and pulled out of the lake immediately, if not sooner," Sam declared flatly.

"I don't see what the rush is, sheriff. It ain't like it's going anywhere," Bray continued. "I mean it gets real cold on that lake, plus it's going to be snowing."

"John!" Sam began. "If I don't see those boats in Castle Lake as soon as the sun comes up this morning then I'm going to get on the horn and I'm going to call in one of those professional recovery teams to do it. Then, when you come in front of the county commission asking for money in the budget next year for the rescue squad, I'm going to point out we already spent it paying someone else to do your job."

"You don't have to threaten me, Sam," Bray responded indignantly. "I'll round up the boys. We'll be there."

Meanwhile, back at city hall, Glenn listened from his raised third story window to the sound of sirens. He wondered with a deep sense of dread if their plan had been foiled. What was happening out there? From the sounds of sirens and the glow of emergency lights, it seemed like the end of the world. Had Bart succeeded in his mission to dispose of Stevie's body or had he been discovered? Was he implicating him in the crime, perhaps even confessing to their indiscretion long ago? Why hadn't he heard from Bart?

The minutes seemed to pass like hours as he waited for word. In the meantime, the mayor took time to clean up any tell-tale evidence that a body had been hidden in his office for an entire day while he lingered at city hall. He also figured his office could use a good airing out since Bart so easily detected the smell of death when he visited there earlier in the evening. The open window was providing him an ear to his city as well as importing fresh air to flush out any smell of rotting flesh that was hanging in the room.

The mayor noted a second round of sirens about thirty minutes after the first group circled the city. The first group seemed to come from the direction of the county jail while the last group seemed to be heading to the west in the direction of Pickett County. Did it have something to do with Bart or was it merely something like a wreck or fire? If only Bart would answer his phone he would know. On the other hand, as mayor he could call one of the city officers and ask but then he didn't want to attract suspicion, especially if the sirens had something to do with Bart.

Tired of waiting after maintaining his vigil for nearly two hours, Glenn decided it was time to head home. Perhaps he could raise Bart later and find out how things went. For now he was going to bid farewell to the office where he had waited all day to ensure no one discovered Stevie hanging in his closet. While he often spent a lot of time in the office, this had been his longest day ever at city hall. He would be glad to get home and take a load off in his nice warm bed. The cold from the open window was starting to chill him to the bone. He could contact Bart just as well from his home as he could from the office through the magic of cellular phones. There was no reason to wait for his cohort's return in the same office where a body had hung all day. The mere thought of it gave the mayor another chill.

"I'm out of here," Glenn said to himself as he grabbed his coat and headed for the door.

His egress was halted in its tracks, however, when he heard movement down the dimly lit hall moments after locking his office door.

"Is someone there?" Glenn asked with his voice shaking. "Hello, anybody there?"

The mayor stood and listened for a few moments before convincing himself that the sound was a figment of his imagination. He figured he had a right to hear noises given the day he just endured. Anyone would be jumpy after spending a day locked in the same room as their friend's decaying body.

Glenn continued down the hall toward the elevator as he pulled on his overcoat. It was frigid outside and he didn't want to catch his death of cold.

His potential cause of death, however, came into question at that very moment as he heard movement in the stairwell located just steps away from the elevator. Someone was coming up the stairs from the bottom floor. Who would be inside city hall at this hour? Glenn had made sure all the doors were locked, double-checking them himself since he didn't want a secretary or custodian to surprise him as he was tossing Stevie's body out his office window.

Glenn hoped against hope the elevator was waiting just on the other side of the door. There was one set of stairs and one elevator that served the old building so his options for a quick exit were limited since the stairs were occupied by whoever was coming up. He knew the chances were whoever was making their way up the steps was friendly. Perhaps it was even a police officer checking on the building.

But, there was that place in the back of his mind that reminded him there was a killer on the loose and that he was a likely target. Law enforcement may not have connected him with the incident at the old Red Dog but he supposed the killer had done his homework and knew he was amongst the guilty.

The mayor's hopes were dashed when he pushed the elevator button and heard the cart activate from down below. His continued pressing of the button did nothing to accelerate the slow elevator's arrival. Meanwhile, he could hear the footsteps round the second landing and continue toward the third floor. He couldn't afford to wait for the elevator. He needed to get away now.

His keys! The mayor fumbled through his pocket for his keys as he began walking quickly toward his office. The footsteps reached the landing outside the third floor. Just as he anticipated the door to be thrust open, the footsteps stopped. The momentary quiet didn't discourage Glenn from sorting through his keys to find the one to open his office.

"There it is," Glenn said to himself as he found the key and started to insert it in the lock.

His rush to refuge, however, was placed on hold momentarily by his curiosity. He knew he had heard footsteps in the stairwell. There was no way, even in his present state, he dreamed that up. But why did they just stop? Perhaps he would call out once before cowering in his office for the rest of the night hoping the old wooden door would protect him from whoever was outside.

"Hello, anyone there?" Glenn called out. "It's Mayor Satterfield here."

Glenn slipped the key in his lock just in case. However, his question was answered by complete silence.

"I said is anybody there?" Glenn asked in a louder voice.

This time, much to his chagrin, his question was answered not by a voice, but instead by a presence. The door at the end of the hall flew open.

He couldn't believe his eyes! It was a man without a face! A form dressed in black, a dark man, his face completely covered or missing, had burst through the door. The scene was surreal as the being seemed to move at almost superhuman speed as he rushed down the corridor toward the mayor.

Glenn couldn't move. His feet were paralyzed with fear almost as if they were stuck in cement. What was in the thing's hand? It was a scythe! The Grim Reaper was coming to get him! He was going to collect his head just like Eddie's!

Finally able to gather his senses and muster movement, he twisted the key but in his rush he snapped the key off in the lock, leaving the key chain in his hand and the rest of his office key jammed in the lock. He was a sitting duck! If only the door to the conference room were open next to his, he might avoid being hacked to pieces. It was his only chance.

Luck was with him as he lunged for the knob. The door swung open, allowing him to duck inside as the form raised the blade over its head preparing for his decapitation.

Glenn felt the creature slam its weight against the other side of the door just as he reached and locked it from the inside. He was safe, at least for the time being. He could call for help from his temporary refuge.

Where was his phone? Panic overtook him as he felt through his clothes and his overcoat, finding nothing. Then it hit him. He had left his cellphone in his suit coat which he now realized was hanging over his chair inside his locked office. He had taken off his suit coat fearing he might get some of Stevie's blood on it when he tossed him out the window. It was a five-hundred dollar suit and it would be awkward explaining to the dry cleaner how blood got on his jacket.

Glenn strained to think of his next move as whatever was on the other side began beating on the door. The old wooden door facing was starting to give way from the power of the blows coming from outside. The door wouldn't hold up indefinitely.

The mayor pressed his weight back against the door hoping to buy a little more time while he considered his limited options. He also hoped, while doing so, the scythe wouldn't come slicing through the door and subsequently through him. He had been fortunate to make it to the safety of the conference room but in doing so he had entered one of the few rooms in city hall without a phone.

He, in his power as mayor, had removed the phones from the meeting room last year, tired of meetings being interrupted by the ringing of the land line. It was bad enough cellphones would constantly interrupt important city meetings without the regular phone intruding on important matters. As such, he banned both cellphones and land lines inside the meeting room. Whatever it was could wait until the meeting was over. What a stupid decision.

Glenn looked around the room as the pounding from the other side of the door echoed through his head like a neverending nightmare. What could he do? Where could he go? Then it dawned on him. He was looking right at it. The window!

He could crawl out the window and climb onto the thin ledge. From there he could make his way back over to his office where there was a pair of phones. He could call for help, that is, if he didn't tumble from the third story onto the concrete below. He could still hear the sound of Stevie's lifeless body slamming onto the sidewalk with a thud.

Glenn knew that while it wasn't a great option, it was his only option if he wanted to live. He couldn't hold off the thing forever. He had to go now.

Glenn shot across the dark room straight for the window

as the thing kept beating on the door. His progress was slowed as he tried to thrust open the window. It was stuck!

"No! You can't be stuck!" Glenn pleaded as he pulled with all his might on the window.

Meanwhile the pounding on the door became even louder. He could hear the wood on the door start to splinter.

"Come on, open!" Glenn pleaded.

The window crashed open as the mayor gave it one last tug. A rush of freezing wind slapped him in the face.

"Here goes nothing," Glenn said to himself as he climbed out the window and onto the small concrete ledge.

Glenn forced himself to slide along the ledge, scooting his feet an inch at a time as the wind whistled through his ears. The concrete ledge was only about the size of his foot and left little room for error. He feared if he didn't put distance between himself and the open window the Reaper's hands would extend out the window and pull him back into the room or push him off the ledge. He could still hear the beating on the door as he inched his way along the concrete. He tried not to look down while the chilling wind buffeted his body. He would be lucky if he weren't swept off the ledge by the wind before he reached his office window.

"Take your time, Glenn, take your time," he encouraged himself as he accidentally looked down.

The mayor was careful to keep himself pressed up as closely as he could to the cold brick on the side of city hall. He knew any lean forward could be his last move. If he could reach the recess in the brick near his window he would have more room.

"Almost there," Glenn continued encouraging himself.

He looked at his destination from the corner of his eye. He was afraid to turn his head out of fear of losing his balance. Instead he tried to keep his eyes on the horizon and his back pressed firmly against the wall.

Then his outstretched right hand found the recess in the brick, telling him he had reached his window. He cupped his hand on the recess, helping pull himself over to the glass. The recess was not quite tall enough where he could stand straight up inside it.

His five minutes of work slowly inching his way to his window now found him faced with two questions. First, was his window locked? And second, why had the pounding stopped at the conference room door? In his concentration during his high wire act over downtown Easton, the absence of the pounding hadn't registered. Had the thing finally busted through the door or worse, had it gone next door? Was it in his office waiting in the dark for him?

He didn't have a choice. He would have to take his chances inside. He hadn't seen a single person or vehicle pass the whole time he was on the ledge and, given the snow and cold, it was unlikely anyone would just happen along. His choices were either to stay up on the ledge and freeze to death, fall off the ledge perhaps to his death or climb into his office and perhaps fall victim to the dark man. He would choose door number three.

Glenn got a quick answer to his first question, as much to his dismay the window was locked. He would have to break it open but in doing so would have to carefully swing his heel to avoid losing his balance. The fact his entire body was going numb would make it even more dangerous.

His first attempt at smashing the window failed. The shatter resistant glass resisted his attempt at breaking and entering. They had replaced the windows at city hall last year to rebuff a gang of BB gun bandits who had been shooting out windows around town. The glass was the only new thing about the building.

He realized his pounding on the glass would likely alert the thing inside to his plans. He would only have a couple of more attempts before it would try to get in his office, that is, if it weren't already lurking inside.

Glenn took a deep gulp of the cold air as he cocked his foot and prepared to make another attempt.

"What are you doing up there?" Bart's voice called up from the sidewalk.

The sound of Bart's voice from below almost caused Glenn to lose his balance. He hadn't seen him approach from the shadows.

"It's in there!" Glenn hissed down, again flattening himself against the brick.

"What's in there?" Bart replied as he was obviously taken back by seeing the mayor tiptoeing thirty feet above the sidewalk.

"The killer - he's inside," Glenn responded in a loud whisper. "He's after me!"

"Stay where you are. I'll be right up," Bart shouted from the sidewalk as he pulled a gun from under his coat.

His rescue mission was short-lived, however as he returned to the sidewalk seconds later.

"The door's locked," Bart yelled back up.

Glenn slowly fished the keys out of his pocket careful to make no sudden movements.

"Here, it's the round one," Glenn announced as he tossed the key ring down.

Bart snatched the key out of the air as it fell. However, even as he prepared to enter the building, he wondered why the door was locked. Would the killer take the time to lockup behind him if he were in the building? Something didn't make sense.

Glenn tried to think happy thoughts as he heard the front door close indicating Bart had entered city hall. Would he hear a gunshot if Bart found whatever it was or would that thing, that dark man, ambush Bart and come back up to finish him? Would there be a point where Glenn would have to choose between taking a leap of faith onto the sidewalk below or fighting off the Reaper?

The mayor rested his head against the brick, keeping his eyes fixed on the building across the street. He could see the pulsing lights atop the city's water tower just on the other side of the small-town skyline. He watched, counting the flashes, trying to take his mind off of the fact he could die at any moment. Where was Bart? Was he already dead?

His question was answered as his office window flew up without warning and a hand extended out grasping his arm in its steely grip.

"Get in here," Bart said as he pulled him through the open window.

The mayor looked wild eyed as he scanned the room, looking for any sign of the dark man.

"Where's he at?" Glenn asked nervously. "Did you find him?"

Bart slammed the window down, closing out the cold as he gave his friend a glare.

"There's no one here …there's nothing," Bart declared. "Look around. We're the only ones here."

"But he was out there," Glenn insisted. "He came at me from down the hall and I snapped my key off in the door trying to get back in."

Bart calmly walked to the mayor's office door and inspected it.

"You mean this door?" Bart asked. "Your office door was unlocked, Glenn."

Glenn rushed over to the door and examined it closely but found no evidence of the key he had broken off in the lock just minutes before.

"That's impossible," Glenn declared.

The mayor could feel Bart's eyes upon him, a look of doubt in his gaze.

"I didn't dream it up," Glenn insisted as Bart continued giving him the odd look. "I'm telling you it was after me. I'm not crazy."

"What was after you?" Bart asked as he put his gun back into his shoulder holster.

"The Grim Reaper - the dark man - something," Glenn responded, the words already sounding unbelievable before he got them out. "I mean he was all in black and he had one of those sickle things. He tried to cut me to pieces I tell you. Don't look at me like that. I know what I saw!"

Glenn knew Bart didn't believe his tale given the look on his face.

"Tell you what, Glenn, it's been a long night," Bart began in a patronizing tone. "Let's go home and I'm sure things will look different in the light of day."

"You don't believe me, do you?" Glenn said incredulously. "I know what I saw. It was here. Why do you think I'd crawl out on that ledge? I'm scared of heights for crying out loud."

Bart looked Glenn in the eye, realizing his friend may be going off the deep end given the pressures of the day.

"I'm sure you thought you saw something," Bart began. "But the bottom line is the door to city hall was locked, your door was unlocked and there's no key broke off inside it. Let's just go home and get some rest then you can tell me everything again in the morning."

Glenn ground his teeth in frustration, knowing Bart doubted his story.

"Let's go then," Glenn growled, snatching his suit coat off the back of his chair.

"By the way, I need a lift," Bart continued. "My ride dropped me off here and it's a little cold for a walk this time of night."

"How'd it go?" Glenn asked.

He'd forgotten all about their mission amid all the excitement of running for his life.

"He's laid to rest," Bart quipped.

"What about our other problem?" the mayor shot back

"Not a problem," Bart responded with a sneer. "I killed two birds with one stone. Let's go get some sleep."

UP FROM THE DEEP

John Bray was a man of his word. His crew put in at Floating Mill at the crack of dawn before taking the short boat ride over to Hurricane Bridge. They were already conducting their first sweep of the black water below the span when Sam arrived following a short cat nap on his office couch.

"There, you happy?" John Bray asked, walking alongside the sheriff who leaned over the side of Hurricane Bridge to watch the squad members below.

Sam sipped his morning coffee as he watched the search effort. He was keeping his fingers crossed they would be able to find something. However, knowing the reputation of Castle Lake, the sheriff knew the odds were against them finding the blue sedan beneath the depths.

"I'd be happier if they found something," Sam admitted.

Bray was a veteran of many search and recovery operations around Hurricane Bridge. His crew was usually called upon to find the bodies of unfortunate swimmers and divers who went missing on the lake. However, in this case, their focus was an automobile. The fact it was larger than a body would make it easier to find but even if they did, raising it would be another matter.

"Well even if we find something there are no assurances we'll be able to bring it up," Bray admitted. "If your car is out past fifty yards from the bank then it's likely went down into the Bottomless Pit and there's no way we can pull it up with the equipment we've got. You'd need a major crane and we won't be able to get one of those in here until the first of the week."

Sam wasn't daunted by Bray's assessment of the situation as he figured it was time for him to catch a break.

"What if it didn't go into the Pit?" Sam questioned.

"'There's a rock shelf near the bank which only goes down about thirty feet," Bray answered. "If your car is on that and didn't go over in the Pit then there's a good chance we can use a heavy duty tow truck to wench it out. But that's a big if. We'd have to be awfully lucky."

"Hey chief, we got something," the voice of one of the squad members sounded over Bray's radio. "We have it on the remote underwater camera here. It looks to be a car."

Bray was obviously surprised by the find as he assumed a vehicle with any momentum would have made it to the Pit. He didn't realize the car was barely creeping along when it plunged off the cliff.

"Is it on the shelf?" Bray called back.

"Yes but just barely," the searcher responded. "We need to get a diver and a hook in here pretty quick or the current may pull it down into the Pit."

"Okay, I've got the wench," Bray began. "Now, what idiot are we going to get to go down there in that cold water and hook it up so we can pull it out?"

Sam gave Bray a smile. He had come ready for such an eventuality.

"Eight-seventeen, this is eight hundred," Sam spoke into his radio. "I need you to come on out here and bring your cold water gear. We found it."

"Ten-four sheriff," replied the officer on the other end. "You'll owe me a big one this time."

"We'll work something out, officer," Sam replied. "Just get on out here and dress warm."

Thirty minutes later an SUV with flashing lights sped up to the scene. Bo hopped out from the driver's side and walked to the passenger door, opening it for his passenger. Being a country boy, he still believed in chivalry.

"Hey gorgeous. What took you so long?" Sam asked as he extended his hand to help his wife out of the vehicle.

Carly was already dressed in her diving gear when she arrived. The skin-tight suit, while covering her from head-to-toe, would do little to cut the chill of the frigid lake. Her time in the water would be limited.

"You better shut your mouth or I'll make you put this thing on," the sheriff's wife replied as she went to the back seat to lug her SCUBA gear out.

Mrs. Delaney was not only the brains of the operation at Castle County Sheriff Department but she was also one of the best divers in the county. She learned her craft back in college and continued her education in advanced diving after graduation. Sam didn't like what he referred to as "big water". He opted to stay on the boat when his wife would go diving on their vacations to the beach each year. The sheriff often quipped it was too difficult to drink a beer underwater, explaining why he would stay on the boat with a fishing rod while she was swimming with the sharks.

"Okay, Mrs. Delaney," Bray began in a patronizing tone as he and the sheriff carried the heavy gear down the treacherous path to the water. "When you get under there you need to ..."

"Yeah, yeah, I know. I need to attach the hook to the frame on both sides and loop it over so it doesn't slip," she interrupted. "This isn't my first rodeo."

Bray was somewhat taken back by being preempted by a woman given he was from a discipline dominated by men.

"Okay, well, it's pretty dark down there so you'll need to ..." Bray began only to be interrupted again.

"Yeah, yeah. Follow the underwater camera cable down to it," Carly said. "You boys just make sure you know how to work the wench."

All Sam could do was laugh as Bray shot him a puzzled

look.

"She'll eat you whole and spit out the bones," Sam warned. "Just stay out of her way and you'll be fine. You do know how to work the wench ... right?"

The recovery base was set up about thirty yards from the dive. It was the only flat place on the bank where the wrecker could park at the bottom of the hilly terrain.

Ten minutes later Carly was in the water, making her way down the cable to the submerged car. Sam would owe her a big one given the fact the mercury was still in the twenties meaning the water temperature was, well, very cold. The hook-up itself took far less time than it did just getting into the water as Carly surfaced five minutes later and gave them a thumbs up.

Sam was chilled just extending his hand to help his wife onto shore. He could only imagine how frigid it was to be completely under the freezing water even with a winter dive suit.

"Was it cold down there?" Bray asked in what had to be the dumbest question Sam had heard in a long time.

Carly shook her head in disbelief as she removed her mask. She pretended she didn't hear the squad director's question. There was simply no response to such an ignorant statement.

"Get me somewhere warm," Carly demanded as Bo threw a parka over her shoulders.

"Get in the cab of the tow truck," Sam suggested. "It should be toasty in there. We left the heat running for you."

The tow truck operator wasted no time starting the wench. The cable strained against the weight of the automobile. A full minute elapsed as the cable hauled the car up from the depths, the trunk finally breaking the surface. It was a blue sedan!

"Bingo," Sam exclaimed as he slapped Bray on the back. "Good work."

Two minutes later the car was on shore. Water poured out

from its open windows quickly revealing no one was in the passenger compartment.

"Do you suppose he ditched the car?" Bo questioned. "Or maybe whoever was in there floated out."

Sam realized immediately upon seeing the open windows that no one drives down the road with their windows down on a night when the low is in the single digits. This told him the car was intentionally sunk. And, being a veteran lawman, Sam knew there was one place they hadn't checked yet. It was a place in which he had found some interesting things over the years – the trunk.

Sam leaned into the driver's window and triggered the trunk as Bo walked around to open the hood. Sam didn't have to move from where he was standing to tell something was in the trunk. All he had to do is watch the expression of his detective's face.

"I suppose the trunk isn't empty, huh?" Sam asked with a sense of dread.

"Good news or bad news?" Bo asked, shooting the sheriff a helpless look.

"Good news. I can sure use some good news," Sam replied.

"Well, the good news is we've found Stevie Grissom's body," Bo responded. "And, better yet, it appears all his parts are with him."

"And the bad news?" Sam winced.

"Rhody Turner isn't going to be making any statements," Bo revealed.

Sam walked with a defeated gait to where Bo was standing over the trunk. He stood viewing the bodies of Rhody Turner and Stevie Grissom for a few moments. It was all too much to digest.

"How?" Sam asked as he slammed his fist down on the car. "How did he get him out? It doesn't make sense. How could our killer convince Rhody to break out?"

"Maybe it wasn't our killer, sheriff," Bo said. "Maybe

our killer has a sidekick. After all, Rhody did say he was going to talk to his old lady."

"Or maybe our killer is a woman," Sam shot back. "How do we know this isn't the work of a female? I mean a woman can be as dangerous as a man. Just look at my wife. If we just knew who his old lady was."

Bo gave the sheriff a grin. He had just remembered a minor detail he forgot to share with his boss given the shock of their discovery.

"Oh, we know," Bo revealed. "While you were snoring on the couch this morning, and yes you do snore, Kendal ran down some leads and found out the identity of Rhody's girlfriend. By the way, have you noticed Kendal never sleeps plus he has that pasty-looking skin? I think he may be a vampire."

Shrugging off Bo's comment about his associate investigator, Sam was anxious to find out more about the identity of the mysterious woman. He hated being the last to know something.

"Do we know if he's paid her a visit?" Sam asked.

"He was supposed to be heading over as I was bringing your wife out here," Bo responded. "I got so busy that I forgot to tell you about it."

"Eight-ten, what'd you find out?" Bo asked over his portable.

The pair waited in the cold for several seconds with only static answering Bo's radio call.

"She's gone," Kendal revealed after the slight delay. "Her landlord let me into her apartment and all of her personal stuff is gone. He said she skipped out yesterday sometime without paying this month's rent too. The girl's name is Tia Wray."

Sam knew immediately the woman was not their killer. The young woman had only recently showed up on the radar screen of law enforcement. Her problems with the law were rooted to her addiction to meth. The illicit drug explained her association with Rhody. The career criminal was long known to prefer younger women since they were easier to corrupt. He also used younger girls to buy the ingredients he needed to make his meth.

"She's a Smurf," Sam noted.

The disappearance of the young woman was disturbing to the sheriff, and not just because she may have helped facilitate Rhody's escape. He realized she was a small-time criminal and was way in over her head. If she had fallen in with the killer unawares, then she might suffer the same fate as her boyfriend.

"Put out an all-points bulletin," Sam ordered. "If anyone comes across her tell them we want her stopped and held."

"Will do, sheriff," Kendal signed out.

"I don't have a good feeling about this," Sam said as he and Bo climbed the hill. "I don't have a good feeling at all."

The thing about small towns is it doesn't take much time for news to spread. The grisly discovery of the bodies of Stevie Grissom and Rhody Turner was the talk of the town before lunchtime. Accounts of the pair of corpses found in the submerged car were already common knowledge long before the newspaper hit the street. The mayor didn't wait on the newspaper to arrive to demand answers from his old friend.

"What did you do?" Glenn shouted as he stalked into Bart's office at the dealership, still strung out from a sleepless night.

Sleep eluded Glenn after he returned to his home that morning. The vision of the dark man materialized in his mind every time he was about to nod off. He probably evaded the blade of the mysterious intruder a thousand times that morning as he played the events at city hall over in his mind. He wondered if he would ever be able to sleep again. He feared that if he did close his eyes, the dark man would be there to collect his head when he opened them again.

"It's all over the street," Glenn continued.

His loud tone prompted Bart to scurry over and close his door so their conversation wouldn't be overheard by a passerby.

"This wasn't what we agreed on," Glenn scowled.

Bart gave his friend a questioning look. He was put off by the mayor's lack of appreciation for his efforts.

"Really Glenn? Really?" Bart responded. "You're going to go there? I did what I had to do for all of us."

"You didn't have to kill him," Glenn incredulously replied.

"What'd you expect me to do? Take him out to dinner and sweet talk him?" Bart responded in a mocking tone. "You wanted me to take care of the Rhody Turner problem and I did – permanently."

"I thought you would pay him off or come to some kind of understanding," Glenn countered. "I never expected you to kill him and stuff him in the trunk of a car."

Bart walked back over and took his seat. His calm demeanor after killing their old friend was disturbing to Glenn. He saw no signs of remorse. Bart spoke of killing Rhody as if he were describing taking out the trash to the curb.

"It was the only way," Bart declared. "He was a loose cannon. Now that he knew he could deal his way out of his problems by giving us up, it was just a matter of time until he put our heads on the chopping block in exchange for a get out of jail free card."

Glenn wasn't buying Bart's explanation. He was still stunned his old chum would resort to murder. But then why should he be surprised since it wasn't the first time. Glenn knew Bart's reputation. He had heard the rumors.

"I still can't believe you killed him," Glenn responded. "You murdered him in cold blood for crying out loud."

Bart wasn't going to put up with Glenn's insolence. The

mayor wanted his problems solved but was complaining when they weren't solved to his liking.

"If I were you, I wouldn't be such a big hypocrite," Bart shot back. "You wanted the issue to go away but you don't have the stomach for how I took care of it. Face it my old friend, you're just as guilty as I am. We are in this together to the bitter end."

"That's where you're wrong, Bart," Glenn disagreed. "I'm not a killer. I have a conscience. I have a soul."

Glenn's comment made Bart chuckle. The mayor's holier-than-thou attitude was almost comical given their history.

"Well I have a soul myself old friend," Bart laughed. "I mean come on, something has to go to Hell when I die. As for that whole conscience thing, I guess they forgot to give me one of those. It makes life a lot easier."

Bart's words chilled Glenn. He realized for the first time that his old friend was a psychopath - a homicidal psychopath.

"I don't want any part of this," Glenn declared. "His blood is on your hands, not mine."

"What about Earl Cutts?" Bart asked. "Whose hands is his blood on? You know blood doesn't wear off a person's hands after only twenty years. Like it or not, your Honor, you're just as much a killer as me. I'm just man enough to admit it."

Bart's statement, while ringing somewhat true, made Glenn's face turn bright red as his anger built.

"I'm not the one who hit him," Glenn hissed.

He looked around to see if anyone were nearby listening to him despite the fact the men were standing alone together in the closed room. Even more than twenty years later, they talked about the Red Dog events in hushed tones.

"It wasn't my idea to torch the place either," Glenn accused. "That was all on you."

Again laughing a maniacal laugh, Bart corrected his

guest.

"Even back then you wanted your problems solved but wasn't man enough to do what needed to be done," Bart began. "You tell me. What would have happened if that little girl we partied with that night went to the D.A. and then Mr. Cutts decided to grow himself a conscience? First off, you wouldn't be the mayor of Easton, that's for sure. No, you'd just now be getting out of prison, branded a rapist for the rest of your life. I'd say that'd hurt your election chances."

Glenn remained quiet for a moment. He was sickened by the knowledge that Bart was right, at least partially.

"You know, sometimes I wish we had just come clean back then," Glenn said soberly. "What we did with that girl was wrong and we made it worse with what we did to Mr. Cutts. Now we're all going to pay for it. All it did was bought us twenty years of regret."

"I can't believe what I'm hearing," Bart countered. "We all had a hand in what happened back then. You're as much to blame for the demise of old man Cutts as I am. It sounds like you're trying to rewrite history at the first sign of trouble."

"The first sign of trouble?" Glenn exclaimed. "There are four people dead, one who you personally killed, and some creature running around trying to collect the rest of us."

"Would you shut up with this talk of creatures and grim reapers?" Bart countered. "Do you have any idea how crazy you sound with that talk?"

"You weren't there last night, Bart. You didn't see what I saw," Glenn responded. "If you'd been there you wouldn't think I was crazy. You'd be wondering what we could do to stop it before it finishes its mission."

"Mission? Really? And what would that mission be?" Bart scoffed.

"Revenge," Glenn responded. "He told us he would get us. He told us he would take us to Hell with him. Can't you see? He's making good on his word."

"That's the most ridiculous thing I've ever heard," Bart said. "He's nothing but a pile of ashes."

"Well I guess we'll know pretty soon," Glenn retorted. "There's four down and three to go."

"Three?" Bart shot back.

"Don't play games, Bart," Glenn replied. "He was as much a part of it as any of us."

"You need to watch what you say, old friend," Bart said, narrowing his eyes at his guest.

"Just stating fact," Glenn said. "Without him we would have never gotten away with it and you know it."

Bart stood up from his desk. The direction of Glenn's conversation was going somewhere he did not like.

"I think it's time for you to go," Bart declared as he pointed to the door.

"I've said what I came to say," Glenn huffed. "You won't be seeing me, for a while anyway. I'm getting out of town until this all blows over. I'm taking me a long-overdue vacation."

"Maybe the grim reaper won't follow you to the beach," Bart sneered as he still stood behind his desk.

"You'll see, you'll see," Glenn assured him as he turned and walked for the door. "He's coming for all of us."

"Oh, one last thing," Bart called out as Glenn reached for the door. "The next time you find a body in your closet at city hall, don't call me."

With that Glenn stepped out the door, slamming it behind him hard enough to rattle the glass. After more than twenty years, their friendship was over.

FROM THE ASHES

Sam sighed as he settled in behind his desk. The veteran lawmen was feeling overwhelmed. Things had changed dramatically over the past week in what had been a relatively peaceful Castle County. At least four deaths were on the unsolved list under his watch and he suspected the number would climb if recent history was any indication.

Adding to the frustration was the lack of leads as to the identity of the killer. His potential witnesses were dropping like flies. He realized the morning's discovery would bring another round of questions from the press. The growing body count would likely catch the collective eye of statewide media. Castle County's problem would soon be on newsprint and television screens across the state if not the nation. What could he tell them? That all this was the work of a killer seeking revenge for a long-past injustice that happened in a place that ceased to exist over two decades ago? There was no precedence for something like was happening. Generally, vengeance is something sought while passions are high, not many years later when cooler heads prevail. Who waits twenty years for payback?

Sam rubbed his eyes as he pushed the message button on his office answering machine, expecting more media inquiries and calls from concerned citizens who feared for the security of their county. Frankly, Sam couldn't blame folks for losing confidence. Their illusion of security was being dashed by the recent unsolved homicides. They elected

Sam Delaney to provide that sense of security. It was a job he succeeded in for twelve years. Now, if things didn't change soon, all those years of work making Castle County a safe place to raise the kids would be forgotten, replaced by a sense of uncertainty.

The messages droned on as Sam wrote down a few numbers to call back while fast-forwarding through others. Most of the messages came from busybodies wondering what was going on. They could read the paper like everyone else. Cliff had used his "dark man" suggestion in his last headline. He could only hazard to guess what would be next.

Sam would soon know the cause of death for both Stevie Grissom and Rhody Turner. Investigator Parks accompanied the bodies to the medical examiner and was under orders to report the preliminary results immediately. The sheriff was pretty certain on the mode of death for Stevie. His throat was cut from ear to ear. However, the reason for Rhody's demise was more subtle as his body, still dressed in his black and white jail top, appeared basically unscathed. The slashes to his arms and legs, he figured, were likely inflicted by the jail's razor wire at the time of his escape. The sheriff hoped the medical examiner would find something, anything, that could jumpstart the investigation. Aside from the long shot that remained in the records of Shelby Mental Health Institute, the sheriff had nothing left unless Bart suddenly had a change of heart. However, Sam had his doubts Bart even had a heart. Regardless, if things continued at their current pace, Bart wouldn't be around much longer anyway. The sheriff just wondered how many other citizens of Castle County would also cease to exist at the hands of the killer.

Sam resisted the temptation to simply press the "delete all" button on his answering machine as he cycled through the tenth message, none of them amounting to a hill of beans. His perseverance was rewarded with message eleven. That message changed everything.

"I have information that you may find of interest," came

the barely audible voice of a man, gasping his words onto the sheriff's answering machine. "I know things that may shed some light on the case you're working on."

It was nothing new for Sam to receive "hot tips" about everything ranging from dogs running at large to the location of Jimmy Hoffa's body. From time to time tips did pan out but often they were the figment of overactive imaginations and manifestations of conspiracy theories. The next words the mysterious voice uttered, however, convinced the sheriff the caller was legitimate. The man, speaking in a feeble voice, was obviously laboring to breathe while leaving the short message.

"I know about the Red Dog," the man continued. "I also know about your four killings there. There will be more."

The caller's dire prediction, while not surprising, still chilled the lawman. There was a sound of certainty in the weak voice.

"You can find me at two-thirty-two Robertson Lane in Harvest Lake," the man noted in his faint voice. "You need to come today. Time is running out for everyone, even me. Ask for Bob Smith."

The cryptic invitation marked the end of the phone call as the man hung up without revealing any more clues as to his identity.

The sheriff, who was ready to grab at straws minutes before, jotted down the address. He wasn't about to look a gift horse in the mouth. There was something about the man's voice that convinced him the caller might be able to tie the recent deaths to events twenty years ago. He was going to take another two-hour trip, this time to the retirement community of Harvest Lake. He trusted he wouldn't drive up to a mental institution this time. At any rate, he knew the person he was looking for was still alive, at least for the time being.

"I'm heading to Harvest Lake," Sam declared as he ducked into the detectives' office.

"If you don't mind me saying, this is an odd time for fishing given the murders and all," Bo pointed out.

"I'm going fishing alright, fishing for information," Sam quipped as he pulled on his coat. "I need you to see the judge up in Shelby and get me a search warrant for Gina Porter's records at SMHI. If we let the judge get away for the weekend, we'll have to wait until Monday and we don't have that kind of time."

Sam headed back out into the cold after issuing his orders, wasting no time pointing his SUV into the wind in the direction of Harvest Lake. Snow was falling once again. The continued cold was allowing the white powder to stick not only to the ground but the roads, even during daylight. The sheriff figured by tomorrow evening the long anticipated winter storm would have Castle County in its icy grip. Forecasters were calling for as much as a half-foot of snow. While that amount might sound like nothing up north, it was cause for panic in Castle County. In a town like Easton, six inches of snow was six inches too much as residents were already scurrying to the stores on their bread and milk runs. It seemed that when snow was in the forecast, most of Castle County became a bunch of doomsday preppers, getting ready for an apocalypse rather than a dusting of powder.

The weather wasn't about to detour the determined lawman from his pilgrimage. He was going to speak with Bob Smith even if he had to walk to Harvest Lake.

The snow would prove a minor hindrance as he motored north to his destination. The early afternoon kept a major accumulation at bay. He figured he wouldn't be so lucky once the sun went down.

Sam spent most of his drive trying to think of questions he would ask the man. He also replayed the man's short message in his mind, realizing the mysterious Mr. Smith mentioned there were four victims. While rumors of the discoveries of the bodies that morning was spreading around

Castle County, Sam was a bit surprised the man up on Harvest Lake had already learned about them. Perhaps he had a local source feeding him updated information.

The sheriff's thoughts were interrupted by a call from Kendal Parks.

"We have the preliminaries on our victims from this morning," Kendal announced. "No surprise on Stevie Grissom. His cause of death was loss of blood. He bled to death from a knife wound that sliced the carotid and jugular."

Sam involuntarily rubbed his throat hearing the detective's description of Stevie's horrible end. Something about a throat-slashing always made the veteran lawman's skin crawl.

"The doc said it was almost like his blood had been drained out," Kendal continued. "He was pretty well empty."

It had taken a lot of blood to paint the foreboding words on Bart's car. Sam expected the blood used for the ghastly work of perverse art was donated by Stevie Grissom. If it wasn't him, then there was another body out there still to be discovered since just a flesh wound couldn't account for that much crimson paint.

"What about Rhody Turner?" Sam asked.

"Are you ready for this?" Kendal asked. "The official cause of death for Rhody Turner is drowning. They found water in his lungs. He was alive when the car went into the water."

"Were there any signs of trauma?" Sam asked.

"Other than some minor injuries, there was nothing," Kendal responded. "It was like he was perfectly healthy until he drowned."

"It's almost like he was stuffed into that trunk," Sam noted. "I can't see Rhody getting put in a trunk without a fight."

"Maybe he got in the trunk voluntarily, sheriff," Kendal speculated. "That would explain the lack of trauma."

If Kendal's suggestion were true then that meant Rhody likely knew his killer, trusting the person enough to put his life in their hands by crawling into a trunk. Did Rhody Turner know the killer? Did his killer have something to do with his escape?

The questions continued to swirl around in Sam's mind like the swirling snow that pelted his windshield as he entered the small town of Harvest Lake.

The remote vacation village was already taking on the look of a Norman Rockwell painting. The snow topped the roofs of the cabins that ringed the large lake around which the town was situated. The beauty was wasted on Sam who was focused on his goal, that being his meeting with Bob Smith.

Sam made the turn onto Robertson Lane and began rounding a hill which overlooked the lake. His tires slipped on the slick incline. Topping the hill moments later, he caught sight of his destination – Harvest Lake Assisted Living Facility. He was at a retirement home.

This time Sam concealed his badge under his jacket before walking inside. He didn't have time for legal wrangling should administration want to get clearance or a warrant. Today he would be a regular visitor for Bob Smith.

Sam was motioned on to Bob Smith's room without a second look from the receptionist. That was a far cry from the panic he started at SMHI the day before. He walked at a fast pace down the hall toward the room. His anticipation built as he nodded to an elderly man working his way down the hall in a wheelchair. Would this be the break in the case he needed or another of the seemingly endless dead ends?

He found the room at the end of hall. The door was partially ajar. The room was dark except for the afternoon light shining through the window which overlooked the lake. A man sat in front of the window, gazing out, apparently watching the snow fall.

"The snow's beautiful isn't it?" Sam began as he stepped

in the room.

The elderly man was dressed in a dark house coat pulled up to his chin. He continued looking out the window without responding to the sheriff.

Was he in the wrong room? Had he been lured on a wild goose chase? Why wasn't the man responding if he was the one who invited him? Perhaps he was hard of hearing.

"Are you Bob Smith?" Sam said in a loud voice as he took a couple of steps closer to the elderly man.

"It's a name as good as any," the man responded.

It was the same voice the sheriff heard earlier on the answering machine. He was in the right place.

"I had a message to come see you," Sam continued, still talking in a loud voice. "Do you mind if I come in and talk?"

The man, summoning his voice with some irritation, took exception with Sam's tone.

"I'm not deaf," Smith declared. "I can hear just fine. Give a man a second to answer next time. At my age it takes a while to catch up."

Sam apologized as Smith gestured for him to take a seat. The mysterious host still faced out the window as he talked.

"I trust you had a pleasant drive up," Smith began. "The lake is really something this time of year. I hear we're going to be getting some snow."

"Um, yes, we're getting it now," Sam agreed. "You said you had some information."

Smith laughed at the lawman's eagerness and his underestimation of the information he was about to reveal. The weak laugh turned into a cough, the mere act of laughing choking the elderly man.

"I don't have just some information, sheriff. I have it all," Smith replied. "I know about your murders and I know why they're happening."

"Do you know who the killer is?" Sam excitedly asked.

"Patience sheriff, patience. All in due time," Smith replied as he turned his wheelchair to face his guest. "I've

RED DOG SALOON

met the killer."

Smith's revelation had Sam chomping at the bit. If Smith had really met the killer as he claimed, his information could blow the case wide open.

"Who is it?" Sam asked. "Who is doing this?"

Smith grinned, the lines in his face suggesting he had spent a lifetime in the sun from his weather-beaten appearance.

"I said I met your killer. I didn't say I knew who he was," Smith clarified. "However, I know for a fact why the murders are happening."

"And how do you know with such certainty?" Sam countered. "You seem to say that with conviction."

Smith furled his brow as he shot the lawman a serious look.

"How else would I know, sheriff? Because I was there!" Smith snapped.

"You were where?" Sam asked.

"The Red Dog," Smith responded. "I was there when it happened. I saw everything. I saw what those pigs did to that little girl."

Sam leaned in toward Smith. He realized that before him was an eyewitness to the two decade old crime.

"Why are you just telling now?" Sam asked. "It's been more than twenty years."

Smith dropped his head and looked down at his feet in shame.

"Because I was a coward," Smith replied. "I've been a coward for twenty years but now my days are coming to an end. I figure I owe it to the girl to let someone know. I don't want to take it to my grave. If I do, I'm afraid I'll never rest."

Smith's candor intrigued the sheriff. The old man was baring his soul after two decades, perhaps making what some would call a deathbed confession.

"Tell me what happened," Sam urged.

His tale would prove to be the most captivating story Sam ever heard. The look on Smith's face told the lawman he was reliving the events of twenty years ago with every word.

Smith's story began at the Red Dog only days before it burned to the ground. The old man recalled that Bart's group was there, being even more rowdy than normal.

"The whole bunch of them was drunk, but then that wasn't anything unusual. That's what they did every Saturday night," Smith said. "They were getting loud and they'd already been in one fight that night. They were looking for trouble, that's for sure."

The whole gang, Smith explained, were in their early twenties back then. Bart was the worst of the group.

"If there was any trouble out there involving his boy, then Sheriff Foster would sweep it under the rug," Smith pointed out. "Bart knew that, so he had no limits. He knew he could do what he wanted and so could his boys. That made them dangerous. They were above the law."

Smith recalled seeing them nearly beat a man to death one evening a few weeks before the incident. No charges ever came of the beating, despite the serious injuries sustained by the patron.

"They were like a pack of dogs," Smith recalled. "If you took on one, you took on all of them. And even then you couldn't win because Sheriff Foster would see nothing bad happened to his son."

Smith walked ahead to the night of the incident. The pain on his wrinkled face revealed the sincerity of his remorse.

"That night Gina Porter was there with a slightly older girl," Smith revealed. "It was Gina's eighteenth birthday so she decided it'd be fun to go to the Red Dog. She'd never been, and like most kids, they thought it was dangerous, kind of a forbidden place good folks weren't supposed to go."

Smith said Gina stayed at the bar deep into the night, drinking with some other patrons despite being underage for alcohol. He couldn't recall if the drinks were bought for her or if she was passing a fake identification. Either way, as the evening progressed so did her buzz as did that of her friend.

"At some point in the evening she became friendly with Stevie Grissom," Smith said. "They sat around talking for probably an hour before her friend decided to leave. That's when Stevie offered to give her a lift home so the other girl could leave with a guy. Accepting that ride was the biggest mistake of her life."

Smith paused to catch his breath. The elderly man strained for air as he progressed through his story.

"An hour later, the bar was empty except for Stevie, the rest of the crew and the girl," Smith recalled. "They were all drunk and one of them, I don't recall which one, began touching the girl. First it was just playing around but then it started getting serious."

Smith again lowered his head in shame.

"She tried to resist but that just made him want it more," Smith recalled, noting Andy walked over and locked the door to make sure no one would walk in on them. "Then they were all on her like a bunch of animals. She tried to fight but they held her down and covered her mouth. She was crying and begging but they didn't care. They were out of control."

Smith's voice took a tone of anger. His false teeth ground together as he continued.

"They raped her, all of them," Smith said with a look of disgust. "It was horrible. I can still hear her screams like it was yesterday."

Moved by the old man's recollection, the sheriff wondered why Smith didn't do something to help the girl. It was obvious Smith was an eyewitness to the crime so he had to be in the bar when it happened.

"Why didn't you do anything?" Sam questioned. "I mean, what were you doing there in the first place?"

Raising his head back up, a sober look on his face, Smith floored the veteran lawman.

"What was I doing there?" Smith asked. "It was my bar."

"But that's impossible," Sam interjected. "Earl Cutts owned the bar at the time."

"Not at all, sheriff," the man responded. "I haven't been Bob Smith all my life. In this case the names were changed to protect the guilty. You know me better by my given name - Earl Cutts."

The revelation was too much for Sam to believe. Earl Cutts had burned up with the Red Dog over twenty years ago. Or had he? The words of Cliff Chapman crossed his mind at that incident. The reporter specifically said that Cutts was "believed dead" given the fact no remains had been found in the ashes of the Red Dog.

"But Earl Cutts is dead," Sam said with a hint of uncertainty in his voice. "Everybody knows he went up in flames with the bar."

Sam's statement brought a smile to the old man's face.

"Yes. That's exactly what I wanted everybody to believe," the man said. "When you don't want someone to find you, what better way to avoid them than being dead?"

Sam was confused by the twist. How could Earl Cutts convince the world he was dead for the past twenty years? Better yet, why would he want people to believe he was dead?

"The only way I could avoid being dead was by making people think I was already dead," he explained. "They would have come back and finished the job if they realized I survived."

"They, I assume, being Bart and his gang?" Sam asked as he slowly clued in to the story.

"Exactly, sheriff. You catch on fast," the man said. "They left me for dead and figured they'd burn up the evidence. They just missed one little detail - they left me breathing."

Could it be? Was this the long-dead owner of Red Dog Saloon sitting before him recounting events of twenty years ago like they just happened?

"Why?" Sam asked as he began to believe he was talking to Earl Cutts.

"I couldn't live with myself," Earl confessed. "I held my tongue that night because I was scared, not just of Bart but his father. The sheriff turned his head to things that went on at the Red Dog so I was beholden to him. And frankly, I couldn't have done anything that night if I'd tried. I was an old man even back then. Sixty-five to be exact."

By the sheriff's quick math that would make the man before him eighty-six or eight-seven. And, by the looks of him, he was every bit of it.

"I couldn't sleep after that, not a wink," Earl admitted. "I'd done a lot of bad things in my life but standing by and watching that, well, I was ashamed of myself."

Earl explained he was not sure what happened to the girl after the incident that night. All he knew is she disappeared from town at some point. He was also unsure if she reported the rape to anyone. He wasn't even sure how she got home that night as she escaped from the bar after the deed was done and the gang went back to drinking. However, about a sleepless week after witnessing the atrocity in his bar, Earl decided to come forward and reveal what he had seen to the district attorney.

"There was a mole in the DA's office," Earl said. "Bart and his boys found out what I was doing and paid a call on me at the Red Dog."

Earl said that much like the night of the rape, the gang came in and locked the front door behind them.

"I told them they would burn in Hell for what they did and I'd see to it even if I had to come back from the grave and drag them there with me," Earl said. "That didn't sit well with Bart. He had his boys hold me while he and Rhody beat me."

Earl said while they held him, blood pouring from his mouth from the merciless beating, he spit in Bart's face. The act of defiance infuriated the gang's leader, prompting him to crack him in the head with the butt of a pistol he pulled from his waistband. The impact knocked the elderly bar owner out cold for a few seconds. However, his head was hard from years of bar brawls and that was what kept the blow from proving fatal.

"When I woke up, I could smell gas and heard the whoosh of flames coming at me," Earl recalled, saying he scrambled away from the heat of the approaching wall of fire. "I was able to crawl to the back door through the flames."

Earl pulled up the sleeve of his night coat. There were scars on his right arm and hand. The scars, he explained, were left by burns he suffered from the fire.

"I got out the back door without being seen," Earl said, noting he threw his false teeth back into the burning building as he formulated a plan to disappear forever. "I knew that if they realized I survived they would hunt me down and finish the job. I knew at that moment I had to stay dead."

Earl revealed he made his way back to his nearby house and gathered up part of his belongings. He then paused to watch the flames from the old Red Dog spire high into the night sky while waiting for his girlfriend. She then helped spirit him away.

"I'd done pretty well for myself," Earl revealed.

He owned a vacation house on Harvest Lake which he had put in his girlfriend's name for legal purposes in case the revenuers came calling about his illegal enterprises at the tavern.

"I was already retirement age so I figured it was time to enjoy my golden years," he said.

The elderly man grinned with pride as he revealed his girlfriend was listed as beneficiary on both the bar and on his life insurance. The settlements were quite lucrative.

"That was more than enough to live on for the rest of our lives," Earl said.

He recalled that he and his girlfriend went on to get

married a short time later and that he had taken her last name.

"I didn't even have to get a new name really," he grinned. "My full name is Robert Earl Cutts. Her name was Rachel Smith. So, when we got married, I just rolled over into being Bob Smith."

Earl explained that Rachel died about five years ago and that he fell into ill health shortly thereafter and was moved into the assisted living facility.

"There hasn't been a day I haven't thought about what happened," Earl confessed. "But I knew that if I came forward, that would be the end of me."

"So you're just trying to make peace before your time is up?" Sam asked. "You know you could live another ten or twenty years."

Sam knew better than that. The man sitting before him looked to be at death's door.

"No, sheriff. As shameful as it may sound, I'm trying to save my skin again," Earl declared. "I guess no matter how old you get you still want to get just one day older."

Earl's statement again left Sam baffled. What did he mean by saying he wanted to save his own skin?

"You see, sheriff, you're not the first person I've told all these things to," Earl continued. "There was a man who paid me a visit a few months ago."

"A man? Was he the killer?" Sam asked.

"I suppose he is," Earl sighed. "It appears to be his work, your murders back in Castle County, that is."

"Who is he? What does he look like?" Sam asked again, sensing he was close to discovering the identity of the killer. "Give me a description. Did you know him?"

"All I know is he was a man who knew everything that happened at the Red Dog that night," Earl replied. "He came and visited me here one evening."

"You mean you can't recall what he looked like?" Sam wondered. "I mean you remember details about stuff that happened twenty years ago. Can't you remember something? Hair color, height? Was he skinny or fat, young or old?"

"Sorry, sheriff. All I can say for sure is he had a deep voice," Earl responded. "In case you haven't noticed, which you obviously haven't, I'm blind. All I can see is shapes and shades in the light. That's why I sit at the window."

His only witness was blind. He was so close yet so far. He had sat there for several minutes talking to the man not realizing he was blind. His detective skills were slipping.

"If you're blind, how do you know you were visited by the killer?" Sam asked. "Maybe he was just curious like me. What makes you so sure he's the killer?"

"Because he came here to kill me," Earl responded.

The old man revealed he told the mysterious man the same story he just told the sheriff. Telling the man what he knew, Earl noted, saved his life - at least temporarily.

"He told me he would kill me last," Earl said.

With that, the old man reached and pulled down the collar of his house coat, revealing a scar on his neck. It was a down payment left during the killer's visit.

"See, sheriff, if you can stop him before he finishes his business in your county, then you're saving my life too," Earl revealed.

His eyes fixed on the scar, Sam was a believer. Earl Cutts' words were now gospel in his mind.

"How many are left?" Sam asked.

"Just two," Earl revealed. "Bart Foster and Glenn Satterfield."

"Mayor Glenn Satterfield?" Sam gulped with his eyes wide. "The mayor of Easton? That Glenn Satterfield?"

"One and the same," Earl confirmed. "He was a rapist and an attempted murderer before he became a politician, not that the two are mutually exclusive by any means."

How could Sam protect the mayor without coming clean and revealing he knew his role in the incident at the old Red Dog? It wasn't like Sam could just stroll in and call the mayor of Easton a rapist. Things had gotten even more difficult.

"And then there's Sheriff Foster," Earl reminded. "My visitor was very interested in him too."

"Do you know anything else that can help me, anything at all?" Sam asked.

"If I knew anything else I would tell you since my neck is on the line," Earl said. "He did know a lot about the girl. He even knew she was at the mental hospital over in Shelby."

The snow was beginning to fall harder outside. The sheriff realized he needed to leave to avoid the chance of being snowed in.

"It's a shame you can't see the snow," Sam said as he started for the door. "It's very beautiful today."

"That's okay, I've seen more than I deserve," Earl said as he turned back toward the window. "The good thing is that at least I won't see him when he comes for me."

NEAR MISS

Sam fought to keep his SUV out of the ditch as he wound back down the hill from the retirement home. Snow was now completely covering the blacktop. The trip was worth it. Not only had he discovered the identities of the Red Dog gang but he also found the rumors of Earl Cutts' death were greatly exaggerated.

He now realized why Rhody insisted on immunity in exchange for his cooperation. The career criminal believed, wrongly, that they had helped murder Earl Cutts. If Sam's suspicions were right, the rest of the gang was also under the impression they had been part of a murder. And, as such, they likely assumed the recent murders of their old gang were part of payback for Cutts' death. They might even think the killings were the work of the ghost of the old tavern owner, back from the grave to collect his tab. They were overlooking their complicity in the rape of the young girl. Sam was convinced it was that unspeakable incident that had brought about the recent killings.

The more he thought about it, the less sympathy he had for the recently deceased members of the Red Dog conspiracy. What was happening was the purest form of justice even though it was delayed two decades. However, Sam had taken a solemn oath to protect the people of Castle County – the good as well as the bad. He had no choice but to find and prosecute someone for the crimes despite his personal feelings. Anything less would be dereliction of duty.

The sheriff resolved to head straight to the mayor's house when he made it back to town. Glenn Satterfield was likely in grave danger and it was Sam's duty to warn him even though he suspected the mayor had already made the connection between the deaths and the Red Dog. Plus, Sam knew Bart was one of Satterfield's biggest contributors, backing the incumbent mayor's candidacy the past couple of elections. Some even believed Bart was bank-rolling the mayor's campaigns in return for special favors that helped benefit both his legitimate and illegal businesses.

Although Bart had never been charged, it had long been rumored he dealt in stolen cars and parts, operating chop shops in neighboring Pickett County along with his alleged dabbling in the narcotics business. The chop shops were beyond Sam's jurisdiction, Pickett County was almost like a lawless frontier where certain crimes were overlooked by law enforcement. Actually, Castle County had been that way before Sam's election as sheriff. Most of its citizens had been oblivious to the illegal acts condoned by his predecessor.

Sam strained his eyes as he steered his vehicle through the blowing snow, following in the tracks of other vehicles, careful to keep a constant speed. The terrain leading from Harvest Lake back to Easton was hilly, creating a hazardous drive on sections of road that hadn't been salted by road crews. He would have to take his time getting back to town. From the looks of things, it would be dark-thirty before he pulled back in to Easton. Sam realized what night time meant recently in Castle County – murder and mayhem. Would the string of murders continue tonight? If Sam had anything to do with it, the string would conclude. Armed with the knowledge of the remaining targets, the sheriff was confident he would have the killer in his jail by sun up.

Sam spent his slow drive back to town formulating a plan on how to catch the killer. His best plan of action was to elicit the help of Glenn Satterfield; however, the sheriff doubted the professional politician would be willing to go along with a plan where he would be used as the cheese to bait the trap. Instead, Sam reckoned, they would use the mayor as the lure without his knowledge. They would wait around and pounce when the killer showed himself. He would enlist the help of the police chief and some of his trusted men. They could cover every entrance to his house and make sure there was no way the killer could get to the mayor undetected. Sure, it would be easier if Glenn would go along but Sam was already resigned that they would have to do it the hard way.

Sam made the call to Chief Denton Wood as he continued his trip back to Easton. The city's chief lawman was stunned by the news of his boss' involvement in the heinous crime but quickly pledged his assistance in the sheriff's plan of action. After all, what better job security could there be than saving your boss' life? Sam agreed to keep the chief's clandestine assistance a secret if the plan never came to pass, but give him the credit if their work saved the mayor's life. It was a win-win scenario for the chief, who, in turn, enlisted the assistance of two of his most trusted officers.

For his part in the mission, Sam would put Bo and Kendal on the case while keeping their mission secret from the rest of his officers. He didn't want news of the joint operation reaching the mayor's ears for fear of retribution against Chief Wood should the plan not go as anticipated. While he trusted his deputies, Sam knew even the most trusted officers tended to talk. All it would take is one slip of the lip to expose the chief to the ire of his boss. Sam was also uneasy given the destruction of Rhody Turner's phone records. He suspected there could be a mole within his department. He had never doubted the loyalty of anyone in his employ - until now.

Sam crossed into Castle County as darkness fell. The return trip took twice as long as the drive up to Harvest Lake. He had already set up his plans for the night over the phone on the assumption he would not be able to gain the mayor's cooperation. However, he would still give Glenn a chance to join forces since it was his life at stake.

The security lights were just coming on at the mayor's home, located on the edge of Easton, as Sam pulled into his driveway. The quickly intensifying snow storm made driving a chore despite the efforts of the street department. The city, not used to major snow storms, had just one snow plow.

The sheriff plodded through the three-inch deep snow in the mayor's front yard. The mayor's large palatial estate sat at the edge of town and was back-dropped by a dense forest. The grand residence reminded Sam of a country plantation with its large columns that greeted visitors.

Glenn had married into money before becoming a multi-term mayor of Easton, tying the knot with the daughter of a wealthy oil man. The marriage ended badly a few years ago but Glenn had been able to make some good investments with his wife's money. And, despite not getting the lion's share of the divorce settlement, Glenn did okay for himself as evidenced by the trappings of wealth that surrounded him. However, given what he knew now, Sam suspected some of that wealth may have come by way of Bart and his illegal endeavors.

It was that money along with generous contributions from his friend Bart that helped finance Glenn's political career - a career the mayor hoped one day would land him in the governor's mansion. He had already put out feelers regarding the gubernatorial race that would be held in two years and had plans to begin fund-raising for a possible bid.

Glenn's aspirations for a higher office were no secret to anyone in Easton. Sam took that into consideration when he assumed the mayor would resist his being recruited into their plan to catch the killer. He realized someone with the mayor's lofty goals could not risk his skeletons being exposed.

Sam waited patiently after ringing the doorbell. He

plunged his hands deep in his coat pockets as the cold breeze whipped across the mayor's grand porch, funneling through like a wind tunnel.

"Sheriff Delaney," Glenn said in a less than pleased tone as he answered the door.

Sam was immediately struck by the mayor's appearance. The normally well-manicured public official, who was rarely seen in public with a single hair out of place, looked like he had been out on a bender. Bags under his bloodshot eyes suggested a lack of sleep while a couple days' growth of beard and his nervous demeanor told the sheriff that the ghost of the Red Dog had already been haunting him.

"Sorry to bother you on such a snowy night," the sheriff began just as he noticed several suitcases sitting by the door. "Are you planning on a trip? You appear to be packed and ready to go."

Glenn rubbed the back of his neck nervously. His eyes darted back and forth as he was obviously not happy about the sheriff's visit.

"Yes, I'm planning to go on a short vacation," Glenn replied. "I thought I'd get away for a while. You know, get a little rest and relaxation."

Sam nodded toward the door. The snow was piling up on the mayor's lawn. The forecasters may have underestimated the accumulation total given the intensity of the snow fall.

"Well mayor, I don't think you're going anywhere tonight," Sam declared. "The roads are treacherous and I'd say they'll be shutting down the interstates in the next little bit. I think we may have a real blizzard on our hands."

"I'd hoped to beat the snow but it rolled in a little quicker than I thought," Glenn replied. "I really wanted to get away before dark, I mean ... before tomorrow."

"Sorry, but I don't think that's happening," Sam said. "No, I think you're stuck here for the night, maybe even tomorrow since I hear it's going to keep on snowing."

Sam could tell Glenn was exasperated by his inability to

get out of town. His procrastination was costing him dearly. He was stuck in Easton.

"But, since you're going to have to delay your trip, maybe we can talk a couple of minutes," Sam said.

"Talk about what?" Glenn asked with a hint of worry in his voice.

"The old Red Dog," Sam replied.

"The Red Dog?" Glenn repeated, acting as if he were confused by the mention of the old tavern. "You mean that old redneck bar outside town? Why would you come over here in the snow to talk to me about that?"

Given the long day Sam had already experienced, he wasn't up to playing word games.

"I've talked to somebody today who says you know a whole lot about it," Sam revealed. "He told me you were there along with Eddie, Andy, Stevie and Rhody one evening about twenty years ago. Oh, and your buddy Bart was there too."

Glenn glared at the lawman. His self-defense instinct kicked in as he felt boxed in by the sheriff. The suddenness of the sheriff's veiled accusation had caught him flat-footed.

"I'm sure you don't know what you're talking about," Glenn retorted. "Who would have told you something like that anyway?"

Sam looked Glenn in the eye, shooting him a slight grin.

"Earl Cutts," Sam responded.

The mere mention of the tavern owner's name left Glenn with a lump in his throat. His face turned pale white as he stood silent for a few seconds with his mouth agape.

"Earl Cutts is dead," Glenn said hoarsely as he cleared his throat. "He's been dead for twenty years."

Sam shook his head, still with a grin on his face.

"I'm afraid not," Sam countered. "I spoke to him earlier today. He's very much alive and he remembers you. He also remembers what you did."

The color returning to his face, Glenn couldn't believe

what he was hearing. How could a man they burned to a crisp in the Red Dog twenty years ago still be alive? Glenn had seen Bart hit the old bar owner in the head, knocking him unconscious and likely killing him on the spot. Then, he and the rest of the gang poured gas all around the building before Bart threw a cigarette, igniting the inferno that reduced the old bar, and Earl Cutts, to ashes.

"You're lying!" Glenn yelled. "Earl Cutts is dead."

"I don't think ..." Sam began as the mayor stepped toward him.

"Unless you've got a warrant, sheriff, you need to be leaving," Glenn insisted, pointing toward the door with an angry look. "I don't know what you're trying to prove but I'd thank you to stay away from me in the future. And, I'd be careful what I said out in public unless you want a slander suit on your hands."

The sheriff had certainly struck a nerve. The mere mention of the Red Dog and Earl Cutts had sent the mayor into a state of panic. He hadn't even made an allegation or cited specifics.

"You're in danger," Sam blurted out. "The same person who killed the others will be coming to get you. Let us protect you."

The sheriff's words gave Glenn a moment for pause as he considered his situation. He knew full well he was in the crosshairs of whatever was out there seeking revenge.

"I can take care of myself," Glenn responded. "Now get out of here before I call the police on you."

Sam gave the mayor a nod as he stepped out the door, pausing a moment as the cold wind hit him in the face.

"Just remember. I tried," Sam said as he tipped his hat to the mayor. "Your blood won't be on my hands."

The mayor stood glaring at the sheriff as the lawman tromped back across the yard, following the footsteps he left when he walked to the door. Glenn considered his options as the sheriff pulled out of his snow-covered driveway and drove out of sight. It was obvious the sheriff knew his connection to the Red Dog. And, if the sheriff knew, then who else knew? Most importantly of all he gleaned from the conversation with Sheriff Delaney was the lawman's claim Earl Cutts was still alive. Had the sheriff been bluffing, making up the story to see if he would bite? What if he wasn't? What if Earl Cutts survived the fire that night more than twenty years ago? It's hard to haunt a person if you're not dead yet.

Glenn stood staring out the window for several minutes, watching the snow fall while trying to decide if he wanted to eat his pride. If Earl Cutts was truly alive, then everything had changed. Who was killing members of the old gang and why? All this time Glenn assumed it was vengeance for their deeds the night of the fire.

"That's it. I'm calling him," Glenn said as he pushed himself to the phone.

"What do you want?" Bart asked in a cool voice as he answered his phone. "I thought we said all we had to say today."

'The sheriff was just here," Glenn said. "He knows, or at least he thinks he knows that I was involved."

"And how is that my problem?" Bart asked.

"That's not the point," Glenn replied. "While he was here he told me Earl Cutts is still alive."

The news caught Bart by surprise. The calculating businessman remained uncharacteristically quiet on his end of the line for a few moments.

"What if he's right, Bart? What if Earl is still alive?" Glenn said. "That means we're not murderers."

Bart smelled a skunk in the works. Why had the sheriff paid a sudden visit to Glenn and dropped a bombshell?

"You realize that is impossible," Bart declared. "He burned up that night. He was dead on the floor. I couldn't find a pulse. He was dead - trust me."

Bart was lying. He had, in fact, bent over the prone frame

of Earl Cutts that night after hitting him in the head with his pistol. However, the bar owner did have a pulse, something Bart kept secret from his partners in crime for all these years.

Bart realized even back then that he would be prosecuted for the attack on the old man unless the others had something to lose. By convincing them Cutts was dead, he enlisted them in his plan to cover up the crime by burning the Red Dog to the ground. Even as the flames swept through the old bar, Bart knew each of the members had a stake in what happened. Their mutual involvement had ensured their silence all through the years - at least until now.

Bart also had an even more sinister motive when he tossed the lit cigarette into the gas-soaked bar that night. He realized with Cutts gone there would be a vacuum in the vice industry in Castle County. The tavern owner dealt in just about anything immoral or illegal. And he was right. Bart took over the drug distribution, promotion of prostitution and stolen goods fencing concessions in the area after Cutts was gone. His decision to eliminate the old man proved to be the best business move he ever made as even now, more than twenty years later, he continued making himself rich by profiting off the vices of others. It was also his less-than-legal enterprises that left him and Sheriff Delaney on bad terms. The lawman knew Bart was dirty but was unable to prove it, much to his chagrin.

Actually, the sheriff didn't know the half of it. The car dealership Bart owned was merely a cover to mask his illegal endeavors. Frankly, Bart could care less if he made one red cent on his car lot as it was just a conduit for laundering his dirty money. At the end of the day, Bart saw himself as some kind of Godfather, heading a small-town Mafia. So long as his drug dealers were dealing, his hookers were hooking and his thieves were thieving, he was a happy man. Anyone who threatened his little crime kingdom would pay dearly. Stevie and Rhody weren't Bart's first contributions to Castle Lake.

While Bart knew Earl Cutts was not dead when he lit the fire, he had assumed the blaze consumed the unconscious tavern-owner thereby silencing the potential witness and business competitor forever. Now, Glenn was on the other end of the line suggesting Cutts survived the inferno that evening.

"The sheriff is just pulling your strings, trying to get you to talk," Bart replied "We need to just keep quiet and everything will be fine."

Glenn sighed loudly on the other end of the line. The sound told Bart the mayor was losing confidence in him.

"Things aren't going to be fine," Glenn retorted. "If things go as they have, one of us is going to die tonight."

Glenn was right. There were four killings in four nights, Rhody courtesy of Bart's own hand.

"Whether you believe me or not, the dark man was out to get me last night," Glenn said in a low voice, still embarrassed to tell his wild story despite the fact he knew it was true. "He will be back tonight for either me, you or ... "

"Or who?" Bart interrupted. "I told you to be careful what you say. He wasn't there. He wasn't part of what we did."

"Regardless, we have to take steps to protect ourselves," Glenn said. "I think we need to talk to the sheriff. We don't have to tell everything; just enough where we can maybe catch the killer."

The very mention of "coming clean" when it came to the Red Dog was not anything Bart would ever consider. What happened there would always stay buried as long as he had anything to say about it.

"Are you crazy?" Bart asked. "We can't tell anyone, and I do mean anyone. We have to stick together."

"I don't know ..." Glenn trailed off.

"I thought you were leaving town until this all blew over," Bart noted. "What are you still doing here anyway?"

"The airport shut down early because of the weather

moving in and then the roads started getting bad," Glenn said. "I suppose that leaves me stuck, for the time being anyway. I'm already packed and ready to go."

Bart quickly formulated a plan given that Glenn would not be able to get out of town, and thereby out of the sheriff's jurisdiction. So long as he remained in town there was a chance he would spill his guts to the lawman in hopes of saving his own neck.

"You need to get out of there," Bart said.

"What do you mean?" Glenn responded.

"I mean that being alone there is just asking for it," Bart continued. "We need to watch one another's back. There's safety in numbers."

Glenn was surprised by Bart's willingness to help him after their blow up earlier in the day. However, when he thought about it, Bart had as much to lose as he did. The dark man was likely gunning for both of them.

"So what do you suggest?" Glenn asked. "Where do we go? What do we do?"

"Well, we start by getting you out of there," Bart said. "Since they know you were involved in the Red Dog mess, they'll be watching you like a hawk tonight, probably using you for human bait. I ought to know. They did me."

The idea of being used as a lure for the killer didn't sit well with the mayor.

"Okay, how do you suppose I get out of here then?" Glenn wondered. "If they're watching the place like you say then they'll be on my tail wherever I go."

"You just get your stuff packed in the car and let me worry about getting you out of there," Bart replied. "Once we get you out, we'll wait until the weather clears, lay low somewhere and then get out of town for a couple of weeks until they can iron out this mess. I could use a vacation myself."

"Sounds great," Glenn said. "But again, how do I get out of here without being noticed?"

"Easy. We'll create a diversion," Bart explained.

"A diversion?" Glenn repeated. "What do you plan on doing?"

"You just be ready to get out of there," Bart said. "You'll know when it happens tonight. When you see your opening, make a break for it and meet me around the back of the dealership. They are keeping the roads fairly clear between there and here so you should be able to make it."

"I'll put my bags in the car right now," Glenn agreed. "What time you think?"

"Sometime this evening before midnight," Glenn replied. "You just be ready to go because we'll only have one chance at it."

With that the men finalized their plans, the mayor to make a break for it after Bart created a diversion to distract law enforcement. However, neither of the "old friends" confessed all of their plans to one another.

"It was just like I figured," Sam said as he met with the task force, the six lawmen gathering in secret behind Easton Elementary School a few blocks from the mayor's house. "The mayor would have none of it so it's up to us. We're just going to have to be discrete."

The plan called for the six officers to take up observation posts in three unmarked cars. The sheriff and chief would observe the front entrance from one vehicle, Bo and Kendal the side and main grounds and Police Officers Kent Stallings and Ryan Goodwin the back and wooded area behind the estate. The city officers would use night vision binoculars to scan the area around the house. At the first sign of anything unusual, the officers, all monitoring a scrambled radio channel, would converge and hopefully capture the killer. Sam warned there was no room for heroes in the mission given the fact their suspect was armed and dangerous.

"How do we know our killer will pick Glenn Satterfield

tonight?" Bo asked. "I mean, he may decide to make a play for Bart."

"Frankly, we don't," Sam admitted. "But I've got a feeling our killer is coming here tonight. When I was in his house a while ago the mayor already had his bags packed. He's planning to fly the coop and if we know that then I'll bet so does our killer. He seems to know everything that's going on before we do."

"What about Bart?" Bo wondered. "We don't have anyone over there now. You pulled them all off."

"He's a big boy. He can watch out for himself," Sam said plainly. "We don't have enough people to be everywhere at once. Plus, somehow I get the feeling whoever it is may be saving Bart for last."

"The best for last huh?" Bo responded.

"Maybe you should have said the worst for last," Sam replied.

Thirty minutes following their clandestine meeting, the officers were in unmarked vehicles and in their observation positions. Sam and the chief were parked unremarkably on the street across from the mayor's house while the other officers were concealed on lots on either side of the property. The officers had unobstructed views to every inch of the estate. If the killer was going to get to the mayor without being seen he would have to be invisible.

The evening went as most stakeouts do, a bunch of waiting and watching. The biggest danger was falling asleep from boredom. The sheriff cranked his vehicle for five minutes at a time, warming the interior before cutting the engine. He wanted to limit the amount of time exhaust was showing from the tailpipe. It was little things like that which could give a stakeout away.

The snow began to accumulate on the sheriff's unmarked minivan, a vehicle he borrowed, without permission, from his wife. What better non-obtrusive vehicle than a teal minivan? The accumulation, Sam reckoned, would better camouflage the vehicle as it sat on the street opposite the mayor's estate.

"I never would have pegged the mayor for something like that," Chief Wood said, breaking the silence in the minivan. "He seemed too high brow, too sophisticated to fall in to a gang of thugs like that."

The sheriff looked through the snow, careful to not take his eyes off the house while he talked with the chief. He knew one lapse in vigilance and there would be a special election for mayor.

"People have their skeletons. Some are just worse than others," Sam responded. "Sometimes folks are capable of doing things you'd never dream they'd do."

"What if it gets out, what they did?" the chief asked. "You know Mayor Satterfield has designs on running for governor. Won't something like this ruin him?"

"I'd say it would, Denton," Sam noted. "But somehow I suspect neither he nor Bart will just step up and admit to what happened. That's why we're lurking in the shadows tonight. Rumor is one thing, proving it is another. So far as I can tell there aren't a lot of people left alive who can provide that proof."

"So they'll get away with what they did?" the chief asked in a disgusted tone.

"Well, Chief, fate has a way of coming around and getting you when you least expect it," Sam replied. "I'm sure the others thought they'd gotten away with what they did, that is, until vengeance came calling. Sometimes a man can get too comfortable with his secrets. I've found very few things stay buried, no matter how deep you bury them."

The lawmen sat silently watching the snow continue to fall, both absorbed in their thoughts. Sam recalled his conversation with Earl Cutts and his assurance the killer had an order to things – an order that would end with the old man being killed last. What terror Earl must feel, waiting in the darkness of his room for death to come to call. Whether it be the killer or the hands of Father Time, his time was near. Sam could sense it during his visit.

The sheriff spied through some field glasses, scanning the white covering which now coated everything giving the landscape a surreal look. He would have problems getting up to Shelby tomorrow to pore over Gina Porter's records. He was bound and determined to make the trip even if he had to go by sled dogs. Sam was convinced there was something in the files that could be the key to everything. Even if they were to catch a suspect tonight, the information in her file could provide valuable evidence.

"Chief! We have some movement near the wood line," Patrolman Kent Stallings said excitedly over the radio.

Sam jumped as the policeman's warning sounded on the radio. Their patience may be about to pay off.

"Can you make out what it is?" the chief asked, pointing for Sam to train his field glasses toward where the policemen were staked out.

"It's something dark," Stallings responded. "Hold on a second. It's moving again."

Sam and the chief exchanged looks, wondering if this could be the killer. Were they about to end the string of murders in Castle County?

"It's a person!" Stallings shouted. "We have a subject dressed in black, a dark man, and he's carrying something moving toward the house!"

"We all need to hold where we are," Sam responded. Let's let him get out in the open so we can surround him."

"What is that, a scythe?" Stallings yelled, not hearing the sheriff's orders to hold his position. "This guy looks like the Grim Reaper!"

"Did you hear? Hold your location until we can get staged!" the sheriff yelled.

His orders went unheeded as he saw the two police officers bolting across the snow, disappearing from view behind the house. They were chasing something.

"Quick! Everyone converge on the backyard!" Sam ordered over the radio.

Sam and the chief wasted no time dashing from the minivan, their advance slowed by the ankle-deep snow.

"He's running for the woods!" Stallings yelled on his portable radio. "Be advised - our subject is armed! He's running for the woods!"

The patrolmen were a couple of hundred yards in front of their closest back up when they followed the black-clad figure into the dense forest behind the mayor's estate.

"I'll follow the footprints. You loop around and we'll catch him in between us," Stallings ordered Officer Goodwin. "Just be careful not to shoot me - you hear?"

Stallings raced along behind the tracks like a hunting dog tracking an animal through the woods. The heavyset patrolman moved quickly through the powder given his size. The tracks were easy to follow in the fresh snow. They read like a road map in the dimly lit forest.

"Freeze!" came the voice of Officer Goodwin just a few feet in front of Stallings. "Hands in the air! Drop your weapon!"

The older patrolman topped the hill to find his younger partner with his gun trained on the man in black.

"I said drop the weapon," Goodwin repeated as he looked down the sights of his gun at the suspect. "I will fire!"

The figure, his face and body covered in black from head to toe, dropped the long-handled weapon in the snow.

"Now on your knees!" Goodwin repeated.

The suspect complied with the officer's orders and slowly went down to his knees. He then placed his hands behind his head.

"We have him in custody!" Stallings exclaimed.

The officer's announcement caused the sheriff's heart to jump as he reached the wood line. This was it!

"Hold on! We'll be right there," Sam responded as he plunged into the forest.

The policemen, not waiting on their backup, decided to handcuff the suspect. They would save the unmasking for their bosses.

"Who are you?" Goodwin asked.

The patrolman pulled out his handcuffs and approached the dark figure while he partner stood covering the suspect. He would slap the cuffs on the dark man to ensure he didn't try to take flight again.

His plan, however, was foiled as the figure, moving like a cat, leapt from the snow landing an elbow squarely to his jaw. The lightning blow snapped the officer's jaw. Screaming in pain as the handcuffs went spiraling into the forest, Goodwin felt himself being drawn in by the man in black as his stunned partner raised his gun.

"Stop right there!" Stallings yelled.

No sooner than the officer made the command, the dark figure pushed his injured partner into him. Stallings' gun went off, the round whistling through the trees above them. The sound of the gunshot gave pause to the other lawmen as they were making their way through the woods about a hundred yards behind.

"Oh no," Sam said as he doubled his pace. "That can't be a good sign."

In the meantime the masked man landed a pair of well-placed blows on either side of Stallings' head. The punches flattened the heavyset officer. The dark man then disappeared into the night leaving the injured officers not knowing what hit them.

Sam and the chief found the policemen moments later, lying side-by-side in the snow. Goodwin moaned as he held his broken jaw. Stallings, blood pouring from a badly busted lip, pointed toward the woods where the man disappeared. Bo and Kendal raced with guns in hand after the tracks.

Sam, now remembering to draw his gun in all the excitement, looked around the immediate area. There in the snow lay a home-made scythe. Its crude construction told the officer this wasn't the work of a grim reaper but instead of a man with some knowledge on how to make a weapon. The blade, the sheriff noticed, was razor sharp.

"All units, all units, we have our murder suspect on foot behind Mayor Satterfield's house heading toward Lowery Lane," Sam called out over the radio. "The suspect is dressed in black and may be armed. Approach with caution. We have two officers down. We will need an ambulance at this location – now!"

A loud scream came from deep in the woods at that moment. It was Kendal Parks!

"Kendal!" Sam shouted as he left the chief behind to care for his injured patrolmen. "Where are you at?"

"Over here, sheriff," the muffled sound of his investigator's voice came a few yards deeper in the woods.

Rounding the heavy undergrowth, the sheriff was met with the spectacle of blood-covered snow.

"What happened?" the sheriff asked in a worried voice as Bo entered the clearing where they stood.

"He came out of the dark," Kendal said, holding his nose as blood poured from around his fingers. "He just appeared out of nowhere and kicked me square in the nose. I never had time to react."

"Get him back to the others," Sam ordered.

The sheriff raised his gun and began to make his way deeper into the woods.

"But sheriff," Bo protested.

"You heard me. That's an order," Sam called back as disappeared into the dark.

Sam moved cautiously through the trees, his gun held at arm's length, ready to fire in an instant. What kind of man could take down three trained officers like they were nothing? What was he up against in this wooded labyrinth? Sam felt at a disadvantage despite being armed with his forty-caliber.

The sheriff wandered through the tenebrous darkness for

several minutes, one snow covered tree looking the same as the last. He kept his eyes trained on the tracks as he navigated his way through the tangle of limbs, bushes and briars.

After five minutes the sheriff caught sight of Lowery Lane. It was the road which ran behind the woods in back of the mayor's estate. The tracks led onto the road and seemed to disappear suddenly. Perhaps the fugitive had a car parked there or maybe he had an accomplice.

Sam stepped onto the road and looked for any additional tracks. There were none. Instead, headlights approached, blue lights activating on top of the car telling the sheriff it was an officer.

"Sheriff, is that you?" came the voice of Deputy Faulkner.

"Did you see anyone?" the sheriff responded. "Did anyone come through here?"

"No, sir," the young deputy replied. "I came this way when you put out the call a minute ago."

Not wanting to let his close encounter go so easily, Sam resolved to go back into the woods on the off-chance the suspect doubled back. The sheriff ordered the officer to patrol the back edge of the woods in case the masked man was still waiting to escape the forest.

"If you see someone, don't you try doing anything alone," Sam cautioned worried for the welfare of the rookie officer. "You get on the radio and you call for back up. Don't even get out of your car. Do you understand?"

Sam disappeared back into the woods after giving his order. He re-traced the tracks through the snow. His mission, however, was for naught as found no further signs of the dark man.

Sam soon came upon the pool of blood where Kendal had been ambushed, telling him he had again covered the trail left by the suspect. The flow was solid enough to where Sam used it like bread crumbs leading him to where the lawmen were gathered. They stood bleeding and injured like they were in a MASH unit.

"Nothing," Sam said with disgust as he holstered his gun.

"At least we have his weapon," Bo said, holding the long scythe like a trophy.

"I'm not so sure he even needs a weapon," Sam said.

The sound of a horn interrupted the sheriff. The sound was coming from the mayor's house.

"What is that?" Sam asked as the horn continued sounding.

"Maybe it's a signal," Bo suggested. "Maybe there's trouble back at the mayor's place."

"Let's go," Sam said as he bolted toward the sound of the car horn.

Sam dashed through the snow, staying mindful the masked suspect could still be lurking somewhere in the trees. He kept his head on a swivel as he hurried through the remaining woods. He and Bo emerged from the forest together, the sound of the horn getting louder as they neared its source.

"There," Sam pointed.

The sound was coming from the mayor's car which was parked in front of his house. Its headlights were on but its hood and windshield were still covered with snow.

The officers cautiously approached the car not wanting to fall into an ambush like their fellow lawmen. Sam pulled his weapon as the men neared the car, the horn still blaring. Looking at his investigator, Sam nodded his head, silently telling him to open the door. It was the worst case scenario.

Inside, Mayor Glenn Satterfield sat in the driver's seat. His face was pressed against the steering wheel, a zip-tie wrapped around his neck. Bo instinctively reached inside and pushed the mayor back against the seat. His eyes were wide open, fixed in terror.

"He's dead," Bo pronounced as he found no pulse.

"No!" Sam yelled, slamming his hand in frustration

against the snow-covered hood. He was still a step behind the killer.

CHALLENGE ISSUED

In three ... two ... one

"This is Hal Greene - Channel Five News - live from Easton where this city's mayor was assassinated last night, the latest victim in the gruesome killing spree believed to be the work of the man dubbed the Red Dog Killer."

The whole scene was surreal as Sam watched the newsman, who appeared to be wearing a half-inch of makeup, begin his live report from the front steps of Easton City Hall. The smooth-talking reporter was just the first of which Sam expected would be a constant parade of news media. The town would soon be full of satellite trucks beaming the developments of the formerly peaceful county around the globe. It certainly wouldn't be a good day for the Castle County Chamber of Commerce or one for the county's sheriff who would soon be on the hot seat.

After all, there were now five unsolved murders on his watch, the last being the slaying of the town mayor. It was funny, Sam noticed, how the other members of the Red Dog gang were considered murder victims while Glenn Satterfield's killing was being called an assassination. All were targeted for the same reason, that being the atrocity they committed together more than twenty years ago, yet somehow the mayor's passing held more importance than the other four combined.

Sam got little sleep after the discovery of the mayor's body. The entire manpower of his department was called in to help sweep the snow-covered landscape for any sign of the killer. Their efforts were in vain. The sun rose on an investigation that was no closer to catching the killer than it was the day Andy Crouch's body was found. It seemed the killer had a knack for eliminating every lead, leaving Sam butting his head against a brick wall, always one step behind. Now, as he stood in the chill of the morning air on the steps of city hall watching the talking head give his report, the trail of the killer was, pardon the pun, cold.

"This horrific chain of events began Tuesday with the discovery of local factory worker Andy Crouch. He was victim of a gruesome ax attack, his body found lying just inside his front door," the dapperly-dressed reporter said, recapping the killings in an overly dramatic voice as if he were narrating a horror film or doing a commercial for a monster truck show at the civic auditorium. "Next we had the slaying of his co-worker and friend, Eddie Young, the following evening, his headless remains found Wednesday inside his home. Then came a pair of grisly discoveries, the bodies of investment broker Stevie Grissom and career criminal Rhody Turner, both found inside the trunk of a stolen car after it plunged into the murky depths of Castle Lake the evening before last. Then our most recent victim, the mayor of the city of Easton, Glenn Satterfield, killed as he sat inside his car in his own driveway."

Listening to it, things sounded bad, really bad. How had Castle County gone from one of the safest places in the country to murder capital?

"The question is, if the mayor himself can be killed in his own driveway is anyone really safe in this formerly peaceful little hamlet?" the reporter posed.

The newsman shoved the microphone into the sheriff's face.

"I have with me the sheriff of Castle County, Samuel Delaney," the reporter continued. "Sheriff, how can the citizens of your county feel safe so long as the Red Dog Killer is on the loose?"

Sam was caught off guard by the reporter's absence of

segue. His lack of sleep left him slow at a time of the morning that he normally wouldn't be awake. How he missed the good old days when he would occasionally get a full night's sleep.

"We're doing everything in our power to ensure the safety of all the people of Castle County," Sam replied nervously as he wasn't used to being on camera. "The people can rest assured that we are following up all leads and leaving no stone unturned in our investigation."

Sam couldn't believe he just said that on live television. The entire thing sounded like some kind of pre-written press release aimed at dodging the question.

"Leads? So does this mean you have a person of interest in this grisly string of unsolved murders?" Hal asked.

"Well, we haven't eliminated anyone at this time," Sam stammered. "We are taking all information we obtain and examining it closely."

"So that means there are no suspects in the case?" Hal surmised from the sheriff's double-talk. "Tell me sheriff; are you any closer to solving these heinous crimes than you were after the first body was found?"

"Well, we ..." the sheriff began, only to be cut off by the cocky newsman.

"And what about the case of Rhody Turner?" Hal posed. "Our news team has learned he was actually a prisoner in your jail before he was able to break out only to fall into the hands of the killer."

"Well yes, he was an inmate in our facility but ..." Sam said, again cut off by the aggressive interviewer.

"Had the security in your jail been better, do you think Mr. Turner would still be alive today?" Hal asked.

"Do I what?" Sam replied, incredulous the reporter would be making such allegations on live television.

"I mean it would appear the Red Dog Killer used a break down in security at your jail to gain access to one of his victims," Hal clarified. "Does that not make the Castle

County Jail guilty in some way in the death of Rhody Turner, perhaps even liable?"

"No, these cases are all ... " Sam began, cut off again by the reporter.

"And what about the assassination of Mayor Satterfield?" Hal asked. "We have information that your department was conducting surveillance in the area at the time and he was killed under your very noses. Would you consider this a cause for concern if you were a citizen of Castle County?"

Sam stood silently, his mouth closed as the reporter again pushed the microphone under his nose. The sheriff looked calmly at the reporter as if he didn't hear the question.

"So you have no answer?" Hal asked.

"Oh, you want me to answer that one?" Sam answered mockingly. "I was waiting for you to answer the question like you did the others. You seem to have all the answers."

"I wasn't ... " Hal began only to have the sheriff jerk the microphone away from him in midsentence.

"I mean I was rather enjoying hearing you interview yourself," Sam declared on live television. "I was hoping if you kept talking you'd solve the case yourself. You seem to be doing pretty good there, Hank."

"It's Hal - Hal Greene," the reporter countered as he snatched back his microphone. "I'm just trying to get answers as to how five people can be killed in five days and yet there's not a single suspect."

"That's simple, Hank," Sam responded. "Our killer keeps killing the people who could identify him. By the way, I didn't say we have no leads. We do, in fact, have several leads which I'm optimistic will lead us to our killer."

"And if they don't?" Hal asked. "And, it's Hal not Hank."

"If they don't, Harold, then I guess you'll be interviewing me a lot more," Sam responded. "Now, if you don't mind, it's time to go follow up on one of those leads I was talking about."

"Sheriff, one last thing," Hal called after the sheriff as the lawman started to walk down the steps of city hall. "What would you like to say to the people of Castle County who are living in fear that a serial killer is in their midst?"

Pausing for a second in reflection, Sam walked back up the steps and looked straight in the camera.

"Two things. First, to the killer. Whoever you are, and I'm sure you're watching, I will find you. Rest assured of that," Sam pledged. "And second, to the people of Castle County, don't believe everything you hear on television. Most of it is a bunch of [bleep]."

News Channel Five was fortunate to have a seven-second delay in its live telecast. The delay gave them just enough time to bleep Sam's last word to the camera. However, those who could read lips had no doubt of the four-letter word Sheriff Delaney uttered.

While Sam was admittedly dancing around the questions during his interview, he told the truth when he said there were leads. His reference was to the still-sealed medical records of Gina Porter, records Sam believed could hold the key to finding the killer. Shelby Mental Health Institute would be his destination. His Saturday was going to be spent going over the records with a fine-tooth comb, looking for anything that might solve the puzzle.

First, Sam would have to drop in on his injured investigator, Kendal Parks. The lawman took one for the team Saturday by coming into the office despite the events of the night before.

"How are we feeling this morning?" Sam asked as he entered his investigator's office on a two-fold mission.

He was there because he legitimately cared for his employees and wanted to check on his officer's well-being. He also wanted to see if the always reliable detective had been able to subpoena the late mayor's cellphone records. Sam had found phone records were good for connecting the dots when it came to linking the Red Dog conspirators together.

"How does it look like I'm doing?" Kendal replied in a nasally tone.

The detective looked back at the sheriff through two black eyes, his Roman nose even more Roman after his encounter with the masked suspect last evening.

"The doctor says it's broke," Kendal revealed.

"It just makes you look even more dignified," Sam quipped as he eyed the bandage draped across the bridge of the detective's nose. "I'm sure it had to hurt his foot too if that's any consolation."

"I'm sure you didn't come here just to discuss the condition of my nose," Kendal noted.

"Well, now that you mention it ..." the sheriff began.

Kendal reached across his desk and held up a paper. He already knew what his boss was looking for.

"It wasn't easy, since it is Saturday and all, but I got it," Kendal revealed, handing Sam a copy of the mayor's phone records. "I haven't even checked it yet. My eyes want to cross when I'm reading."

Sam immediately pored over the records. A familiar number at the bottom of the page drew the sheriff's eyes. It was the last call made before the mayor's death. It was Bart Foster's number, the call lasting around five minutes.

"He called Bart Foster right after I left," Sam declared. "I bet I'd just walked out the door when he called him."

"Is that really a big surprise since we know they were in this together?" Kendal asked. "I'm sure there are a lot of calls on the list between them."

Kendal was right as a closer examination of the records netted numerous communications between the mayor and Bart Foster. However, it was the final call that intrigued the sheriff.

"Did you ever wonder how our suspect was able to double back so quickly and just happen to catch the mayor in his car with his bags all packed?" Sam asked his detective. "I mean, the timing would have to be perfect to pull that off.

That's not to mention that the guy would have to have superhuman speed."

"Well I can vouch for that superhuman speed," Kendal countered, rubbing his nose. "It was like he appeared out of thin air."

"What if there are two?" Sam asked. "What if our killer has a partner?"

Kendal nodded his head, realizing the sheriff's suggestion wasn't that far-fetched. Perhaps the man they chased in the woods that evening was simply a decoy meant to lead the officers on a wild goose chase while his partner was murdering the mayor.

"That could be, but then we're still at square-one since we don't have even a single suspect," Kendal noted. "But logic would tell us if we catch one then we can catch the other. Care to venture a guess as to the identity of our second person?"

"What if it was Bart Foster?" Sam asked. "Hear me out for a second. All this time we've been assuming our beloved car dealer is a victim waiting to happen but what if he's not. What if he and the killer have mutual interests? What if this isn't about payback after all? What if this is about eliminating anyone who was there that night?"

"Go on," Kendal urged the sheriff.

"Maybe we've been wrong about the motive all this time," Sam continued. "Maybe instead of looking at Bart as a victim, we should be treating him as a suspect."

"But everyone knows Glenn and him were tight," Kendal countered. "I mean Bart was always one of Glenn's main contributors at election time."

"True, but that might be part of it," Sam replied. "It was common knowledge Glenn intended to run for governor next election and something so perverse from his past would have derailed his candidacy. Now, this next part may sound a bit far-fetched, but what if Glenn and Bart combined to get rid of the rest of the witnesses?"

"But that wouldn't explain why Glenn was killed," Kendal pointed out.

"Unless Bart thought he was also expendable being the only remaining witness," Sam said with a serious look. "Maybe Bart realized Glenn would throw him under the bus at the drop of a hat if he knew it would protect his political career. Or, maybe it came down to something as simple as Bart suspecting his old buddy was going to kill him too so he just acted first. One thing we know for sure, Bart was the last one to talk to the mayor."

"Great idea, sheriff, but highly unlikely if you ask me, which you did," Kendal said. "But, if history is any indicator, we may find out tonight. If Bart ends up dead I think we can scratch him off our suspect list."

"If Bart ends up dead then our cases may never be solved," Sam declared as he glanced at his watch. "But that's for later. Right now I need to get on the road for Shelby. You got the warrant?"

"Let me know what you find," Kendal said as he handed the sheriff the search warrant for SMHI.

Bart woke refreshed after enjoying one of the most restful nights of sleep in a long time. The prospect that a killer was out there stalking him did nothing to disturb his rest. His ace in the hole gave him the confidence to sleep like a baby. His mind, for the first time in many years, was totally unencumbered. The ghosts of his past were buried once and for all.

It wasn't that Bart had a death wish. Actually it was quite the opposite. The wealthy entrepreneur had a lot to live for. It was for that reason Bart had his ace in the hole. Well, actually he had a pair of aces, both with fifty-thousand reasons to make sure his rest was uninterrupted.

As many people suspected, Bart was not exactly a wholesome All-American boy. On his way to amassing his small fortune, Bart had fractured a few laws and made a few friends in the criminal underworld. Therefore, when he had "dirty work" to be done, he knew who to call. In this case, he called a pair of particularly dangerous individuals, their former deeds proving their worthiness to be chosen to watch his back. And, given there was someone out there apparently intent on cutting Bart down in his prime, the businessman made his cohorts a business proposition, offering a bounty of fifty thousand dollars cash to the person who kills the killer. Bart knew his two hand-picked body guards would kill their own mothers for that kind of money. Therefore, watched over by his pair of cut-throats as he slept in his man cave in the back of his dealership, Bart's slumber was one of peace.

Bart glanced at his clock, the red digits telling him it was ten in the morning. He couldn't recall how long it had been since he'd slept that late. It had truly been a restful evening. He paused for a long stretch as he rose from beneath the covers. Rubbing his eyes and giving one last yawn, Bart threw his feet over the edge of the bed. The shock of the cold floor on his bare feet snapped him wide awake. He quickly found his house shoes, insulating his feet inside them as he stood up and made his morning walk to the bathroom.

However, something caught his eye as he was about to enter the bathroom for his morning constitutional. On his bureau in front of the mirror sat something covered by a large black cloth. What could it be? Bart hadn't been drinking last night, other than his normal gin and tonic before bed, so it wasn't anything he had put there. And, it certainly wasn't there last night when he had taken his Rolex off, laying in front of the mirror where it was still laying by the covered package. Maybe one of his body guards put it there since there was no way anyone else could have gotten into his locked room, let alone got past his guards.

Walking over to the package, Bart wasted no time snatching the cover off its contents, revealing what was beneath. He was not prepared for what he was about to see.

It was the perfectly preserved head of Eddie Young! An expression of terror was still on his face. His eyes were fixed almost as if he was still looking at his killer.

Bart fell backwards, the horrific scene robbing him of breath as he stumbled onto his bed. He couldn't tear his eyes from the disembodied head which sat like an ornamental bust on his vanity.

"Robert! Holden! Get in here!" Bart yelled as he kept his distance from the head almost as if it would rise up and come after him. "Do you hear me? Get in here now!"

There was no answer to his frantic cries despite his posting of both guards outside his door the night before. There was only one way in and one way out of his bedroom at the dealership. Where were they? He was certain they wouldn't desert him. There were fifty thousand reasons they should be running through the door to answer his shouts.

"What's that?" Bart said to himself as he noticed something protruding from Eddie's mouth.

Bart pushed himself off the bed. A cautious look revealed it was a piece of paper. There was just enough of the paper hanging out of the mouth to catch his attention. Was the paper meant for him? Bart stood looking at the head for a full minute, trying to decide whether or not to pluck the parchment from the severed head. In the end, his curiosity overcame his fear as he forced his body forward, his trembling hand extending toward Eddie's skull. Then, holding his breath, he grabbed at the paper, careful not to touch the blue lips that held it.

Much to his surprise the exposed piece was only the tip of the iceberg as an entire piece of note paper was dispensed out of the mouth of the severed head. A green liquid clung to the parchment. Its mere appearance made Bart gag as he could only imagine what kind of bodily fluid it was.

However, his momentary nausea was trumped by what he saw on the paper. On the top of the note, written in neat handwriting, was his name. The note was for him. And, above his name was the logo of his dealership. The note stuffed in the mouth of Eddie Young had been written on company stationery perhaps taken from a pad which was lying on the same bureau where the head sat still staring at him. Had the killer written the note while inside the same room where he was sleeping? If so, why was he alive to read the note? There was only one way to find out.

Bart sat back on the bed and smoothed the paper out on his bed, using a pair of dirty socks to wipe away the green fluid. It was then Bart realized what he was reading was not merely a note but a letter written to him.

Bart,

If you are reading this then I obviously resisted the urge to slice your throat while you slept, an urge made doubly tempting by your incessant snoring. In case you are wondering, I had no option but to snap the necks of your "bodyguards." You will find them neatly tucked away in one of the trunks of your pre-owned vehicles outside on your sales lot. As a means of morning calisthenics, I'll leave it to you to figure out which one, something you'll hopefully do before someone takes it on a test drive this morning. You have such a knack for getting rid of bodies I figured you wouldn't mind disposing of two more although I hear Castle Lake is getting kind of full.

Before I move on to the main thrust of my correspondence, I would first like to thank you for your assistance in the elimination of Rhody Turner. Scheme as I might I couldn't for the life of me figure out a way to get our criminal friend out of the lock up so I could kill him personally. Meanwhile you were able to do it with relative ease, your abilities in the area of homicide impressive to say the least. If it weren't for the unavoidable fact that I must kill you I think we would have quite a bit of fun swapping notes when it comes to the art of killing. Yes Bart, we are both killers, cut from the same cloth. The only difference between you and me is I feel a shred of remorse when I kill while you feel nothing. It would appear despite my heritage that I somehow found a bit of conscience.

Now to the rub, since I guess you're in a hurry to find those bodies on your lot. I spared you for a reason this morning. I need you to do me a favor before I kill you, something that I suspect you will do without thinking twice. I also want to meet you face to face, perhaps have a short conversation before I complete my task.

Tonight, nine o'clock at the old Red Dog. I think you know where it is. I'd warn you to come alone but seeing all your friends are dead already I suppose that would just be overkill. Don't be late!

Yours truly, Ben

P.S. BRING THE HEAD!

Bart stared blankly at the parchment for a minute, considering his own mortality given the foreboding prediction of his death by the man calling himself - Ben.

"I'm not going out like that," Bart sneered as he wadded the paper in his hand.

Bart angrily threw the wadded note at Eddie's head. He yelled defiantly at the skull as if it was listening to his ranting.

"I don't know who you are, Ben, but you've messed with the wrong man. You don't know who you're dealing with!" Bart screamed.

Bart would make the meeting with the mysterious Ben but it would be on his terms.

DARK REVELATION

It was refreshing just to get away for a while. The constant questions from the press and the public at-large were starting to get under the sheriff's skin. His two hours alone in his SUV as he motored toward Shelby were about the only quiet time he had enjoyed since the world seemed to unravel less than a week ago. The snow-covered landscape served as a catharsis for the lawman. The several inches of powder that fell the night before had transformed the countryside to pure white. The roads, thankfully, were clear for the most part, cut like black trails through the otherwise pristine winter covering.

While it was out of his hands, at least for the time being, Sam felt partially responsible for what was happening. After all, the people of Castle County had placed their trust in him when they sent him back for a fourth term of office. The fact he was unable to stem the tide of homicide in his hometown was weighing heavily on him. It had become his toughest test - a test he intended to pass even if it meant working night and day.

However, in the back of his mind, he realized there was an expiration date with the case. If he was right, and he was certain he was, the murders were revenge for the incident at the Red Dog more than twenty years ago. What would happen once the last of the victims were gone? Would the killer disappear leaving the cases unsolved forever? Or, in a worse-case scenario, had the killer acquired a taste for murder? Were the recent homicides only the beginning of a reign of terror by the mysterious killer? Would the killer keep on taking victims until he was caught? The sheriff's last question was given legitimacy with the call received just as he hit the Shelby city limits.

"Tell me nothing else has happened," Sam declared as he answered his phone.

"I wish I could, sheriff," Bo responded. "Some hunters found Tia Wray this morning."

Sam slammed his hands on the steering wheel. He could barely contain his frustration. People were dying everywhere in his county.

"She was at the bottom of a bluff near the state park," Bo continued. "It looks like she's been there a couple of days."

"Were there any signs of trauma?" Sam asked.

"It appears she was strangled," Bo responded. "The killer probably used a ligature to choke her from behind and then just dumped her on the side of the road."

The death of the young girl was especially disturbing to Sam since her death marked the first victim, as far as he knew, who was not at the Red Dog the night Gina Porter was raped. The killer had departed from his normal method of operation, that is if the girl's death was the work of their killer and not a copycat. At this point, the sheriff wasn't so sure all the deaths were the work of one person. The killing of Tia Wray didn't seem to be part of the killer's method of operation.

Her death cut the sheriff deep given her young age. The girl's life had been sidetracked by drugs. That was something she could have overcome had she been given time. Now, she wouldn't have that chance. Her life was ended because she became involved with the wrong man, or perhaps, wrong men.

Sam would never realize it but his gut instinct was spot on with the exception of the motivation that drove her the day she died. It wasn't loyalty to Rhody Turner or her addiction to drugs. Instead, her motivation was old-fashioned greed.

Just weeks before the jailbreak, Tia contacted Bart asking his assistance in springing Rhody from the county lock up. Rhody figured his old friend owed him a favor since he had maintained his silence about the Red Dog for so many years. At that time they had all assumed they were not just guilty of rape but also of premeditated murder for what they thought was the death of Earl Cutts. It was actually the death of the bar owner that was the motivation behind their continued silence since the statute of limitations for rape had expired. There is no statute of limitations for murder.

The career criminal realized he would be going up the river for a long time on his most recent drug charge. That was what prompted him to use his trump card when it came to leveraging Bart's assistance in his escape. However, Bart, despite his criminal enterprises, was not inclined to stick his neck out for Rhody since he would hate to see his many shady dealings come crashing down for being a party to a jail escape. Bart made a calculated decision to deny his old friend's request when it was first made. This was despite Tia's physical bribe which he readily accepted, opting to chance no one would believe Rhody's version of the Red Dog events. However, with the Red Dog killings came the realization there would be people who would give credence to the criminal's story. The businessman also knew Rhody would be quick to trade him and the mayor for a lighter sentence. He couldn't just wait around and take that risk. Bart was a man of action.

That was when he contacted Tia and agreed with the plan that called for Bart to provide a vehicle and transport out of the state. Bart was standing next to her, listening to her every word, when she made the call to the jail the day of the escape. In exchange for her cooperation and her agreement to forever leave Castle County, Bart promised her twenty-five thousand dollars in cash along with a car of her choice. She readily accepted his generous offer, her greed overcoming her concern for Rhody's well-being. However, in doing so she failed to realize that once the escape was set in motion her usefulness was over. In fact, she became a liability.

When it came to Bart, his liabilities didn't last long. Tia was dead within an hour of her call. The businessman kindly offered his trusting accomplice a ride to her apartment where she packed and loaded her baggage in his car. Her return inside her apartment to check for anything she may have left behind was her final mistake. Bart made short work of the petite young woman. She never heard him approach from behind before he strangled her with a dog chain inside her apartment. Bart prided himself on the kill since he used what was available to him to commit the murder. The dog chain was lying outside the house after Tia untied her dog, letting it go free since she wasn't planning to take the canine with her when she fled town. Anyone could kill with a gun. It was adapting to one's environment that separated the truly gifted from the rest.

He resisted stuffing her in the same trunk her boyfriend would end up in that night, opting to dispose of her body immediately by tossing her remains off the side of the rarely traveled country road. He would later throw her belongings in a dumpster. While not needing an excuse for his actions since he had no conscience, Bart rationalized killing the young girl by telling himself she would have been quick to point the finger at him once the body of her old boyfriend was found. Killing Tia Wray wasn't personal, it was just business.

Not knowing of Bart's involvement in Tia's death, the young girl's murder made Sam realize he could leave no stone unturned during his visit to SMHI. He had to find an answer or at least a clue as to the identity of the person who was leaving the trail of bodies behind. Right now he had nothing, absolutely nothing. The killer could be a total stranger or his next door neighbor. The sheriff knew there was no such thing as a perfect crime. There had to be something he could seize on, something that would flip on the proverbial light bulb.

With a feeling of desperation, Sam pulled into the parking lot of the mental institution Gina Porter once called home. Had she left a clue as to the identity of the person who was wreaking vengeance on her behalf?

Sam immediately caught the eye of the receptionist, the same woman he met during his first visit. She gave him a knowing nod and picked up the phone.

"He's here," Sam heard her say.

"You can go on back. Ms. Marks is expecting you," the receptionist invited.

Sam gave the receptionist a smile as he walked to the administrator's office where Agnes Marks was waiting. She had been forewarned about his visit by the call he made just before he left Easton that morning.

"I have what you're looking for," the middle-aged administrator announced as Sam walked through the door.

The administrator pointed to a box full of folders sitting on her desk. She had collected the files shortly after the sheriff left following his first visit, anticipating his return.

"I think I rounded up everything," she said. "I actually had it ready the day after your last visit. I looked for you to be back a little quicker."

"Well, we've been kind of busy back in Easton," Sam responded wryly as his intents had originally been to come back the next day with the warrant he now handed the administrator.

"Yes, I've heard," Agnes replied with a smile crossing her face. "I caught your interview on Channel Five this morning."

Sam couldn't help but blush since he felt, in hindsight at least, that he went too far that morning especially given the fact it was on live television. He was usually in better control of his emotions. He was normally the level-headed one instead of the cowboy. The pressure, he figured, was getting to him.

"Hey, don't worry. I think that Hal guy is a jerk too," Agnes said as she patted the sheriff on the shoulder. "Just give me a shout if you have a question. I've got some errands to run around the facility. I hope there's something in there that can help you."

Sam settled down at Agnes' desk and began shuffling through the voluminous files in the box. He donned a pair of reading glasses that he recently began carrying in his front pocket. It was just another sign of his advancing age. It was more of an irritation than anything. Just the same, he avoided letting people see them on his nose. He would conceal them when he could, quickly whisking them off his face once he was through reading. They would sit on his nose for a couple of hours this afternoon as he read the book of Gina Porter's life.

The files revealed Gina had been in and out of mental health care for much of her life. Her last four years were spent under in-house care at SMHI. The trigger, the doctors wrote, for her mental illness was her victimization at the age of eighteen. The exact details for her lapse into insanity were not contained in the paperwork.

Diagnosis ranged across a litany of mental illnesses, most psychologists agreeing that post-traumatic stress syndrome had brought about other neuroses and mental issues. They also agreed her instability could be traced back to one event - an event that so traumatized her that she would never be the same.

Sam learned she never got married. Her distrust of all men was understandable given what she went through. She left home shortly after the incident and never returned to Castle County again, not even to visit her parents. Both of her parents were now deceased. Her ties with her parents had been permanently damaged as the result of what occurred that night. Her reluctance to reveal what happened to her drove a rift between them. Sam figured her parents went to their graves never realizing what happened to their daughter. Had she been ashamed to tell her parents what happened, perhaps fearing they wouldn't believe her? It was all so sad.

The medical records, while illuminating, provided no clue as to anyone who would be seeking justice for what happened to her. Actually, it was quite the opposite since she had apparently gone to great lengths to conceal the crime, whether it was out of shame or fear. She was an only child, her parents were gone, and she made no close friends during her life so far as Sam could tell. What was he missing? Was he barking up the wrong tree? It would seem there was no one who would be her avenger.

"How's it going?" Agnes asked as she ducked her head in the door. "You've been poring over them quite a while."

Sam finally took off his glasses and rubbed his eyes. A slight headache was starting to form in his temples.

"She was one messed up lady," Sam admitted. "But then who can blame her - poor kid."

"I agree, sheriff. It's a crying shame someone didn't pay for what happened," Agnes noted. "It's not in the paperwork but many of us kind of knew what happened that triggered her problems. We just didn't know the exact details.

"Oh, they're paying now," Sam countered. "It just took a while."

"I guess it's true what they say about Karma," Agnes agreed as she began boxing up the files that covered her desk.

"So tell me, did she have any visitors, anyone who she talked about a lot?" Sam asked.

"No, not really. She spent most of her time alone," Agnes said. "She was a very quiet woman and kept things to herself. That was probably a lot of her problem."

Frustrated by the lack of leads, Sam began helping the administrator clean up the files he spread across her desk.

"What about journals, diaries, and things like that?" Sam asked. "Maybe something of that nature would have something in it."

Agnes placed the last of the files in the box, shaking her head at the sheriff's question.

"No, we don't have anything of that nature anymore," Agnes replied. "All personal items were given to her next of kin."

"Next of kin?" Sam asked as he recalled reading that her relatives were all deceased.

"Why yes - her son," Agnes replied as she picked up the box full of records.

"She has a son?" Sam asked with his eyes wide. "I didn't know she had a son."

"Neither did we," Agnes said as she paused. "She didn't tell anyone, kept it secret like everything else. Then he came walking in one day, nice-looking young man. He looked like he'd been in the service, very well-mannered, polite and clean cut."

"Did he see her often?" Sam asked.

"Well, no," Agnes responded. "She died the day after he first came in to see her. He was the one who found her, poor dear. It was horrible, finding his mother like that. I can only imagine what that did to him, a young impressionable boy."

"Do you know his name or where he is?" Sam asked, excited by the prospect of finally having a suspect.

"Well he gave us an address but it wasn't legitimate because everything we've sent there has come back incorrect address," Agnes noted. "The last time I saw him was the day his mother was buried."

"What about a name, do you remember a name?" Sam asked.

"I can't really remember," Agnes admitted. "I see a lot of family in here so sometimes things slip but maybe Helen will remember. She's our receptionist you've met. As I recall she was kind of sweet on him when he came in. Like I said, he was a rather handsome young man."

Agnes called the receptionist into her office. The young

woman timidly entered.

"Helen, by any chance do you remember the name of Ms. Porter's son, the one who came in right before, well, you know," Agnes asked.

"Yes ma'am. Well, I know his first name," Helen said, looking at the sheriff.

"It's Ben. His name is Ben".

SOMETHING ABOUT BEN

The war never ended for Ben. It had simply moved closer to home and became more personal. That was the thing about war. At least over there, most of the time killing was just business, not personal. It was a job, a condition of his employment, an oath he took days after graduating high school.

A bored pizza-faced teen, he was ready to get out from underneath mom's apron as soon as he was handed his diploma. Easton was no place to live, to spread one's wings. He spent his teenage years imagining the day he would escape the mind-numbing malaise of his hometown. He knew his destiny was outside the bonds of Castle County. However, he would learn neither fate nor Castle County would be quick to let him go. It was as if both required a favor of him before turning him loose. Actually, it was much more than a favor. Their request was asking him to go above and beyond.

But then he was used to going above and beyond during his relatively short time with the special forces. He had already completed more hazardous missions than most seasoned veterans do in a career. His superiors recognized his special skill set during his training. They directed his career into an area better suited for his abilities. That area was killing. Ben was one of the best. He was a natural despite his youthful looks which earned the nickname Baby

Face Ben amongst his squad of specially trained professionals. Anyone can pull a trigger, toss a grenade or push a button on a joystick guiding a drone. However, only the truly gifted in the killing industry, Ben learned early on, can take care of business without depending on the normal tools of the trade, using their hands or whatever is available in arm's reach. He was trained to adapt.

That training was put to the test early in Ben's career. It was one of those rare occasions when things crossed from being business to being personal in an instant.

Ben had been in-country for only a couple of weeks. The young soldier was assigned to a special team charged with finding and neutralizing Taliban deep in the mountains of Afghanistan. That's when it happened, at a time he least expected. His first test wasn't deep in the Afghani frontier or in some remote mountain pass; it was in the mess hall as he was eating his lasagna. He had just sat down and began to pump ketchup on his lasagna when the yelling started. The voice was in a language he didn't understand but the tone was unmistakable. A moment later a shot rang out to his right. The head of one of his comrades at arms seemed to explode. Blood splattered across the table where the soldiers were dining. It was a rogue Afghani security officer bent on cashing in on his seventy-two virgins while taking out a few G.I.s along the way.

Ben instinctively reached for his sidearm which he was supposed to carry at all times. It wasn't there. He had disobeyed the order, leaving it in his arms locker in his rush to enjoy the lasagna. Now, the screaming traitor was taking aim at other soldiers as they dove for cover. His first victim was slumped dead across his plate of food. Ben had to adapt and adapt quick. Taking advantage of the traitor's hesitation in pulling the trigger again, Ben looked around for something to arm himself with. Seeing nothing available, he grabbed the butter knife he was using to cut his lasagna. Ben ran toward the armed man with the dull knife cocked back ready for battle. The Afghani traitor, who was preparing to squeeze off another shot, never heard him coming.

The butter knife sunk deep into his eye socket, the dull metal burying itself to the base of its handle in his skull. His shooting spree was over. The traitor was dead before he hit the floor.

Ben stood over the dead officer like an animal over its kill. His brothers-in-arms looked at the dead gunman with the butter knife protruding from his eye socket trying to understand what had just happened. It wasn't a story one could read in the local paper even though his actions became lore within the battalion. Many a soldier would tell the tale of Baby Face Ben slaying an armed terrorist with nothing but a butter knife. It got to a point that many believed the story to be only legend. However, Ben and those who witnessed his bravery knew it to be true.

Despite his unique abilities when it came to killing, Ben was the type of person most people naturally liked, that is if they weren't on the other side of the battle lines. His disposition was one of a mild-mannered young gentleman. He was soft spoken and always addressed those his senior as "sir" and "ma'am." It was obvious he was well-raised.

But, perhaps his best quality was one that people never saw except by the product of his actions. It was his sense of justice or the old fashioned idea of good triumphing over evil. It was the whole reason he dreamed of joining the military even as a child. It wasn't about the killing, it was about setting things right. It was about beating the bad guys. The Golden Rule was at his very core. The philosophy was instilled in him by his mother his whole life.

Now, as he pulled into the snow-covered driveway just outside Easton, Ben was one step closer to setting things right. He aimed to ensure good triumphed over evil. It would all be over, one way or another, in just a few hours.

Ben looked over his shoulder as he tromped through the snow. He walked with purpose onto the porch after assuring himself no prying eyes were watching. He wasted no time knocking on the door.

"Hello," the man said as he opened the door, a bit surprised to see his visitor. "What can I do for you?"

"You can come with me," Ben declared.

Without another word, Ben's fist flashed out like a missile, catching the man in the midsection. The vicious blow doubled-over the surprised man right into Ben's knee. The knee-shot caught his chin, knocking him out cold.

Ben quickly threw the unconscious man back on the floor and closed the door behind him in case someone passed by. He then pulled out the duct tape he had in his coat. He bound the man hand and foot with the tape before using a piece to cover his mouth.

"A million and one uses," Ben mumbled to himself as he surveyed his quarry.

Ben found a bedspread and wrapped the bound man inside it. He didn't want anyone to see him toting the unconscious man to his car.

Returning to the door, Ben peered through the window to make sure no one was traveling down the road. Traffic was sparse given the horrid weather conditions. Convinced no one was looking, Ben threw the man over his shoulder and carried him to his car, laying him in the backseat still wrapped in the bedspread. He then pulled out of the drive less than three minutes after he arrived. His mission, at least this part, was completed with no complications. As for his well-wrapped passenger, his inconvenience would only last a few hours.

Ben navigated the back roads with his mind wandering back to what led him to this point - the point where he had an unconscious hostage in the back of his car. It was still surreal to the soldier, how things had turned out. How fate had brought him back to Castle County.

Just three months before, Ben was on the other side of the

world engaging the enemy in their own backyard, seeking out "the bad guys" where they hid deep in the mountains of Afghanistan. However, a call from home put his war abroad on hold, bringing him back to Castle County. It was his mother. Her condition had deteriorated.

Just a week after trekking through Taliban territory, he stood outside his mother's hospital room in Easton. He dreaded his present mission more than any mission he ever undertook during his three years in the service of his country. His mother's battle with cancer was coming to an end. She had valiantly fought the disease for nearly a year. Despite his missions around the globe, Ben made time to come back and visit with his ailing mother while she underwent treatments. His last trip home was about four months earlier.

Along with being his mother, Elizabeth was also the only immediate family he had left in the world aside from her ex-husband, Trent. He had left them seeking his fortune in Hollywood when Ben was just seven. Ben called Elizabeth mother. He called Trent, well, Trent.

Elizabeth was the only mother Ben had ever known.

Back during his last visit to Easton, hopes were high she might beat the disease, the prognosis for the forty-four year old somewhat promising after months of chemotherapy. He went back to active duty believing things on the home front were improving. He couldn't be more wrong.

Word came ten days ago that his mother would not be making a recovery. Her condition was determined to be terminal by her doctors. Hospice had already been called to make her comfortable in her last days. The cancer had come back with a vengeance. Its progress was hopelessly aggressive. Ben was granted extended leave given his status as her only surviving child. He was furloughed from active duty for one hundred days in order to take care of his mother and set her affairs in order after her passing. Ben found it would take nowhere near the hundred days allotted to him.

His mother's condition had deteriorated beyond his worse imagination when he arrived home.

The woman he found when he returned to Easton was not the same woman he left just four months before. Now bed ridden, Elizabeth, who was active and chipper despite her chemo when he last saw her, now was under a hundred pounds. Her frailty left her unable to rise from her bed to give her only son a hug. He barely recognized the woman that it seemed, just yesterday, was teaching him to ride a bike, pushing him in his swing set and even teaching him how to throw a baseball. Elizabeth was both his mother and his father when he was growing up.

It all made him feel so helpless. A feared warrior able to vanquish all enemies, he was powerless to do anything against the horrible disease that had stricken his mother. What if he had stayed in Easton instead of joining the service? Would things have turned out differently? Had he abandoned his mother in her time of need? Ben tried not to blame himself for selfishly following the beat of his own drummer. His departure from Easton came with the blessing of Elizabeth when he enlisted.

"You have to live your own life, Ben," she told him when he joined the service. "You just go make me proud in whatever you do."

And Ben had made his mother proud. Elizabeth bragged about her "soldier boy" to all her friends at city hall where she had worked as the mayor's secretary until her health deteriorated to the point where she had to take an extended leave of absence. She had chosen not to remarry after Trent left. Instead, she dedicated her time to raising Ben, her job at city hall and her involvement in volunteer work - the latter of which she always stressed to her son. The Golden Rule that Elizabeth instilled in Ben as a boy still guided him as a grown man. It had such an influence that he took it as his first tattoo, one of many he planned to get, telling his life story in ink.

He held his mother's frail hand as he sat at her bedside, the words 'Unto Others' emblazoned on his forearm. Sadly, he figured she would never see the tattoo as her time was near. Ben was sent into her hospital room to say his last. But, in the scheme of things, she didn't need to see a tattoo to know her son was living what she taught him.

However, her focus on the final day of her life was on a secret she had kept. Sure, she could have let Ben find out about it in paperwork she left behind detailing everything but then that would be the coward's way out. She had taught her son to never be a coward.

"There's something you need to know," Elizabeth said in a barely audible voice, her breathing labored as Ben sat at her bedside watching her fight for air to speak. "It's about your mother."

"I know. You've told me," Ben interjected.

Ben realized Elizabeth was not his natural mother even though she had raised him from a baby. She had adopted him as an infant after his mother was killed in an accident. He was told before he was even a teenager to spare him the shock of learning he was adopted if he were to find out later in life.

"No, you don't understand," Elizabeth continued. "Your mother ... she's alive."

"What do you mean?" Ben stammered. "Alive? How? I mean, why?"

"She had no choice," Elizabeth said. "It was something horrible, something she couldn't tell. She made me promise not to tell you. She wanted me to raise you as my own. And I did that, Ben. You're my son. You'll always be my little boy, no matter what."

"But why are you telling me now?" Ben asked as he still held to his mother's hand.

"I couldn't leave with this on me," Elizabeth said opening her eyes, her look sincere as she glanced down seeing her son's tattoo for the first time, the sight bringing a slight smile. "You have a right to know. What you do with it is up to you."

"But why wouldn't she want me to know she was alive all this time?" Ben pressed. "What could be that horrible?"

"Some things are best kept secret," Elizabeth replied as she squeezed his hand tighter. "She had her reasons. What they are, well, that will be up to her to tell you."

Elizabeth cast her eyes toward her bedside. She was too weak to raise her hand to point.

"In the music box, the one you used to love to listen to when you were a little thing, there's a piece of paper with her name and address if you want it," Elizabeth said. "Just remember son, be careful what you ask because you may just get answers you don't want to hear."

The revelation that his birth mother was still alive combined with the terminal illness of the only woman he had ever called mother was overwhelming, even for the battle hardened veteran. How could he live his whole life without even a suspicion that his real mother was alive? What about his father? Was he alive too?

"What about my father?" Ben asked.

His mother sat silently, her eyes closed again. The question was obviously disturbing to her.

"You have no father," Elizabeth said coolly. "I've already said too much, more than I should have."

"But ..." Ben began.

"Enough about these things. I've cleared my conscience," Elizabeth said. "Let's talk about pleasant things in the time I have left."

And talk they did, the next hour spent strolling down memory lane, recalling the good times, laughing and crying as they reminisced. Ben was there when she breathed her last. He was still clutching her hand as she passed. He would later recall it was both the best hour and worst hour of his life.

Ben resisted the temptation to open the music box for the

next couple of days as he took care of his mother's final arrangements. A steady stream of well-wishers came for visitation at the funeral parlor. His mother was a beloved member of the community given her work with various benevolence groups that helped the needy of Castle County. Her face was also well-known in social circles given her work at city hall where she served as administrative assistant to the mayor for his entire administration.

She had been one of his first hires when he was elected. The job kept their small family afloat shortly after Trent left them high and dry. Mayor Glenn Satterfield was one of the well-wishers that passed her casket during visitation. He offered his sincerest condolences, extending his clammy hand to Ben as he rambled on about how sorely Elizabeth would be missed. While the income she brought home from her job at city hall kept them off welfare, Ben had never cared much for the mayor. There was something about him he just didn't trust even as a child. Now, as an adult, the feeling was doubly strong.

Perhaps it was a sixth sense or perhaps he was just a good judge of character. However, being the soft-spoken gentleman his mother had raised, Ben smiled and accepted the mayor's hand, thanking him for coming to offer his condolences. As far as he knew, the mayor had done nothing to hurt his mother during the years she worked for him. In Ben's book, the fate that would befall anyone who hurt his mother would be far worse than any pain and suffering he had inflicted during combat. Something like that wouldn't be business, it would be personal. You don't mess with a man's mother.

The cold November rain fell the day they buried Elizabeth. A sea of black umbrellas surrounded the graveside as the minister offered a few last words. Ben stood over her casket as they lowered it into the ground, tossing a single white rose into the open grave as the rain dripped off his brow. His mother was gone.

It was later that day Ben allowed himself to again think about the things Elizabeth told him from her death bed. Should he open the music box or should he go on with his life and ignore the fact his birth mother was still alive? After all, she had lived anonymously for all these years, taking no actions to contact him. Why had she given up her own child? And what of the horrible secret Elizabeth referred to? How could anything be so horrible that a mother would give up her baby without looking back?

Ben sat alone at the kitchen table at his family home after the funeral. He eyed the music box for several minutes trying to decide what to do. He was still soaked to the bone, a towel draped over his shoulders and a hot cup of coffee in his hands cutting the fall chill.

"This is silly," Ben mumbled to himself as he grabbed the box and opened it.

He froze as the song began to play. The familiar tune sent him back in time to his childhood when he would listen to the music box. It was a care-free time, a time when everything was good with the world. How he missed those times.

Resisting the urge to cry, Ben seized the piece of paper from the box. He took a breath and opened it – Gina Porter, 1043 Walker Street, Shelby.

There it was in black and white. His birth mother lived just a couple of hours up the road. He realized he had to go. If nothing else, he wanted to find out why she abandoned him as an infant. Besides, it was a short drive and he had ninety days until his return to active duty. Why not meet his mother? He would drive up the following day.

As was the case with Sheriff Delaney three months later, finding out the address was to Shelby Mental Health Institute was quite a surprise. Elizabeth had left out that piece of information. However, he had come this far so he may as well at least go in for a few minutes. What could a short visit hurt?

Ben was pleasantly surprised by the reception he got from the cute brunette working the front desk. Her flirty smile made him feel welcome. He could tell she liked him on first sight, something that didn't bother the young soldier one bit.

"Hey, do you have someone by the name Gina Porter here?" Ben asked the receptionist.

"Yes, she's a resident," the girl responded.

"Do you have visiting hours or something like that here?" Ben continued. "Do you like have to make an appointment or something like that?"

"No, not at all," Helen responded with a slight giggle. "Our residents can have visitors anytime during regular hours. Who should I say is here?"

"Tell her Ben is here to see her," he replied. "She'll know who you mean."

Helen made a call and pointed Ben down the hall.

"She'll see you," Helen announced as she gave Ben directions to her room.

Ben was surprised by what he found in the facility. Instead of screaming lunatics wandering the halls, he found well-kept rooms and pleasant surroundings, a couple of patients actually pointing him to Gina's dormitory when he got turned around in the hallway. He had traversed the rugged mountain peaks and passes of Afghanistan at peril of ambush every turn yet he couldn't navigate his way down the halls of a mental institution.

Ben paused for a moment outside her door as he recalled Elizabeth's warning that he should beware of the answers he may find.

"Gina Porter?" Ben asked in a quiet voice as he pushed open the door.

Sitting crossed-legged in a chair, a drawing pad on her lap, Gina continued scrawling away. She didn't bother looking up at her visitor.

"You shouldn't have come," she declared

unceremoniously, her disheveled long dark hair covering her face. "Elizabeth broke her promise."

"Elizabeth is dead," Ben revealed as he stepped into the room and closed the door behind him. "She died from cancer a few days ago."

"I'm sorry. I didn't know," Gina said apologetically.

She paused her drawing for a moment and looked off into space like she was recalling her old friend.

"She was a good person," she said simply before she returned to her drawing.

Waiting for a moment in awkward silence, Ben cleared his throat in hopes of attracting her attention. She continued her drawing.

"She told me that you were my birth mother," Ben declared.

His statement caused her only a slight pause before she again went about her drawing.

"Well, is it true?" Ben asked.

The question prompted Gina to look up for the first time. Peering at Ben from underneath her long dark bangs, her face wrinkled beyond her years, Gina responded in a cold tone that sent a shiver down Ben's spine.

"You wouldn't be my son if it weren't for her," Gina said. "I wanted to get rid of you before you were born but she talked me out of it."

Ben was speechless. His mother had just admitted she wanted to abort him while he was in the womb. His life was spared only by Elizabeth's pleas.

"But why? How could you even think about something like that?" Ben asked incredulously.

"Because you were conceived out of evil!" Gina hissed. "You are demon spawn."

Ben was shocked by the venom that was spewing from her mouth. Her wild eyes and her shrill tone told him she was eaten up with hatred.

"What do you mean?" Ben asked.

"There's some things best left alone," Gina replied.

Ben stepped over to where Gina was sitting and took the sketch pad from her hands. Laying it aside, he looked directly into her brown eyes.

"I have a right to know," Ben stated squarely. "Elizabeth said there was some horrible incident that made you give me up when I was a baby."

"Careful what you ask. You may just get the answers you don't want to hear," Gina said as she returned Ben's gaze.

Her wording was eerily akin to what Elizabeth told him on her death bed. However, Ben didn't care. He wanted answers, no matter the consequences.

"I'm a big boy now," Ben countered. "I think I can take it."

"You were a child of rape!" Gina screamed, standing up, as she growled her words out from between clenched teeth. "I was raped when I was just a teenager and got pregnant with you. I couldn't keep you knowing every time I looked at you I'd remember what those animals did to me. Frankly, I was afraid what I might do to you. I couldn't trust myself."

Ben hadn't seen that coming. Her explanation made him take a seat as he digested what he just learned. Three days ago he was just another adopted child living your average life. Now he was speaking with his birth mother who was telling him he was an unwanted child of rape.

"You said they did this to you. What do you mean?" Ben wondered.

"There were six of them," Gina said as she sat back down. "It was at an old bar called the Red Dog. It burned down a short time later, I guess about twenty-two years ago. I was there for my eighteenth birthday when it happened. They were all drunk and forced me to do things - terrible things."

Ben shook his head in disgust. He tried to fathom what kind of monsters would do something so heinous to a young girl.

"Your mother, well Elizabeth, she was with me that night," Gina revealed. "We were having fun until she left with her boyfriend. One of the guys at the bar was supposed to take me home but things got out of hand after she left. She always felt guilty for what happened, kind of like she was partially responsible since she was my older friend. She felt like she abandoned me that night. I think that's why she volunteered to take you, partly out of a feeling of responsibility for what happened."

Ben put his head in his hands and ran his fingers through his short hair. The answers, just as Elizabeth predicted, were painful.

"What happened to the men who did this to you?" Ben asked angrily.

"Nothing. Absolutely nothing," Gina snarled.

"What do you mean nothing?" Ben asked. "How can you just rape someone in a bar and get away free and clear?"

"No one would believe me," Gina tearfully revealed. "Some of them had connections and they were able to get it buried. Then the sheriff came to see me and suggested I should keep my mouth shut if I didn't want bad things to happen. Then the bar burned down a couple of days later. They wanted to get rid of the owner because they were afraid he would tell what he saw."

"He saw what happened?" Ben asked.

"Yes, he watched," she replied. "He was there the whole time but did nothing. I guess they were afraid he would have an attack of conscience and do the right thing so they burned the place down with him in it."

"So they killed him?" Ben asked.

"They thought they killed him," Gina said with a wry smile. "I found out a few years ago they didn't get the job done. He's still alive."

Ben stored the information about Earl Cutts away for later use. A witness was still alive - a witness who had seen everything yet didn't lift a finger to help.

"You said the sheriff warned you to be quiet. Why would he do that?" Ben asked.

"Because his son was the ringleader," Gina responded. "You've probably heard of him. He runs the big car lot in Easton. His name is Bart Foster. His father is the former sheriff, Bill Foster."

Ben was floored by Gina's revelation. One of Easton's biggest businessmen was a rapist and attempted murderer.

"So it went to high places," Ben whistled.

"You have no idea," Gina retorted. "Some of Easton's most famed citizens were involved. What would you say if I told you Mayor Glenn Satterfield was one of them too?"

"I'd say I never trusted him, from the very day mom went to work for him," Ben snapped back without hesitation. "There was something about that guy. I just couldn't put my finger on it before."

"He no doubt hired Elizabeth hoping to buy her silence about what I'd told her," Gina said soberly. "They were evil, Ben. All of them. And they'd do anything not to be exposed for what they did."

"Why don't you expose them?" Ben asked. "You still can. Go public and let people see them for what they are."

Gina smiled, rolling her eyes as let out a laugh.

"Yeah, like that'd do any good," Gina said. "Who would believe me after all this time? Haven't you noticed? I'm certifiably crazy. Better yet, what are the chances, given what they tried to do to old Mr. Cutts, that I'd ever live to tell the story if they knew I was coming forward? From what I hear your honorable mayor wants to be governor so I doubt he'd want it to get out that he likes raping young girls."

"I won't let them hurt you again," Ben promised.

"I'm sure you wouldn't," Gina said reaching out to pat Ben on the arm, touching her son for the first time since she held him in her arms immediately after giving birth to him. "But it's too late."

"It's never too late!" Ben exclaimed.

"No Ben, it's too late for me," Gina replied. "The only thing that would make me happy now would be to see them all dead and in Hell. They've ruined my life and messed up yours. They deserve to burn in the everlasting flames for what they did. For some sins there is no forgiveness."

Ben couldn't disagree with her wish. The group had earned themselves a special place in torment.

Gina went on to explain that after she gave birth to him, she "ran away" and got as far from Castle County as possible.

"It wasn't like my home life was all that anyway," she revealed. "My father left when I was little and my mom wasn't exactly a candidate for mother of the year. I guess you could say I was from the wrong side of the tracks."

Gina admitted she hated Castle County after what happened.

"I wanted to be anywhere but there," she admitted. "I couldn't get away far enough."

She broke ties with everyone she knew in her hometown, including Elizabeth who she entrusted to raise her son. She even became estranged from her mother as she seemingly fell off the face of the Earth for several years.

"It's all a blur," Gina said. "I went from place to place, never staying anywhere very long."

It was a few years ago, while she was institutionalized at a facility on the west coast after another one of what Gina referred to as her 'episodes', that her mother was contacted. From there her mother rekindled their relationship and convinced her to move closer. That was when she became a resident at SMHI.

Shelby was as close as Gina would move to Easton, her hatred of her hometown just as intense as it was the day she left it behind forever. The reunion was short lived, however, when her mother died a couple of years ago, snatched away suddenly by a heart attack. Her death left Gina alone, again, her only living relative not even realizing she existed - that is until now.

"It would have better if you never knew I was alive," Gina declared

"No, now I know the truth," Ben disagreed. "And you know what they say - the truth will set you free."

"I'll never be free," Gina said resolutely. "Never again."

"Tell me who they were - all of them," Ben demanded.

"I didn't want you to get involved in any of this," she responded. "They are dangerous."

"They have no idea what danger is," Ben responded coldly. "I want you to write down on your pad their names and everything you know about each of them."

Gina did as she was told. Her son's forceful instance and perhaps a deep-down hope they would get their just deserts convinced her to reveal all. Even though it had been over twenty years, she hadn't forgotten one detail.

"That's all of them. Everything I know," Gina said as she handed Ben the sheet of paper bearing all the conspirators names. "Now what?"

Ben sat in deep thought for a moment, trying to decide where to go from there.

"Now I guess we get to know each other," Ben said. "After all, you are my mother and we have twenty-one years to catch up on."

"I'm surprised you'd have anything to do with me after how I left you," Gina responded.

Just as he had done with Elizabeth earlier in the week, Ben spent the next hour catching up, this time with his birth mother. He told her about his career in the service. He could see the pride in her eyes as he talked about his time in the military, leaving out some of the more graphic missions he had completed.

They ended their first meeting with Ben promising to come back the next day for a visit.

"Can I bring anything?" Ben asked, realizing Gina likely never had any visitors.

"Well," Gina began quietly. "I haven't had a drink in years. They don't allow alcohol in here. I mean, after all, it is an institution."

"So you want me to smuggle some alcohol in like I'm going to the prom?" Ben clarified.

"Maybe some wine or Champagne? We could toast to new beginnings," Gina suggested.

"Well, okay, but if I get busted you're going to have to bond me out," Ben smiled as he patted her on the shoulder before heading out the door.

Ben spent that evening doing what the military called target acquisition. He found the whereabouts of each of the six on the list Gina wrote for him. As luck would have it, bad luck for them anyway, they all still resided in Castle County. He also acquired intelligence on a seventh person she had not included on her list - a person Ben held equally responsible. He would find the whereabouts of Earl Cutts later. For the time being, he was simply intelligence gathering, nothing more.

After his reconnoitering, Ben spent the rest of the evening sitting in silence alone at Elizabeth's house, recalling the good times he spent there as a child. He also wondered what life would have been like had his birth mother not given him up. Did the men who victimized his birth mother have any idea what they had done? It simply wasn't fair they were allowed to go on with their lives all these years as if nothing ever happened. They needed to pay for their transgressions. The question was, as Ben sat deep in thought, how he would exact justice on them. He had already resolved not to return to duty until he held them accountable for their actions. The only question in his mind was how far would he go?

Ben awoke the next morning at nine o'clock, sleeping later than he had in years. Civilian life was already making him soft. After doing some chores around the house, since he would place his childhood home on the market when he returned to the service given he had no plans to return to

Easton, Ben pointed his car toward Shelby. He recalled Gina's wish and stopped to pick up a bottle of wine on the way.

He was greeted by the friendly smile of the receptionist when he arrived at SMHI. The cute girl gave him a knowing look.

"You didn't tell me you were Ms. Porter's son," Helen said as he walked up to the front desk with his backpack slung over his shoulder containing the contraband.

"Well, I didn't know I was until a few days ago myself," Ben responded with a grin. "I didn't want to freak everyone out here with some long-lost son story."

"She was very excited," Helen revealed. "She's told everyone that will listen that her son came for a visit."

Helen's revelation gave Ben a warm feeling inside, knowing he had lifted the spirits of his birth mother.

"Excited doesn't always mean it's a good thing," came Agnes' voice as she emerged from her office. "Whether you realize it or not, your mother is a very disturbed woman."

"We spoke last night," Ben replied. "She seemed fine."

"She certainly isn't fine," Agnes countered. "She has life-long mental issues, many which center on you."

Agnes had just sucked all the happy out of the room, replacing it with her gloomy diagnosis.

"With that said, your sudden appearance in her life could be really good or really bad," Agnes continued. "We just have no way to know yet. I just hope it is positive because, if it is, that could help lead to her improvement."

"Maybe even her recovery?" Ben asked in a hopeful tone. "Is there any chance she might be able to live on the outside some day?"

"I'm afraid she will never completely recover," Agnes replied. "The scars are too deep. All I ask is that you watch her closely during your visits and let me know about any changes you see."

Assuring Agnes he would do what was best for her, Ben

RED DOG SALOON

gave them a wave as he strolled down the hall to Gina's room. She sat scribbling on her pad when he walked in. However, instead of continuing her work as she had on his first visit, she quickly put away her pad, placing it underneath where she was sitting.

"I told you I'd be back," Ben announced.

"And so you did," Gina replied with a broad smile.

"And guess what I brought?" Ben announced in a quiet voice so no one would overhear as he pulled out the bottle of wine. "Was 2012 a good year?"

"It sucked for me," Gina retorted. "But I'll drink to it anyway."

Laying the bottle on the table, Ben, who was straight-edge having rarely ever taken a drink, discovered wine bottles contained corks.

"Houston, we have a problem," Ben said. "I don't think I'm going to be able to get that out."

Gina gave him a disappointed look.

"Tell you what, I'll go down to the desk and sweet talk the receptionist and maybe she will give me something to open it with," Ben said as he started out the door.

"Ben," she began. "I just want you to know that I love you."

Ben didn't know how to respond to her statement. It caught him out of left field. He wasn't a touchy-feely kind of person so such words of endearment were strange to him.

"I'll be back in just a minute." Ben responded.

Feeling almost guilty that he didn't return her declaration of endearment, Ben strolled back down the hall. He was greeted by the smile of the receptionist when he approached the front desk.

"Back so soon are we?" Helen asked.

"Yeah, she was busy doing something so I thought I'd come down and chat with you for a second," Ben said.

He was covering the true purpose for his visit to the front desk since he figured it was against the rules to drink alcohol in the rooms.

"Well I'm honored," Helen responded. "So what should we chat about?"

On second thought, perhaps Ben would kill two birds with one stone. Helen was a good looking girl and he hadn't been on a real date since high school. The military had been his steady date for over three years.

"Well, we could talk about going out and getting some dinner tonight," Ben suggested.

"Are you asking me out?" Helen clarified, her eyes already telling Ben the answer to his question would be resounding yes.

"Well I suppose I am," he responded with a smile. "Maybe dinner and a movie? You do like movies don't you?"

"Yeah, scary ones are my favorite," Helen said with a grin still on her face.

"It's a date then. Tonight around seven?" Ben asked.

"That sounds great," Helen replied.

"Hey, while I'm at it, and I know it's kind of against the rules here, but would you have anything that a person could get a cork out of a bottle with?" Ben asked.

"Well it's against the rules for a reason and not what you think," Helen responded. "It's not the alcohol but the glass."

"What?" Ben asked as a sick feeling suddenly settled in the pit of his stomach.

"Your mother, well I don't know if you know this, she's classified as a high suicide risk," Helen revealed. "She's attempted suicide on several different occasions since she's been here. That's why she's in a special pod away from anything she could use to harm herself."

The color left Ben's face. Helen immediately realized something was wrong.

"You didn't leave the bottle in the room with her did you?" Helen asked in panicked tone.

Ben didn't bother answering as he bolted down the hall.

Helen banged on Agnes' door before she followed.

Ben ran faster than he had ever run but it wasn't fast enough. Arriving at the door he found it blocked, an obstruction preventing him from opening it. A look inside confirmed his worst fears. On the floor lay his mother amid an expanding pool of blood. The broken wine bottle was beside her. She had used the jagged glass to slash her own throat.

"Mom! Mom!" Ben screamed as Agnes and Helen joined him, all three throwing their combined weight against the door, finally getting the chair that blocked it to give way.

Their arrival was too late. He would again stand over his mother's casket and cast a white rose into an open grave. He had lost two mothers in less than a week. This time he was truly alone.

He left SMHI following the funeral carrying only a single box to represent Gina's entire life. While it came as no surprise that much of her belongings were sketches and drawings since that was her hobby, the subject of her art did surprise him – they were drawings of him at various times of his life. She had kept up with him, perhaps through letters or even e-mails from Elizabeth. Despite giving him up at birth, she had never forgotten about him. She had been watching his life from afar, afraid to get involved lest her secret be revealed.

Unknown to the Red Dog conspirators, the ending of Gina Foster's life also meant the end of their lives. Ben resolved to memorialize his birth mother the best way he knew how – with revenge.

"I love you too mom. I love you too," Ben whispered to himself, refusing to shed a tear, knowing he had waited too late to say the words.

SINS UNFORGIVEN

The revelation that Gina Porter had a son changed the game for Sheriff Delaney. The mysterious offspring automatically climbed to the top of his suspect list. Actually, he was the only one on the list since the lawman had no one he could call a suspect when he arrived at SMHI a few hours ago. His next move would be to locate Gina's son so he could either eliminate him as a suspect or perhaps link him to the crimes.

"So what was your impression of their relationship?" Sam inquired of the facility administrator. "I mean, were they friendly or was it a stormy thing between them?"

Agnes straightened the folders in the box as she digested the sheriff's question.

"Frankly, I don't think they even knew what their relationship was," Agnes replied. "From what we understand, Ben didn't even know his mother was alive until a few days before he showed up here."

"Who raised him then? I mean if his mother didn't, he had to be raised by somebody," Sam wondered aloud.

Agnes began rifling through the box of records, finally finding what she was looking for a minute later. She thumbed through the pages before handing the folder to the sheriff.

"From her records it would appear a friend raised him," Agnes noted. "She never revealed the identity of who adopted him but from what the record says, whoever it was lived in Easton since that's where he was raised."

"He did tell me he was staying in Easton," Helen interjected "He didn't say where though. We never got that far before his mother's death. He seemed so nice."

Helen dropped her head as she recalled that fateful day. She darted her eyes up at Agnes to see if she had overstepped her bounds.

"He was here when she killed herself," Agnes explained. "Actually, he brought in a bottle of wine, which is against regulations here for safety reasons since she was a suicide risk. She broke the bottle and used it to cut her own throat. I think he felt responsible."

Agnes sat down at the desk as she continued to look over Gina's records, dedicating her time to the pages where Gina referred to her child. In the meantime Sam continued speaking with Helen only to find her knowledge of Ben was limited to the short conversations they had during his pair of visits nearly three months ago.

"I can tell you the person who raised him was a friend that was with her the night she was molested at that bar," Agnes said as she scanned Gina's clinical records. "But once again, there's no name."

Sam thanked the women for their help. Their information had at least provided him something to go on. He had spent more time than anticipated at the institution and, glancing at his watch, realized he needed to get back to Castle County. It would already be after sundown by the time he made it back and if history was any indicator, someone would die tonight unless he could prevent it.

The snow had continued during his time at SMHI. The roads were already beginning to frost over again despite the salt road crews had caked on the blacktop. It would take the full two hours to get home but in the meantime the sheriff would let his cellphone do some work for him. His first call, however, got him information he didn't want to hear.

"Bart has disappeared," Bo declared "He must have taken one of the cars on the lot this afternoon."

That meant Bart was on his own. That might not be a bad thing since their attempt to protect the mayor the night before had failed miserably. After all, Bart had avoided the killer this long, whether it was by luck or design.

His next call was a long shot but he had to try.

"Cliff, I need you to do some research for me," Sam told the old reporter as the sheriff was leaving the institution's parking lot in Shelby. "I need you to go up to your paper archives and look up the story around the time of the Red Dog fire."

"Are you on to something, sheriff?" Cliff asked.

"I may be," Sam admitted. "I need to know exactly how long ago the Red Dog burned down plus, if you can, and I would owe you big, I need to find out the name of the girl who was with Gina Foster that night."

"So you do have a suspect?" Cliff queried.

"If you can come up with that name, I may just have one," the sheriff confirmed. "This is top priority. I need you to do it right now and call me back. I'm driving in from Shelby."

Cliff assured him he would diligently research his question but couldn't guarantee he would be able to recall the girl's name.

"You get the exclusive when I break this," Sam assured the reporter as he hung up.

The light was already getting dim behind the light gray snow clouds. Darkness would soon fall on Castle County.

Bart found the car in which Ben concealed the remains of his security force. Both men had their necks turned backwards. The macabre scene reminded him of an owl's neck. Just as Ben had said, both of his body guards had their necks snapped. Ben was a real expert. He was able to stalk and kill two cut-throats with relative ease. They were two of the toughest thugs Bart knew. He had hand-selected them for their ruthlessness.

The one thing they lacked, however, was intelligence. That was Bart's strong suit. He was always the leader. Most importantly, he was smart enough to have others do his dirty work. But, when others would shy away, Bart wasn't timid about getting his hands dirty. He had done his own wet work that night at the Red Dog. He had also killed with his own hands when he slipped the zip tie around Glenn's neck the night before.

Bart was no fool. He knew it was either him or Glenn. He realized Glenn would do anything to protect his reputation and, with the rest of the old gang gone, he could ensure the secret was buried forever if Bart was no longer around. In Bart's book, he had simply beaten the honorable mayor to the punch.

While he would never know it for sure, Bart's reckoning was right. Glenn had ulterior motives for accepting Bart's generous offer for refuge the night before. Concealed in his back waistband was a thirty-eight caliber pistol, a gun police found when they moved his body from his car after his murder. Glenn had planned to eliminate his old friend in his sleep with a double tap to the back of the head. He would then leave for holiday as planned, the dark man blamed for the murder. It was a perfect plan except for the fact Bart beat him to the punch. He had used the distraction caused by the dark man to surprise his old friend. He had choked the life out of him before he could get his hand on his gun.

Bart believed if he could outsmart the veteran politician, who was every bit as crooked and calculating as he was, he could outsmart the dark man. Sure, the mysterious killer could have easily cut his throat the night before, but he didn't. That would be his biggest mistake. Bart vowed the dark man would rue the day he declared war on him. Furthermore, the killer had showed his hand, arranging their clandestine meeting allowing Bart to scheme how he would turn the tables on the killer and be the sole survivor.

Bart stuck to the back roads despite the continued snow. He didn't want to risk picking up a tail from law enforcement if he were to return to the main roads. He realized he was being watched, again. He wanted it to be just him and the dark man - no one else. The meeting, of course, would not be on equal footing if Bart had his way. The crafty reprobate was already formulating a foolproof plan to eliminate his antagonist.

The sun had long since set. Bart roamed the side roads without passing a single car in almost an hour. It was about time to head toward his appointment. His attention, however, was grabbed by a light up ahead shining through the blowing snow. It was a church with a single car parked outside. He recognized it to be that of Father Dan O'Brien, priest of the only Catholic church in Baptist-dominated Castle County. He recognized the low-mileage, good-as-new, lightly-traveled dark blue four-door sedan that was parked outside. Bart had sold it to him just months before.

In a move that surprised even himself, Bart guided his car into the church parking lot. Aside from rare visits on Easter and Christmas, Bart rarely darkened a church door, figuring he may be struck down by lightning by merely taking a seat on one of the hardwood pews. But, given the mission before him, he could use all the help he could get. Plus, for the first time in his life, Bart realized his own mortality. A voice somewhere deep inside was asking what happens after life ends. Bart had been able to keep that voice muted until now.

"Maybe he isn't here," Bart mumbled to himself as he timidly mounted the church steps and pushed open the door.

"Anybody here?" Bart asked.

He walked between the pews and nervously eyed the large crucifix that sat behind the choir loft. He was ready to turn around and walk out.

"Someone here for confession on a night like this?" came the voice Bart immediately recognized as that of Father O'Brien. "You must have done something really bad."

The smiley face of the priest appeared from behind the choir loft where he had been placing song books for mass the following day.

"Ah, Bart. You're a sight for sore eyes," the father said in a faint Irish accent followed with a hint of a chuckle. "Tell me you haven't come to confess to selling me a lemon because I don't know if there's forgiveness for that."

Bart didn't know what to say since the father was right on both matters. First he had done something really bad and second, the car he sold him was in fact a lemon.

"I was just in the neighborhood and thought I'd stop in and maybe make sure things are right between me and the man upstairs," Bart said coolly.

"Ah, confession is good for the soul, my friend," the priest said. "Let me get on my confession-hearing stuff and I'll meet you in the confessional. It's right over there."

Glancing at his watch as he plopped down in the confessional chair, Bart realized he would have to make a quick confession of his long list of sins since time was flying and he had an appointment to keep. Maybe he could get blanket forgiveness on the whole lot of them. The priest joined him moments later, taking a seat on the other side of the curtain.

"So how do we do this?" Bart asked.

"Well, my son, you tell your sins and ask for forgiveness," the priest explained. "Then I tell you what to do and if there is penance required."

"Does what I say here, stay here?" Bart asked. "I mean there could be stuff that is pretty bad ... just saying."

The priest laughed on the other side of the curtain.

"This isn't Vegas, but yes, it stays here. And by the way, I've heard it all," the father replied. "There's nothing that would surprise me."

The priest couldn't be more wrong. Bart's list of sins were large by any standard. Plus, even as they spoke, a pair of corpses lay frozen solid in his trunk outside.

"What if I'm not sorry," Bart asked, his question surprising even Father O'Brien. "I mean, do you have to be repentant to get forgiveness?"

"Well yes. That's how it works," the priest responded. "How can you be forgiven if you aren't sorry for what you've done?"

"Can you forgive me for something I'm about to do?" Bart asked.

"No, my son. I don't think I can do that either," the priest replied. "What are you about to do that's so bad?"

"I'm sorry father. This was a bad idea," Bart said as he stood up and left the confessional. "I need to be going. I've got to be somewhere in a few minutes."

Father O'Brien emerged from the confessional and watched as Bart walked briskly toward the door.

"Come back when you get things straight," the priest called after the unrepentant soul.

"Tell you what father," Bart said as he paused before going out the door. "If things go my way tonight, I'll be at church tomorrow."

With that Bart turned to leave.

Sam's phone rang just as he passed the Castle County line. His eyes were starting to cross from straining them into the blowing snow that pelted his windshield.

"Well I think I've got what you want," Cliff revealed. "I went back and looked up the old story and let me tell you, I was kind of surprised. Do you realize it's been nearly twenty-two years since that old bar burned down? Time flies doesn't it?"

Time had flown, yet, in a way it seemed to Sam it had just happened yesterday. He could still see the Red Dog in his mind's eye just as if it was still standing.

"What about the girl?" Sam asked.

"Well that's a funny thing," Cliff began. "I couldn't for

the life of me remember her name, that is, until I went back and looked up the fire."

"And?" Sam interjected, hoping to get the old journalist to the point.

"And, I kept turning through the pages, looking at the old stories from back then," Cliff continued. "That's when I came across a wreck that happened a few weeks after the Red Dog burned."

"What's that have to do with anything?" Sam wondered.

"Well if you'll listen for a second, I'll tell you," Cliff replied. "So anyway, there was a girl involved in the wreck. She had to be flown out, got hurt pretty bad. It was the girl who was with the Porter girl that night at the bar. I remember thinking that to myself back then, connecting the two. It's funny how a memory works, isn't it sheriff?"

"Yes, hilarious," Sam said. "What was her name?"

"I've got it right here in front of me so I wouldn't forget," Cliff replied as he looked at his notes. "Her name is Elizabeth Warner."

"Is she still around Easton?" Sam asked excitedly.

"That I wouldn't know," Cliff responded. "There's not a lot of Warners around so it shouldn't be hard to find out."

"That's true," Sam agreed. "I'll do that as soon as I get to the office."

"So you ready to tell me what you've got going on?" Cliff asked. "I mean, I spent my Saturday night doing your research."

"Trust me, if this works out you will be the first to know," Sam said thanking the reporter as he pulled up outside the sheriff's office, anxious to look through the phone book.

Sam found six listings under the name "Warner" in the Castle County phone book. None of them were for Elizabeth Warner. He realized there was no guarantee any of them would have any relation to the woman he was looking for but then he was due for a bit of luck.

That luck seemed far away at first as, one by one, the listings failed to pay off. The sheriff had pretty well lost hope as he dialed the last listing, one for Randolph Warner.

"Hello. Is Elizabeth there?" Sam asked.

"Who is this?" Randolph Warner replied in a stern voice.

"I was calling for Elizabeth Warner," Sam repeated. "Do you know her?"

"I don't know who this is but I don't appreciate what you're doing," he responded in an angry tone. "Now who is this before I hang up?"

The man's response made Sam's heart jump. He may have just hit pay dirt.

"I'm sorry. This is Sheriff Sam Delaney," he explained. "I'm trying to reach Elizabeth Warner."

The tone on the other end changed.

"Sheriff Delaney. I'm sorry I didn't recognize your voice," Randolph said. "I was afraid it was someone playing a sick joke or something."

"So you do know Elizabeth Warner then?" Sam clarified.

"Why yes. She was my daughter," Randolph said, the sheriff quietly pumping his fist as he stood up from his chair.

"Do you suppose I could talk to her or get a number or something?" Sam asked.

His request was met with silence on the other end of the line. Randolph didn't know how to respond to the sheriff's request.

"I'm sorry sheriff, but that'd be impossible," Randolph began. "Elizabeth died three months ago."

"Died?" Sam repeated aloud.

"Yes. She had cancer for quite a while," Randolph said in a hushed tone. "She fought it hard but lost her battle."

"I'm sorry," Sam apologized as he racked his brain trying to place her seeing Castle County wasn't exactly a metropolis. "I didn't know. Did she have any children?"

His question was met with a slight chuckle from the other end of the line. Sam found that odd given the subject matter of their discussion.

"Yes she does. He was adopted as an infant and she raised him as her own," Randolph responded. "I figured you knew that."

Sam was confused. What would make Randolph think he would know about his daughter or her son?

"How would I know that?" Sam asked.

"Because you just hired him a couple months back. He works for you," Randolph responded his words causing the sheriff to catch his breath as he heard the sound of his own blood pumping in his ears. "He isn't a Warner though. Maybe that's why you didn't recognize the name. He goes by his adopted father's name – Faulkner. He's your deputy Ben Faulkner."

Sam dropped the receiver, his mouth agape, ignoring Randolph calling out wondering where he had gone.

"Sheriff! Sheriff! You there, sheriff?" the far off sound of Randolph's voice continued as the receiver swung back and forth on its cord beneath the sheriff's desk.

"That's how he did it," Sam whispered to himself.

It was obvious now why there were no clues found at the scenes of the first two crimes. Deputy Faulkner had been first on the scene at both the Andy Crouch and Eddie Young murders. The CSI team was looking for strange prints, those that couldn't be accounted for. Prints belonging to the sheriff and his deputies were discounted since they were "supposed to be there." It was also apparent who doctored the phone records, something that had bothered Sam given his suspicion he had a mole in his department. The deputy had been able to hack the system, or more likely figure out the sheriff's passcode, to erase Rhody's conversation with his girlfriend on the eve of his short-lived escape. And, he had done it all to avenge what they had done to his mother so long ago.

Forgetting he had just been talking on the phone with Randolph, Sam clicked on his intercom to dispatch.

"Is Ben Faulkner on duty tonight?" Sam asked as he stared blankly at the wall, still in a state of shock.

"Yes sheriff," the dispatcher responded. "He's out on a call right now."

"Where?" Sam questioned.

"He's out on a call of shots fired," she responded. "It's in the vicinity of the old Red Dog."

FAMILY REUNION

Bart wept as he fell to his knees in the snow looking into the face of his father. Only a wire held the former sheriff to the pole, keeping his lifeless body from falling face down in the powder. Bart's eyes adjusted to the dim light. He could see the gaping holes where his bullets had ripped through his father's body, exiting out his chest. The form he thought was the dark man through his night sight was actually his own father. He had been tethered to the pole like a condemned man before a firing squad. Bart had in fact hit his target when sniping from the top of the hill, striking the center of mass with every squeeze of the trigger. The first shot had likely proved fatal to the long-time lawman.

Bart wouldn't be afforded a formal period of mourning as the sound of a voice behind him interrupted his macabre gaze into his father's dead eyes.

"Put your hands behind your head and kick the gun away from you!" Deputy Ben Faulkner ordered in a firm voice, his gun trained at Bart's head. "Do it now, sir!"

Recognizing the young deputy, worried the gun might go off by accident if he made a false move, Bart did as ordered. He slowly rose from his knees before kicking his rifle away.

"I can explain, deputy," Bart began. "It's not what it looks like. It was the killer who did this. He called me here and killed my father. It was the dark man. He's still here ...somewhere."

Bart's explanation fell on deaf ears as the deputy stood

silently with his gun still trained on him.

"Well, aren't you going to do something, officer?" Bart said, looking down the barrel of the deputy's gun. "He is still out here. He could kill us both. Don't you hear what I'm saying?"

The deputy remained silent despite Bart's emotional plea. The night was so quiet he could hear the snow hitting the ground.

"Did you bring the head?" the deputy asked calmly.

"What?" Bart stammered.

"I asked, did you bring the head like I told you," Ben repeated in a calm voice. "Eddie Young's head. I loaned it to you this morning. I'd like it back."

Bart couldn't believe his ears. The young deputy was the dark man!

"I won't ask you again," Ben repeated as he cocked back his gun's hammer.

"It's in my bowling bag in the car," Bart replied quickly. "Who are you? Why are you doing this?"

"Let's just say I'm a man who cares," Ben replied. "But, while we're playing twenty questions I just have to ask - do you have a soul?"

Bart couldn't fathom the deputy's query. Here they stood in the middle of a vacant lot, the cold freezing them to the bone, his father riddled with bullet holes, his blood still running onto the snow and he was asking if he had a soul.

"I've killed a lot of men," Ben confessed. "It's just part of my line of work, nothing personal. But I've never seen a person who would kill their friends at the drop of a hat like you. You're pure evil."

Bart claimed ignorance to the deputy's assertion. He wasn't about to confess his long list of wrongdoings.

"I'm sure I don't know what you're talking about," Bart replied.

"Come on Bart. It's just me and you here. No one else," Ben began. "I'll share if you'll share. You know, they say confession is good for the soul."

"I wouldn't know about that," Bart countered, his eyes darting to the ground, his attempts at absolution minutes earlier at the church a miserable failure.

Ben wore a wry smile on his youthful face as he looked knowingly down his barrel at Bart.

"Your friend Andy - I almost backed out," Ben confessed. "I showed up at his place not knowing what I'd do. I'd planned it all out, how I was going to get rid of all of you. I mean he had it coming but I still wasn't sure when I got there. It was actually pure bad luck on his part."

"Bad luck?" Bart asked timidly.

"Yes, I suppose you could say that," Ben thoughtfully responded. "Frankly, the fact he had a wood burning stove cost him his life. I was walking up to his house when I saw the ax lodged in a piece of wood out front so I grabbed it. I mean I couldn't shoot him in the face with my sidearm."

"I suppose not," Bart agreed.

"So anyway, I walked up his steps and was standing there, in my uniform mind you, holding the ax in my hand trying to decide if I wanted to go through with it," Ben recalled. "That's when he opened the door. I figure he was heading to work or something because he was dressed in his factory shirt. He left me no choice. I was standing there with an ax. He forced my hand so I killed him. The good news for him is that he never knew what hit him."

Bart stood silently considering the deputy's confession to the murder - a murder which had started the house of cards to fall.

"Your turn," Ben said.

"I don't know what you mean," Bart replied.

"Yes you do," Ben retorted. "I was there the next night outside Eddie Young's trailer."

"What?" Bart snapped back, still trying to deny his guilt.

"Imagine my surprise," Ben began. "I go there with plans to get Eddie and I hear gun shots so I turn off my headlights and just sit there and watch. And what do you suppose I see? Is it coming back to yet, Bart? I see Eddie stumbling out of his trailer, running around in the snow like a drunken maniac with a gun in his hand and then I see someone dressed all in black sneaking into his trailer. That's where I got the whole idea to dress in black when I went out hunting. You were the original dark man. I'm just a copycat."

Bart realized his crime was witnessed by the deputy. He thought there were no witnesses to his murderous deed that night.

"Eddie was a drunk," Bart declared. "He was in a panic. He figured he was next. I knew it was only a matter of time until his drunken tongue got us all, so I took the liberty. He'd filled up my voice mail with crazy messages. Pretty soon, I knew he'd be calling other folks and it wasn't exactly like you sent out a schedule of when you'd pay him a call so I couldn't take the chance of him spilling his guts."

"The liberty of killing your friend?" Ben clarified. "You cut his head clean off."

"I don't know if you'd call him a friend," Bart said pointing out the two rarely spoke since the Red Dog burned down. "As far as the head thing, that was just a lucky swing."

"You could have been shot," Ben countered. "He did have a gun you know."

"He couldn't have hit the broad side of a barn in his condition," Bart replied, cracking a grin despite his situation. "If you ask me, I did him a favor. Left to his own deserts he would have died from cirrhosis of the liver."

Ben shook his head in disbelief at Bart's coldness.

"I guess I should thank you for leaving his head," Ben said. "When I went in after you left it was just lying there, staring at me. Now it'll serve as the prime piece of evidence against you."

"So you're planning on taking me in?" Bart asked in a hopeful voice.

"Then there's the little matter of Stevie Grissom," Ben continued as he ignored Bart's question. "I really would have felt bad killing him, given the way he's turned his life around and all. Of course, again, you didn't give me that opportunity."

Bart again grinned at the deputy's grasp of the situation.

"He was on the edge of telling the sheriff everything," Bart replied. "His wife had his stones. I had to take advantage of the situation. We followed him from his house, me and my two colleagues who you stuffed in my trunk. When he got out at the store I crawled in his back seat and waited for him to leave. It was easy after that. He never saw it coming."

"See, confession is good for the soul," Ben said. "And while you're confessing I have to confess that I followed you from the parking lot to the place you thought you'd hidden his vehicle. Just like the night before, you'd beat me to the prey."

"I was going to come back the next night once Rhody broke out of jail and kill two birds with one stone," Bart admitted. "But the car and the body were gone so I had to make arrangements for another vehicle to pick up our escapee."

"The car is still there. I just pulled it down the trail from where you hid it in the woods," Ben noted. "I, as you know by now, removed the body of the late Stevie Grissom and deposited him into the closet of the Honorable Mayor Satterfield later that night. I had to let you know someone was watching. He was still bleeding when I got there. You left a fresh kill."

Ben looked for a twinkle of regret in Bart's eyes. There was none.

"And then there was Rhody Turner. I have to admit I hadn't a clue how I was going to get to him but you are very good at what you do," Ben noted. "Oh, and you're welcome for my getting rid of the recording of his conversation with

Tia. I couldn't take the chance of the sheriff implicating you in the escape, um, and the murder - or should I say murders - since you're the one who killed Tia too. I hate that worst of all since she really had nothing to do with all of this. I couldn't have you locked up in his jail like Rhody was. I have a schedule to keep."

"The girl was expendable," Bart snapped.

"You are a real piece of work," Ben said shaking his head in amazement and disgust.

Bart took Ben's words as a compliment. He was impressed by his own ability to adapt to the static situation and eliminate those who posed a threat.

"It's my turn," Bart declared, wondering about Ben's motivations. "You never told me why you're a man who cares. Are you kin to Earl Cutts, maybe a grandson or something? He wasn't exactly man of the year you know. He did some bad things, some very bad things."

Ben couldn't help but laugh at Bart's ignorance.

"You really don't get it do you?" Ben declared through his laughter. "This isn't about Earl Cutts. Besides, you did a bad job killing him since he's still alive. It looks like he's the only one you didn't kill given the head count you've amassed in under a week, most of them your friends. I barely had to lift a finger. I feel like Tom Sawyer and the picket fence."

"Alive? Impossible!" Bart snapped. "I saw him burn up right here."

"You're wrong," Ben corrected. "I just spoke with him a while back. He's very much alive, at least for now anyway."

Bart searched his mind for the source of the dark man's venom. What had caused his murderous rampage? Could it be?

"Was it that whore?" Bart blurted out before realizing the consequences of his words.

"What did you say?" Ben asked, not believing his ears.

"This isn't all about that whore we had fun with that

night?" Bart replied.

His words were barely out of his mouth before he felt the crack of the deputy's gun across his nose. The impact knocked him to his knees.

"Don't you ever call her that again!" Ben screamed, resisting the overwhelming urge to fire a round from his forty-caliber into Bart's eye. "She was my mother!"

Bart grimaced as he saw his blood pouring onto the white snow. His nose was likely broken. He reached under his nose to stem the flow.

"I hit a nerve didn't I?" Bart said.

Bart struggled to his feet, finally daring to look toward the deputy. The taste of his own blood gave him a sudden surge of courage much like a wounded animal.

Ben stood quietly for a moment, biting his lip as he fought his trigger finger which was twitching around the cold steel. Then he broke his silence, a sneer crossing his face.

"It's a hell of a thing killing your own father," Ben stated with a smirk, nodding toward the dangling corpse of Bart's father. "Like I said, I wanted you to do a favor for me. I don't kill women, children or old people. I figured you couldn't resist the temptation to shoot me in the back. I was banking on that and you didn't disappoint me."

Gathering his courage, figuring he was going to die anyway, Bart straightened up and looked Ben in the eye.

"You wouldn't know, would you?" Bart said spitting blood at Ben's feet, his words bringing still another smile from the lawman's lips. "You wouldn't know what it's like to kill your own father."

"No, I wouldn't, but I figure I'm about to find out ... dad," Ben replied.

Bart stood bleeding in the steady snow. He couldn't believe his ears.

"You'd be surprised what you can find out when you have nothing but time on your hands," Ben began. "Surely you had to wonder why I saved you until last when I could have killed you at my leisure. I wanted to meet my dear ... old ... dad."

Bart couldn't find the words to either beg or defy.

"I'd always wondered where I got the ice water in my veins," Ben continued. "Now it's obvious. You're the coldest person I've ever met. You gave me the killing genes ... dad. I don't know whether to thank you or blow your head off. Is it a blessing or a curse?"

Bart flipped the blood off his hand, splattering it onto the snow as he eyed his son.

"I mean you killed them before I could. Eddie, Stevie, Rhody and even Glenn," Ben went on. "Even I couldn't believe you were cold-blooded enough to kill your best friend, well, your only friend actually. It seems the sheriff didn't keep me in the loop on their little stakeout at the mayor's house that night. I almost got caught while you were killing your friend. I hated having to hurt the officers but I couldn't let them take me in while you were still walking around free."

"The honorable mayor would have killed me," Bart said spitting out another mouthful of blood. "I just beat him to it is all."

"Yeah, I suppose he would have," Ben agreed. "And the funny thing is if you hadn't come back when you did that night at city hall I would have taken care of him myself. He was about to take a terrible spill onto the sidewalk from three stories up when you showed up. It's a good thing you didn't open his closet that night when you came back or, well, we wouldn't be here having this conversation."

Bart realized the fact he was hearing the deputy's confession likely meant he wouldn't live to repeat what he'd heard. The dread of death, Bart reckoned, would be worse than death itself.

"What are we doing out here chatting like it's a family reunion?" Bart asked. "Get it over with already. A big man you are, shooting an unarmed man. I guess you got that from your mother's side of the family, huh?"

His father's words brought a laugh from Ben. He had waited months for this moment.

"Oh, you're not going to be unarmed," Ben laughed. "We're going to do it just like they did back in the good old days. A showdown at the Red Dog Saloon except this time it's not at high noon."

Bart looked incredulously at his son. While ending many lives himself, Bart had no taste for a fair fight.

"I didn't kill your mother," Bart responded, hoping to escape his fate. "She was very much alive when she left that night."

"Oh, you killed her alright," Ben declared with a crazed look in his eye. "You killed everything that was good in her that night. It just took her twenty-two years to finish dying. Now you're going to join her, well, figuratively anyway, since I suspect you're going to a far different place."

Bart snarled despite his hopeless predicament.

"The way I figure it, your mother was a tramp so she'll be right there with me," Bart snapped. "Maybe me and your precious mother will have a happy reunion."

Ben resisted playing executioner. He simply smiled as he pulled out another gun from under his coat.

"It would give me nothing but pleasure to take my knife and cut you limb from limb and make you suffer a slow, painful death," Ben said. "But then if I did, that'd make me just like you - a heartless killer who delights in inflicting pain on others. I'm not like you, dad. I'm not like you at all."

Ben extended the gun to his father while his own gun was still trained at his head.

"You can go to hell!" Bart exclaimed as he defiantly extended his middle finger to his son.

It was the wrong move as the appendage disappeared in an instant as the sound of the deputy's gun set his ears ringing. Pain tore through Bart's body. His son had blown off his middle finger.

"Looks like you'll have to draw with your left hand now," Ben said calmly as Bart watched the blood pump from where Bart's middle finger used to be. "Here, do it before you bleed to death. Ten paces and then we fire."

Fighting off shock, Bart reached out to take the gun from his son, realizing he had one last chance at redemption. Ben had made a fatal mistake handing him a loaded gun. He wasn't going to make it a fair fight.

"Just one bullet," Ben said as his father took the gun in his hand. "You got just one shot."

Taking the gun in his hand, the pulsing pain from his right hand numbing his mind, Bart gave his son a defiant grin.

"It'll only take me one shot," he winced through the pain.

It was at that instant the sound of a siren could be heard approaching in the near distance. The sound distracted Ben just for an instant. It was the break Bart was hoping for. He raised the gun and fired.

Click. The gun didn't fire as Bart pointed it point-blank at his son's head. Click ... click ... click. Bart repeatedly pulled the trigger to no result. The gun wasn't loaded.

"I just had to be sure," Ben said.

There would be no showdown at the Red Dog. Ben, this night, would serve as his father's executioner. He pulled his trigger, putting a bullet between Bart's eyes. The real dark man was dead.

No sooner had his father's body hit the ground than he was bathed in the blue lights of the sheriff's cruiser. He reached down and retrieved the unloaded gun Bart had tried to use moments before and concealed it under his coat.

Ben went from playing the role of executioner to that of nervous rookie deputy in an instant as the sheriff ran up behind him. His gun still pointed toward the prone body of Bart Foster, Ben looked nervously at the sheriff.

"I pulled up and found his father like that, strung up with

RED DOG SALOON

bullets all in him," Ben began. "Then he comes running at me with a gun. I had to shoot him."

"I understand deputy," the sheriff began. "Are you hurt?"

"No, sheriff. I think I'm okay," Ben replied believing the sheriff was buying his tale. "He didn't get a shot off."

His performance ended quickly with the sound of the sheriff cocking the hammer back on his gun.

"I need you to toss the gun in front of you and put your hands behind your head, deputy," Sam said in a firm voice with his gun pointed at his officer.

Ben stood in shock for a moment, considering his options.

"I won't tell you again, deputy," Sam warned.

"I'd never hurt you," Ben declared as he tossed his gun into the snow and placed his hands behind his head. "You've got to believe me. You're a good man, too good really."

The two lawmen stood looking at one another in the vacant lot of what used to be Red Dog Saloon.

"They had it coming. They were past due, long past due," Ben volunteered, his explanation causing no change in the sheriff's expression.

"The things they did to my mother, they were unspeakable," Ben continued after not getting a reply from the sheriff. "They were going to get away with it if somebody didn't do something. Where's the justice in that?"

The sheriff looked at the bodies littering the snow-covered field and then turned his gaze back to his young deputy.

"Here's how this is going to work," Sam said as he slowly lowered his gun. "I'll expect your resignation on my desk first thing Monday morning."

Ben stood in shock for a moment. He couldn't believe what he was hearing.

"After that you leave Castle County forever, and I mean you don't ever come back here," Sam said with a determined look in his eyes.

He was letting him go despite knowing he was involved in the killings.

"Why?" Ben simply asked.

"I had a mother too," Sam replied. "I assume there's evidence that will tie Bart to all this?"

"Yes, more than enough," Ben replied realizing there would be no problem pinning the murders on his now deceased father, especially given the fact Bart had committed most of them himself anyway.

Giving Ben a knowing look, Sam nodded toward his patrol car.

"Get on out of here before I change my mind," Sam ordered.

Ben paused for a moment. He was tempted to tell the sheriff the whole story. Or, at least, thank him for letting him go.

"I said get on out of here!" the sheriff shouted.

It was a word to the wise for Ben as he headed toward his patrol car which was parked next to where the sheriff had parked.

"And one last thing," Sam called out as the deputy was about to disappear into the darkness. "You let time take care of Earl Cutts. He was going to do the right thing back then. Agreed?"

Ben nodded in agreement before stepping into the darkness and heading to his patrol car. He had never planned to return for Earl in the first place. He didn't kill old people.

"And my cruiser better not have a scratch on it," Sam called out into the darkness as he now stood alone with the bodies of Bart and Bill Foster, father and son breathing their last on the same evening.

Hearing Ben pull away, Sam made a call for an ambulance and the crime lab team which was staying at a hotel in Easton, deciding to stay in town for the next murder which they figured would come sooner than later. They would pull double duty this evening. Actually, once they checked Bart's trunk, it would be a night's worth of work for the lab boys.

The quietness was cathartic for the sheriff as he stood in the vacant lot waiting for the distant wail of sirens. Time had in fact flown. It seemed like just yesterday when he picked up the young girl as she walked alongside the dark highway leading toward town from the old Red Dog. Sam flashed back twenty-two years as he stood alone in the snow.

He had been in on leave from the Army visiting Carly, who he would soon marry. He figured he would go out to the Red Dog one last time for a drink. He knew once he was married Carly wouldn't allow him to frequent such places. He reached the bar only to find it closed. That was unusual since the tavern generally stayed open to all hours, especially on weekends.

He could see it like it was yesterday. The young girl's clothes were torn, her hair disheveled, and her makeup smeared as she wept uncontrollably.

"What happened?" Sam recalled asking the girl, her shoulders heaving from her deep sobs as he continued toward town with her in the passenger seat of his old Camaro.

"Where do you live?" he asked, noticing some blood on her arms, her lips visibly swollen.

"I can't go home like this," the girl said through her sobs. "Just take me to a phone."

Sam did as the teenager tearfully requested and found a payphone in downtown Easton.

"Do I need to call the police?" Sam asked as she climbed out of his car.

"No, please don't!" she begged. "Don't tell anybody. I'll be okay. Let's keep this our secret."

With that, the girl walked over to the phone and lifted the receiver, waving him to leave. While he obliged her wishes, he had never forgiven himself for leaving, for not doing more to help the young girl.

He never learned her name that night but he knew it now - It was Gina Porter. He had his suspicions when her picture was pointed out in the annual by his wife. He now knew it for sure.

While his role that night was more of an act of omission rather than commission, it still bothered him. He should have done something more to help her. Perhaps if he had taken initiative things would have turned out differently.

For Sam, this night would be a night he would never forget. It was a night stranger than fiction. For Sam's grown children, they would remember it as the evening their father called them in the middle of the night just to tell them he loved them.

EPILOGUE

With the head of one of the murder victims found in his bowling bag inside his car which also contained the bodies of two of his business associates not to mention his finger prints all over the smoking gun that killed former Sheriff Bill Foster, it was easy to pin the reign of terror on Bart.

The way the story bearing the byline of Cliff Chapman read in the local paper, Bart suffered from paranoia believing his old friends were going to inform on him and turn state's evidence for the murder of Earl Cutts. Therefore, giving in to his delusional thinking, he went about silencing the potential witnesses. He even killed his own father before dying in a shootout with Deputy Ben Faulkner. It was an open and shut case that never had to go to trial since Bart had already received the death penalty at the hands of the young deputy. No one was the wiser.

A smaller story later in the week revealed the young hero who brought down the crazed killer had resigned his post, opting to return to the military, saying law enforcement work proved too dangerous for him. No one knew it but he had never left the service in the first place. He took the deputy job with the sheriff while he was just on leave. The sheriff would improve his background checks for future hires.

He reported back to active duty the next week. He and Sam would never speak again, Ben true to his word to never again set foot in Castle County.

Press conferences, television appearances and paperwork

monopolized Sam's time for the next several days giving him little time to even breathe. The public was fascinated by the nightmare which had visited his small town. However, like other hot headlines, the press found another story, another flavor of the week, leaving Castle County to return to its peaceful self even as the snow from the historic snow storm melted away.

It was then Sam made a two-hour drive to tie up the one loose end. It had been only a week since his visit so he remembered the way to Earl Cutts' room. Pausing at his door, the sheriff rapped lightly. The door swung open at his touch.

Like déjà vu, the sheriff found Cutts again sitting at his favorite place by the window overlooking the lake where he had fished his retirement away. Ben had been true to his word, leaving the old man in the hands of time.

Walking over to the old man's chair, Sam announced his presence, his voice getting no reaction. Realizing something wasn't right, the sheriff walked over to the old man's perch at the window. Earl Cutts was dead, the victim of the world's most notorious serial killer - Father Time. The Red Dog had claimed its last.

ABOUT THE AUTHOR

Roger Duane Sherrill is an award-winning professional journalist serving as crime and courts reporter for the Southern Standard newspaper in McMinnville, Tennessee since 1990. He is a 1988 graduate of Tennessee Tech University where he was conferred a degree in Political Science. He has won numerous state awards for news writing as well as news photography during his long career. He has also taken awards for his weekly humor columns, Taking a Stand as well as Family Man. He often draws on his experience working the crime beat in writing his stories, most of which are set in small towns such as the one where he has spent most of his life.

Made in the USA
Coppell, TX
10 September 2021